GROUND TO A HALT

GROUND TO A HALT

CLAUDIA BISHOP

WHEELER
CHIVERS

This Large Print edition is published by Wheeler Publishing, Waterville, Maine, USA and by BBC Audiobooks Ltd, Bath, England.

Wheeler Publishing is an imprint of Thomson Gale, a part of The Thomson Corporation.

Wheeler is a trademark and used herein under license.

The text of this Large Print edition is unabridged.

Other aspects of the book may vary from the original edition.

Set in 16 pt. Plantin.

LIBRARY OF CONGRESS CATALOGING-IN-PUBLICATION DATA

Bishop, Claudia, 1947–
   Ground to a halt / by Claudia Bishop.
     p. cm. — (Wheeler Publishing large print cozy mystery)
   "A Hemlock Falls Mystery" — T.p. verso.
   ISBN-13: 978-1-59722-543-4 (softcover : alk. paper)
   ISBN-10: 1-59722-543-6 (softcover : alk. paper)
   1. Quilliam, Meg (Fictitious character) — Fiction. 2. Quilliam, Quill (Fictitious character) — Fiction. 3. Hemlock Falls (N.Y. : Imaginary place) — Fiction. 4. Women detectives — New York (State) — Fiction. 5. Murder — Investigation — Fiction. 6. Sisters — Fiction. 7. Psychics — Fiction. 8. Hotels — Fiction. 9. Large type books. I. Title.
PS3552.I75955G76 2007
813'.54—dc22   2007013497

BRITISH LIBRARY CATALOGUING-IN-PUBLICATION DATA AVAILABLE

Published in 2007 in the U.S. by arrangement with The Berkley Publishing Group, a member of Penguin Group (USA) Inc.
Published in 2007 in the U.K. by arrangement with the author.

U.K. Hardcover: 978 1 405 64222 4 (Chivers Large Print)
U.K. Softcover: 978 1 405 64223 1 (Camden Large Print)

Printed in the United States of America on permanent paper
10 9 8 7 6 5 4 3 2 1

To My Readers,
with warmest thanks for all the time
you've spent
in Hemlock Falls

CAST OF CHARACTERS

At the Inn at Hemlock Falls

Sarah Quilliam-McHale owner-operator
Margaret Quilliam her sister, and chef
Doreen Muxworthy housekeeper
John Raintree business manager
Elizabeth Chou a chef
Peter Hairston sommelier
Cassie a waitress
Dina Muir receptionist
Lila Longstreet a guest
Millard Barnstaple a guest; president, Vegan
    Vittles
Priscilla Barnstaple a guest; Millard's wife
Victoria Finnegan an attorney
Robin Finnegan a guest; her husband
Maxwell Kittleburger a guest; president, Pet-
    Pro Protein
Olivia Oberlie a guest; pet psychic
Rudy Baranga a guest; a food wholesaler
Max a dog

And various waiters, groundskeepers, sous chefs, et al.

In the Village of Hemlock Falls

Myles McHale investigator
Elmer Henry the mayor
Adela Henry the mayoress
Jerry Grimsby a chef
Marge Schmidt businesswoman
Betty Hall Marge's partner
Pamela Durbin owner, Pamela's Pampered Puppy Palace
Davy Kiddermeister the sheriff
Howie Murchinson town attorney and justice of the peace
Miriam Doncaster the librarian
Esther West owner, West's Best Dress Shoppe
Harvey Bozzel advertising executive
Bernie Hamm owner, Heavenly Hogg's
Quincy Peterson a sixth grader
Maria Kowalski a first-grade teacher
Harland Peterson a farmer

And Others

Lt. Anson Harker NYS Police
Lt. Simon Provost Tompkins County Sheriff's Department

8

CHAPTER 1

The morning breakfast crowd at Marge Schmidt's All-American Diner was in agreement: Quincy Peterson was destined to come to a bad end.

It was not, Sarah Quilliam mused, as she extricated her curls from the wad of Double Trouble Watermelon Bubblegum that Quincy had stuck in her hair, that the citizens of Hemlock Falls disliked the Peterson family. Nor were those villagers who dropped in at Marge's every morning for coffee and Betty Hall's famous cinnamon buns spiteful just for the heck of it. Quincy's antisocial behavior was notorious. The diner crowd usually had an accurate finger on the village affairs. There was the incident of the Superglue and Nadine's angora cat at Nickerson's Hardware store. The stink bomb at the School Board meeting in May. The mustache in permanent marker on the statue of General C. C. Hemlock's horse in

Peterson Park. And currently, Quincy's fascination with all of the places that chewed bubblegum would stick in a more or less everlasting way.

"Told ya not to help with this field trip, didn't I?" Marge Schmidt poured Quill a second cup of coffee. There was a subterranean we-told-you-so sort of chuckle from the villagers seated near Quill's table.

Quill carefully pulled out the last bit of gum from her hair and balled it into a paper napkin. Quincy was seated directly across from her. He smiled. It was quite a nice smile. You'd never guess from his angelic looks that he was a demon in the guise of a six-year-old. Quincy stuck his tongue out as far as it would go, revealing another wad of gum. Quill grabbed protectively at her hair, and resisted the impulse to shake the kid by his ankles until he turned blue. "Yes, Marge," she said rather crossly, "you did tell me not to do it."

"So why *did* you?" Marge persisted. Marge resembled a smaller version of a Sherman tank. Her neck swiveled in a turretlike way, and her small, bullet-sharp gaze was uncompromising in its directness. She was a very good friend to Quill and her sister Meg, but she wasn't the most tactful person around.

There was something different about her

today. Quill's visual memory was excellent. Marge had tinted her hair a brighter (rather brassy) ginger color. An inexpert smudge of blue eyeliner creased her upper lids. She wore a sequined t-shirt under her bowling jacket.

Marge avoided Quill's inquiring look and directed her blue-rimmed, unwavering stare at Quill's stomach, which was slim and flat in a well-cut cotton skirt. "Getting used to being around kiddies, maybe?"

Quill, recently and precipitously married to Myles McHale (to the astonishment of the entire village) felt herself turn pink. "Of course not."

This was a fib. She was thirty-six, and her biological clock was chiming loud and clear. Her sister Meg's interest in Quill's possible pregnancy was even more persistent.

"You heard about John," Marge said with an air of approval. "He and Trish had their first. Little girl."

"Oh, yes," Quill said. She could feel her face light up. John, who had moved from being Quill's business manager to her accountant as her own expertise grew, was coming to visit them Saturday with the new baby.

"He's quite an example," Marge pointed

out. "Bachelor for years. And now lookit 'm."

"I'm here because Maria called me in a total panic this morning," Quill said in a flustered way, "flu's decimated the teachers' aides. There wasn't anyone else to call. She was in a pickle."

Marge snorted. "You put yourself on the volunteer list, though. Didn't ya? Told ya this kind of thing wasn't your bag. Didn't I?"

Quill sighed and glanced at her watch. The school van was running late. Marge's All-American Diner was the collection point for the first-grade field trip to the Heavenly Hogg's Pig Farm. A dozen or more six-year-olds were distributed around the restaurant like restless chickens, waiting for Maria Kowalski and their ride. Quill, along with two harried school aides, was chaperoning the trip.

"What could I do? Poor Maria tried everyone else. By the time she got to me she was desperate. It's midweek and things are a little slow at the Inn, and I thought, why not? How hard can it be to take care of a bunch of . . . stop that immediately, Quincy." She reached across the table and removed the glass sugar jar from his sticky grasp. She peered doubtfully at it. "How

12

full was it, Marge?"

"Near the top."

"Well, it's only a quarter full now."

Marge, whose barracuda instincts had helped make her the richest woman in Tompkins County, gave Quincy the benefit of the glare that had reduced corporate raiders to jelly and snapped, "What'd ya do with the sugar, kid?"

Quincy said "Phuut!" and sprayed spit and sugar all over the linoleum-topped table.

"Do you suppose he ate it all?" Quill rubbed her temples with both hands. "If he ate it all he's going to go into glucose shock, or something."

"You wish," Marge said unfeelingly. "At least he'd be unconscious. I tell you what, you take him on over to the ER at the clinic and dump him there. It'll be the smartest move you'll make all week."

"I want to go to the ee-rr," Quincy said.

"You'll be fine," Quill said. "I mean, you feel okay, don't you?"

"If I don't, do I get to go to the ee-rr?"

"Is your tummy upset?" Quill looked at him anxiously. "Do you feel dizzy?"

"What IS the ee-rr?" Quincy persisted, "I want to see it."

"No, you don't," Marge said.

"Yes, I do."

"No, you don't"

"Yes, I DO!"

Marge thrust out one meaty arm and clamped her palm over Quincy's mouth. "Shut up, you."

"Watch out!" Quill said hastily, "He'll . . ."

"Ow!" Marge snatched her hand away.

". . . bite," Quill finished.

Quincy smacked his lips in a thoughtful way.

The door to the diner swung open. Quill turned in her seat. "Thank goodness. There's Maria." She rose, slung her purse over her shoulder, grabbed Quincy gently by the back of the neck, and waved at the grade-school teacher. Maria Kowalski propped the front door to the diner open and waved cheerfully back. She was a comfortable-looking woman in her mid-thirties, with a round, open face, dark eyes, and dark brown hair drawn back in a practical ponytail. She was dressed for the warm September weather in sandals, a droopy skirt, and a white cotton blouse untucked at one end.

"I see you made it, Quill!" she called.

Quill nodded.

"Terrific!" Maria's gaze swept around the diner. "People!" she shouted. She clapped

14

her hands briskly together, "People! The van's right outside at the curb. Line up nicely, please." She frowned, suddenly, amid the general scraping of chairs and the surge toward the door. "Quincy? I saw that. Quill, if you could just pay a leetle bit closer atten . . . Quincy, if you pinch Emily one more time, that's it for you, young man. No trip to see the nice little pigs. You'll have to stay with Miss Quilliam up at her nice Inn for the rest of the day."

"Cool!" Quincy said.

Quill, a little pale at the thought of Quincy in the same general area as her volatile sister, Meg, nudged him out the door and into the line waiting to board the van. He wriggled impatiently under her grip. "Do you know," Quill said kindly, "that you can pet the piglets at the farm? They have goats, too."

"Who cares about stupid old pigs?"

"Well," Quill asked reasonably, "what *do* you care about?" She nudged him into the van and guided him toward a seat. Quincy sat, and cocked his head in a considering way. "Killer Two," he said, finally,

Quill sat gingerly next to him. "Killer what?"

He rolled his eyes dramatically. "It's a Play Station game . . ." he paused. The word

15

"stupid" hung in the air, unsaid. "They made me leave it at home. It's supposedly not educational. Wrong! It's *very* educational." There was a great deal of indignation under the sugar on his cheeks.

"No Play Station games," Maria Kowalski said over the back of the driver's seat. "School rules. They aren't educational." She raised her voice to a genteel shriek. "Everybody buckled in? Everybody snug as a bug in a rug?" A chorus of juvenile "yesses" greeted this repellent foray into simile. "Good!" Maria beamed. "All right, people. Here we go!"

The van pulled away from the curb and proceeded down Main Street at a sedate thirty miles an hour. Quill who rarely, if ever, proceeded anywhere in a car at a poky thirty miles an hour, looked out the window at the village, as if seeing it for the first time. Ten years ago she and her sister Meg had gotten lost on their way to Albany from New York City and decided to settle here.

Quill considered a moment. They'd driven into Hemlock Falls on June twelfth. So it was ten years and three and a half months, exactly. Meg had been suddenly, agonizingly widowed. Quill had been six months divorced. Both of them had felt, instantly, that this place would provide a peaceful haven

16

from the stresses of the city.

Built over one of the famous shale gorges left by the glaciers millennia ago, Hemlock Falls was a village the twenty-first century had passed by. Trappers on their way to Canada had settled the village itself more than three hundred years ago. By the early 1800s, Hemlock Falls had grown to a more than respectable size. Prosperous farmers erected cobblestone houses along Main Street. Wrought-iron street lamps were converted from gas to electricity. Each year, the Ladies Auxiliary filled the stone troughs in front of the stores with a spill of red, pink, and white geraniums. The village attracted wealthy summer visitors from Buffalo and New York City. The prosperity that began just after the Civil War lasted up to the Great Depression.

When Meg and Quill first chanced upon it, the village had lapsed into the quiet decline that characterized much of upstate New York in the latter half of the twentieth century.

But then they'd seen the beautiful old copper-roofed building that had become their Inn.

Quill twisted around in her seat and looked up the hill. The Inn at Hemlock Falls sat glowing in the early autumn sun. The stone walls were a welcoming creamy gold. The sight of the velvet lawns sweeping to the lip of the waterfall and the inviting sprawl of the stone buildings lifted her spirits, as it always did. The yellow-green leaves of the surrounding trees were the first signs of true autumn to come; in a few weeks, the entire place would be cupped in a riot of red, orange, and yellow.

She became aware of warm breath on her cheek. It smelled of peanut butter.

"What're you looking at?" Quincy demanded.

"My sister and I own that Inn up there. I like to look at it in the sunshine."

Quincy leaned over her shoulder, his sticky hand on her bare arm. "In what?"

Quill blinked.

"What's it *in?*" Quincy said impatiently.

"An Inn is a sort of small hotel. We have twenty-seven rooms. Guests come and stay with us. My sister is the chef. Cook, I mean."

"I know what a chef is," Quincy said. The word "stupid" hung in the air again. "Like a cook, right? Only it costs more." He blinked at her. His eyes were very blue. "Are you the big sister?"

"Yes," Quill admitted. "Do you have a big sister?"

"Yeah." Quincy settled back into his seat. "She's stupid."

Conversation languished. The van rolled smoothly down Route 15. In this part of New York, wine had supplanted much of the more traditional farming. Fields of heavily fruited grapevines alternated with acres of corn and soybean. They passed a buggy drawn by a horse sweating in the mild heat, an Amish farmer at the reins. A clutch of draft horses drowsed outside a shabby red barn.

Something in the tired posture of one of the old mares caught her interest, and Quill pulled the sketchbook she always carried with her from her purse and began to draw. The scent of peanut butter drew her from her absorption.

"You draw pretty good," Quincy said, his chin digging into her right shoulder. He gazed critically at the sweeps of charcoal. "I could do that, I bet."

"I'm sure you could," Quill said equably.

"That horse looks pretty sad."

"Do you think so?" Quill was mildly flattered. It was one thing to get insightful reviews from the critic of *Art Today* (which her paintings did, frequently), quite another to get them from a six-year-old. "You're a pretty noticing kind of guy."

Quincy looked smug. "Yeah. I guess I am."
Quill went back to her sketch.

Quincy rose onto his knees and looked at the van from back to front, frowning in a challenging way. He poked Quill in the ribs.

"Please don't poke me, Quincy."

"I thought maybe you didn't notice that Mrs. Kowalski has a zit on her cheek."

Quill took a breath, let it out, and went back to her sketch. She shaded the hollows under the mare's eyes. Quincy resumed his eagle-eyed perusal of the van. He grabbed the top of the stick of charcoal and wiggled it back and forth.

"Quincy." Quill dug into her purse for her eraser. "Please do *not* do that again."

"I thought maybe you didn't notice that Mrs. Heldegger wears a wig." He paused. "I guess it's on account of she's bald."

Six-year-old boys have piercing voices. Quincy's was more piercing than most. It cut through the general babble like the "wrong" buzzer on a game show. Mrs. Heldegger, a totally blameless school aide who indeed wore a wig due to female pattern baldness, flushed a painful shade of red.

"Stop that," Quill hissed.

Quincy scowled. "I was just noticing, like you said I should."

"I said no such thing." Quill avoided Mrs. Heldegger's reproachful eye.

"Yes, you did."

"No, I didn't."

"Yes, you DID DID DID!"

"For heaven's sake, Quill!" Maria Kowalski cast a worried look in the rearview mirror.

The van took a sharp right, and bumped down a dirt road. "Look, Quincy," Quill said desperately, "see that nice big sign? With the nice bright pink pig painted on it? We're here! At Heavenly Hogg's Pig Farm. There'll be a lot of great animals to notice here."

Quincy's snarl was full of contempt. "Even a bad noticer can notice a big fat pig right in front of your face."

The van came to a halt in an asphalt parking lot. The lot was immediately south of a series of long, low red barns. A bricked pathway ran beneath a post-and-beam archway up to a white clapboard farmhouse. The front door opened, and a large weathered man in rubber boots stomped down the path to the bus. The wind shifted. Quill caught the odor of pig. Maria Kowalski waved both arms and hollered, "Halloo, Bernie," and the rubber-booted man hallooed back and shouted, "Get them little guys lined right up, will ya?"

"This here," Bernie Hamm said some twenty minutes later, "is the weaner bin."

Quill headed the line of curious first graders. Maria Kowlaski brought up the rear. There were five stops on the pig farm tour. The weaner bin was the fourth. Quill was fascinated in spite of herself. The farm was clean, bright, and well swept. The pigs were healthy and happy.

The first stop had been a gulp-inducing view of Hamlet, the farm's prize boar. Hamlet, Bernie proudly informed them, weighed upward of a thousand pounds. The animal took up the better part of an eight-by-ten pen, and responded with a friendly grunt when Bernie scratched his back with a stick. The second stop was a straw-filled pen three times the size of the first, occupied by three pregnant sows. A hand-lettered sign listed their names: Daisy, Maybelle, and Gloria. Gloria had a perky checked bow tied at the base of her tail. Next was the birthing pen, with three more sows lying peacefully on their sides, each suckling what looked like way too many little piglets for any mother to handle. The fourth was the weaner bin, filled with several dozen scampering gilts that had given up mother's milk for mash.

The first graders hung over the plywood wall in an impatiently shifting row. The little pigs scampered merrily around the pen, rooting between the slats on the floor with happy grunts. Bernie Hamm slung one booted leg over the low barricade, scooped up a small pink specimen, and tucked it under his arm. The kids crowded around him, scratching the piglet's nose and rubbing its little ears. It made Quill feel quite sentimental. Her sister might be right. Children could add a lot to one's emotional life.

"And this here's the cooler." Bernie took a left turn down the graveled aisle. Quill hurried to catch up, Quincy at her heels. The rest of the children straggled behind, still enraptured by the piglets. Bernie came to a halt, a radiant smile of pride on his face. "Just installed 'er last month, Quill," he said. "Big improvement in the fridge we had here before."

"It's a cooler."

"Yep. She'll hold forty carcasses at once."

Quincy pushed his way between Quill and Bernie and flattened his nose against the glass. "Hey!" he said. "I'm noticing something right now!" He looked up at Quill with a happy sigh. "There's a lady in there with the pig guts!"

Quill gazed intently at the row of carcasses through the frosted glass door. She took a deep breath. Then she spun around and grabbed Quincy by the shoulders. She shoved him in Maria's direction. "Tell Mrs. Kowalski to get everybody back on the bus."

Quincy opened his mouth to protest. Quill looked at him. He turned without a word and trotted back to the rest of the class.

Bernie removed his John Deere tractor cap, scratched his head, and shoved it firmly back onto his skull. "Now what was *that* all about? Most of these kids are farm kids, Quill. Ain't none of 'em not seen a carcass before."

Quill turned her back to the cooler and took several deep breaths. "Not that kind of carcass, Bernie."

"What?"

"That's Lila Longstreet lying on the floor in there."

Bernie paled. He turned and peered shortsightedly through the glass door. Then he threw the door open and stepped in. He stepped out again, his face the color of goat cheese. "Oh migosh."

"We need to call the sheriff," Quill said steadily. "Is there any hope? I mean, should we . . . ?"

Bernie shook his head dazedly. "Head's smashed like a durn pumpkin." He ran one huge hand over his face. "Oh migosh. You say you know her?"

"She was a guest at the Inn." Quill paused. "But she checked out yesterday."

Bernie nodded heavily. "I guess she did, Quill. I guess she did."

CHAPTER 2

"How'd you know it was Lila Longstreet?" Meg demanded. "Nope. Don't tell me. Let me guess. The hair."

"What was left of it," Quill said with a shudder.

"How do you suppose she got that particular shade of white-blonde anyhow?"

"That's a really stupid question." Quill put her head down on her desk and closed her eyes. "She bleached it, of course."

"Sorry. I thought maybe that'd be sort of a diversionary tactic." Meg made a face. She'd changed shampoos that morning. The new product made her short dark hair stand up around her face like a blown dandelion. It was warm for September, and she hadn't yet given up her summer attire of shorts and t-shirt. Between her ruffled hair and her clothes, she looked about six years old.

Quill shuddered.

"I probably just made you think about it

more. Do you want to talk about it? I mean, any more than you have already? Which was just about enough, if you ask me. But I'm here for you, sis."

"I absolutely do not want to talk about it."

Meg curled herself into the corner of the couch that faced Quill's desk. Quill loved its fabric. It was bronze with splendidly bold chrysanthemums. At the moment, she wished the flowers weren't so blood-colored.

"It was awful. The worst part was keeping the kids from figuring anything out. No. The worst part was finding poor Mrs. Longstreet. No. It was all the worst." She took a deep breath. It was hard to get enough air.

"Do the pet food people know about it yet?" Meg asked after a long moment.

"The pet food people," Quill repeated. She clutched her forehead. "Oh, shoot. The pet food people."

Lila Longstreet was — had been — the executive secretary of the tiny International Association of Pet Food Providers. The IAPFP convention had occupied several of the suites at the Inn for the past two days.

"Someone must have told them," Quill said hopefully. "Davy Kiddermeister is supposed to take care of that, right?"

Meg made another face. Davy Kiddermeister was sheriff of Hemlock Falls now that Quill's husband, Myles McHale, had accepted an investigator's job with the federal government. Davy wasn't a bad sheriff, just slow to perform the more distasteful law enforcement duties. Since most of the police work in a village the size of Hemlock Falls was pretty routine, nobody held this reluctance against him. But there was little likelihood that he'd broken the news of Lila Longstreet's death to the IAPFP's president, Olivia Oberlie, a mere two hours after Quill had discovered the body. If he'd done anything at all about it, he'd sent a letter.

"Everyone knows Lila checked out yesterday, so no one's expecting to hear from her right away," Quill said tentatively. "Maybe I don't need to rush out and tell Olivia just yet. Lila made such a fuss about leaving yesterday that even Mike knew she'd left and he," she added a little crossly, "wouldn't notice if we'd lost the roof. Even though it's his *job* to notice if we've lost the roof. Which brings up another thing, Meg. We're going to have a problem with the insurance inspection this year. I don't think we can put off redoing the wiring any longer . . ."

"Quill."

". . . and the estimate from Peterson's

Roofing is just outsized. I was thinking . . ."

"Quill! Could you get to the point, here?"

"I was!" Quill, crosser than ever, shoved the stack of current bills into the top drawer of her desk and slammed the drawer shut. "Okay. Fine. Forget about the budget. We can forget about paychecks this month, too. Of course, if the wiring blows and the lights go out we can forget about the guests, which makes the paychecks moot, so who cares, anyway?"

"This body was bad," Meg said sympathetically. "You always go off on a tangent when things are bad."

"It was bad." Quill agreed. She got up and walked to her window. "Murder is always bad."

The office fronted the drive. Normally the view outside it soothed her spirits. She shoved the drape aside and looked out. September in upstate New York was one of her favorite times of year. The lawn running down to Hemlock Gorge was a luxuriant green, the grass so thick she wanted to bury her hands in it. Water plunged over the waterfall at the lip of the gorge with steady cheerfulness. Late-blooming roses made pockets of sunlit yellow and warm peach in the gardens Mike tended so carefully. This morning, she'd looked up on her way to the field trip to remember how lucky she was to have this kind of beauty in her life.

This afternoon, she wasn't so sure.

Meg scratched the back of her neck. "Is it officially murder? I mean, did Davy actually say so?"

Quill went back to her desk and sat down with a sigh. "Not officially, no. But he wouldn't say anything to me before he filed whatever it is he has to file for the investigation."

"So maybe you don't have to tell Olivia that someone hated Lila Longstreet enough to bash her over the head. Maybe you just have to tell her there was an accident. Let the police take care of the rest. Why should you have to handle the gruesome part?"

"Except that someone *did* hate Lila enough to kill her. And she hasn't been in Hemlock Falls long enough for anyone we know to do it. Which means the murderer is one of our guests. And from what we've all seen of Lila we'd be hard put to find anybody at the pet food convention that *didn't* have a motive."

"That's for sure," Meg murmured.

"Which means," Quill said, smacking her hand onto her desk blotter for emphasis, "that the murder investigation is going to start and end right here. It'd be highly disingenuous of us to tell Olivia this was an accident when she's going to find out pretty darn quick that it isn't."

"Highly disingenuous, huh?" Meg said dryly. She tucked a chenille pillow behind her back and swung her sneakered feet onto the coffee table. "You always get wordier when you're upset, too. Have you noticed that?"

"So we need to bite the bullet and inform Olivia," Quill said briskly. "Tell you what. Why don't you invite Olivia into the kitchen and settle her down with some hot tea? You can break it to her more gently that way."

"Me?" Meg straightened in indignation. She ran one hand through her short dark hair, which made it even messier. "Why am I any better at this than you are?"

"Because you're shorter than I am?" Quill offered in a tentative way. "Shorter people are less intimidating." She thought about the numbers of eight-inch sauté pans Meg threw across the kitchen every month. "Never mind. Forget that."

"I already have."

"Okay. Try this. Olivia's bound to have really creepy questions about what happened. You can just say you don't know, because you don't. I, on the other hand, obviously know too much, since I'm the one that found the body. It'll be better for Olivia's nerves this way."

"You're the manager of this place, not me," Meg said flatly. "And chief among the manager's duties is informing guests about the sudden death of other guests. I'm the chef and I'll go so far as to make that pot of tea — and throw in a couple of scones. But *you* tell Olivia somebody murdered Lila."

"Wait a minute," Quill brightened "It's remotely possible that it was an accident, isn't it? Do you suppose something huge and heavy *fell* on her, Meggie? Those hog carcasses weigh a ton."

"Was she under one?" Meg asked in a practical way. "No, she wasn't. You said she was lying just to the right of the cooler door, with her head . . . or what was left of it . . ."

"Cut it out."

"Sorry. Her head was just inside the cooler and her feet were pointing toward the back. You said it looked as if she'd been dragged in by the heels and left there. You also said there were smears of blood and br . . ."

"Cut it *out*."

"And umm . . . gray matter on the lintel and the concrete path to the cooler. Which you discovered *after* you found the body when you were looking around waiting for the police."

She certainly had. She'd had to throw out her one pair of comfortable shoes as soon as she'd returned to the Inn.

"Now, you may be a big, fat baby about bodies . . ."

"Hey!"

"Well, we've seen a few of them in our time, haven't we? And you're still squeamish. Maybe it's because you're, you know . . ."

"I know what?"

Meg smiled hopefully at her.

"Pregnant? No. Not a chance." This, plus Meg's unsentimental reference to the several homicide cases the sisters had solved in the past, exasperated Quill so much that she added, "Shut *up!*" with the intensity of Quincy at his most obnoxious.

"But you are a wizard at remembering the details of a scene. Any artist is."

Quill glanced involuntarily at the charcoal sketch hanging over the couch. It was a preliminary of a piece of hers that hung at MOMA, a portrait of the two of them, sitting on the grass near the waterfall.

"So you can forget about trying the accident angle with Olivia. Unless you want to weasel. The only thing about weaseling is that the fib's bound to come out later. You'll look like an idiot or a fibber. Take your pick."

"I'm just going to tell her that Lila died unexpectedly. That we're truly sorry . . ."

"We're in the minority then," Meg interrupted blithely. "I don't think I've ever seen a meaner bunch of conventioneers in my life. It's weird. You'd think pet food people would be, I don't know, nice. Most people who love pets seem to be. But will they be sorry poor old Lila's dead? I think not."

"They're not all mean, Meg."

"Victoria Finnegan and that bozo disbarred husband of hers?"

"See?" Quill said. "Robin's a sad sack, sure. But he's not mean."

"He has," Meg said darkly, "a weak chin. And his wife's a shark. What's that quote when it's at home? 'First thing, we kill all the lawyers.' "

"One of Shakespeare's Henrys," Quill said. "The fifth? No, the fourth."

"As for the other pet food people . . . yuck."

Quill nodded reluctant agreement. "Now, Maxwell Kittleburger and Millard Barnstaple — I have to agree with you there." *Fortune* magazine had put Maxwell Kittleburger on its "Ten Toughest Bosses" list. He hadn't climbed to the top of the pet food manufacturer's heap by being a nice guy. And Millard Barnstaple was just plain sneaky. He gave Iago a good name. Like Iago, Millard smiled and smiled and yet was a villain. Or maybe it was Casca, Quill thought. Whomever.

On the other hand, Priscilla Barnstaple's malice was direct and unambiguous. It was odds on which of them was worse, sneaky husband or hammer-handed wife.

"Pamela Durbin's not so awful," Quill ventured.

"Maybe not," Meg said grudgingly. "But she named that pet store Pamela's Pampered Puppy Palace. Phooey. And she plays up that Southern belle stuff to the max. She tried it," Meg added in a dangerously calm way, "on Jerry."

"Who resisted, I'm sure." Quill sighed. "Okay. I'll go talk to Olivia. And then I won't have to think about it anymore. We won't have to think about *them* anymore."

"We'll have to think about the murder no matter what. We know it has to be one of the IAPFP crowd. And if we've got a murderer at the Inn, we're going to have to do everything we can to find out who it is. I mean, I love Davy. But . . ."

Quill nodded. They all loved Davy. But as an investigator, he ranked right up there with Inspector Clouseau.

"And when is Myles coming home? He could handle this with one hand tied behind his back."

This was true. Myles' career at the NYPD had brought him job offers across the country. He'd retired instead to the undemanding sheriff's job in Hemlock Falls. Iraq changed his mind. He'd taken on undercover work. Quill never knew where he went when he left on assignment.

She shook her head.

Meg addressed the ceiling. "We don't know." She lowered her gaze abruptly. "Which brings up something else we need to talk about, sis. You never seem to know where Myles is or when he's coming home. He's never there enough for you to get pregnant. And you've been married less than . . ."

"Stop," Quill said.

"You knew he was going to have to travel with this job but . . ."

"I said 'stop,' " Quill said in an even tone. "And I mean it."

Meg, uncharacteristically, shut up without further argument. Then she said, "Hey! Maybe Olivia already knows about Lila, being a psychic. Heck, maybe she knows who the murderer is. We won't have to investigate this case. We'll just ask Olivia for a reading."

"Olivia's a pet psychic, as you know very well. She's never claimed to be psychic about humans, just animals. Besides . . ." There was a tap at her office door. Quill broke off in mid-sentence. It was Dina's tap, brisk and prolonged, so Quill didn't bother to yell "come in." Their receptionist would barge in anyway.

"Hey, Quill, Meg." Dina slammed the door open, and shut it carefully behind her. She perched on the arm of the couch. She had either come straight from one of her classes at nearby Cornell or she'd been in the village; she'd replaced her usual jeans with the calf-length black skirt she assumed for her receptionist duties, but she still wore her gray sweatshirt with the tiny Cornell logo right in the middle.

"Hey, yourself," Meg said. "Are the guests checking out in a mighty swarm?"

Dina blinked once behind her round red-rimmed glasses. "Because that Lila Longstreet's dead, you mean? No. Not yet. As a matter of fact, they never do."

This was true. Crime seemed to attract guests rather than repel them. Quill had never quite understood why.

"Although that isn't what I came in for. I

came in to ask for an Inn at Hemlock Falls t-shirt. I left mine at the dorm. And to tell you that I can work tonight after all. Davy canceled our date."

Quill went to the credenza and pulled out a size small t-shirt, which would swamp Dina, who was a size four, dripping wet. She handed it over. Dina unselfconsciously pulled her sweatshirt over her head and replaced it with the tee.

"Do *you* think anyone's told the pet food people about the death?" Quill asked. If Dina knew, it'd be because Davy had told her. And if Davy had told her, it was useless to hope that the rest of the village hadn't heard already. Davy was a reluctant sheriff on occasion, but he was conscientious to a fault. The news would have gone over the police scanner before he made a private call to Dina. One out of three Hemlockians had police scanners in their pickup trucks. Come to think of it, the proportion was probably higher than that. "Did you talk to Davy?"

"I talked to Davy. But I talked to some of the guys in the village, too." Her brown eyes widened. "It's awful."

God only knew what kind of garbled story Olivia may have heard already. Driven by guilt, Quill leaped to her feet. "I'd better go find Mrs. Oberlie. It'd be terrible if she heard some horrible version of what happened."

"What could be more horrible than what did happen?" Dina asked.

"Not much, I admit," Quill said. "But it must have been quick. I hope so at least."

Dina shook her head. "Getting ground up into pork sausage? How quick could that be?"

"Cripes," Meg said. "you didn't say anything about *that,* Quill."

For a long moment, Quill found herself speechless. Finally, she managed, "That is absolutely not true."

"It isn't? That's what I heard when I got into town this morning."

"That is utterly ridiculous. She was hit over the head. With a blunt instrument of some sort."

"Really? For Pete's sake. I should have known it was a crock," Dina said disgustedly. "I stopped down at the Croh Bar for a cup of coffee before I came to work and the place was full of people talking all about it."

"The coffee's better here," Meg said shrewdly. "You stopped at the Croh Bar for the gossip. I should go down there myself. I'll bet Quill didn't tell me everything."

Dina shrugged. "Well that's what everyone

39

was talking about. Sausage, they said. Betty already'd taken it off the breakfast menu by the time I got there. Which was a good idea. It certainly put *me* off sausage for a while." She bit her lip regretfully. "But you say it's a crock."

"It most certainly is a crock!" Quill said heatedly. "Who in the world started that rumor? That's just revolting!" She grabbed her hair with both hands and tugged at it. It was red and springy and flew up in a wild halo around her head. "Ugh! If that gets around we're going to be swarmed with media."

"You're right about that," Meg said sunnily. "I can see the headlines now: 'Secretary Ground to a Halt.' "

"Come to think of it, Davy didn't say anything at all about the sausage part, so it has to be bogus," Dina said with an air of finality. "And I heard about the murder first from him."

Quill frowned at her. "Well, you just put the kibosh on that particular rumor. Good grief. I've really got to find the IAPFP people now. Where are they, Dina?"

"The Tavern Lounge," Dina said. "At least, Mrs. Oberlie is. When the pet food people broke for lunch, they never went back to meeting again. And the conference room's a disaster area, by the way. According to Doreen."

"Oh?" Quill frowned. IAPFP had booked the conference room for the entire week. Although the Monday meeting had been loud and contentious, the six conventioneers had left the usual sorts of mess in the conference room: used coffee cups, overflowing wastebaskets, crumbs on the floor. What more could they have done to the conference room? Quill was suddenly reminded of the three-day visit of the members of the Church of the Rolling Moses some years before. "Uh-oh. They didn't rip the white boards off the wall to make a replica of the tomb at Gethsemane? Did they?"

"Nope. Just broke up chairs. And dented the Sheetrock a bit. Nate says that Mr. Barnstaple and Mr. Kittleburger started mixing it up."

"Mixing it up?" Quill repeated.

Dina struck a boxing pose. "You know, throwing punches at each other. And smashing the chairs. Stuff like that." Dimples appeared in Dina's cheeks. "Doreen got out her mop."

"Good," Quill said. Their seventy-two-year-old housekeeper was formidable when roused. "Did that break it up?"

41

"Nope. Doreen was about to whack Mr. Kittleburger a good one, but Mrs. Oberlie put a stop to the whole shebang and everybody sort of skulked off. Except Mrs. Oberlie. She went to the Tavern Lounge and started slugging back gin. She's still there, as far as I know. And that little dog of hers, too."

Gin? Quill glanced at the clock on her rosewood desk. It was just after one.

"So," Dina said. "What do you want me to do first?"

Quill blinked. "Be the receptionist, I guess. Was there something else?"

"I could spend some time at the Croh Bar and squelch that sausage rumor." Dina pushed her glasses up her nose and regarded Quill with sparkling eyes. "Or I could maybe get started on helping you with the murder investigation. You know what I found online the other day? I found this little dingus that you can use to bug a room. They'll ship it to us overnight, if you want."

"No investigation," Quill said. "We're leaving this one up to the police. At least for now," she amended. "And for heaven's sake, don't even think about bugging the guests' rooms. It's a class D felony, or whatever."

"Of course we're investigating this," Meg

said briskly. "We'll never get rid of these horrible guests if we don't. Dina, I think I'll go down to the Croh Bar and squelch that sausage rumor and see if I can pick up any other good rumors. You can come with me if you want."

Quill looked from one to the other in panic. "You two aren't really going to take off for the Croh Bar? There's too much to do here."

"Bugging the rooms, for instance!" Meg said. "Dina, how many of those little dinguses could we buy?"

"Funny," Quill said. "As in not-at-all-funny. If we're going to investigate, we'll do it the legal way. Tech-free snooping. Well." She rose to her feet reluctantly. "I'm going to find Olivia Oberlie. And I would appreciate it, Meg, if you would send some tea. Coffee's even better. If she's been swilling gin for a couple of hours, she'll need it. And I'd appreciate even more, Dina, if you would . . ."

"Gotcha," Dina said cheerily. "Croh Bar it is. Just kidding," she added hastily. "Sorry. I forgot what a horrible day you've had."

"I certainly have," Quill said glumly. "And it's just going to get worse."

CHAPTER 3

Ground into sausage
Ugh.

Quill walked slowly down the slate-floored hall that led from the reception area to the Tavern Lounge. There wasn't any doubt in her mind that there'd be a murder inquiry. Within hours, the Inn would be filled not only with the homicide team from nearby Syracuse, but a clutch of reporters, TV cameramen, and garden-variety thrill seekers. She knew — from past, equally distressing cases — that the furor would die down within days. The wayward attention of the public would turn to other crimes in other places.

She had learned, too, that it was a rare guest who actually canceled reservations under circumstances like the one she and Meg faced now. But there'd be an effect. The kitchen staff would get cranky. The meals would be late. The housekeeping staff would get wound up and call in sick. The guests would get drunker than they usually did, and the wait staff would get harassed and threaten to quit. The inquiry would be a huge disruption.

Quill hated huge disruptions. Her idea of a perfect day was one in which absolutely nothing happened.

She and Meg had to solve this murder, and quickly, too.

Quill stopped just short of the entrance to the Tavern Lounge and thought it over. The IAPFP convention was due to disband on Friday. This was Tuesday. It was pretty unlikely that the police would get through all that they had to do in three and a half days. The coming weekend was fully booked with a whole new set of guests. And if the police were going to hold over any of IAPFP's members for questioning, not only would other accommodations have to be found for the incoming guests but the possible suspects-in-residence would get angrier as the investigation wore on. And Meg was right. The members of the IAPFP made mink look like cuddly house pets. Unless someone uncovered the identity of the murderer pretty darn quick, it was going to be a heck of a week.

A sweaty hand at the back of her neck

startled her back to the present.

"Gotcha!" Rudy Baranga said gleefully. "Guess I snuck up on *you,* little lady."

"Mr. Baranga," Quill acknowledged, coldly. "Is there something I can do for you?"

Rudy Baranga was built like a muscular pear. He had a small, balding head with a few strands of dyed black hair swept artfully across his scalp, and shoulders that sloped into a substantial belly. In Quill's private hierarchy of Horrible Guests, he was a Grabber, just one step up from the Lascivious Snickerer. He was also one of the six members of the International Association of Pet Food Providers she currently had under suspicion of the murder of Lila Longstreet.

Quill eyed him severely. He was a meat wholesaler, she recalled, a supplier to the manufacturing members of the IAPFP. And Pamela Durbin, owner of the infamous Pampered Puppy Palace, had intimated that Maxwell Kittleburger depended on Rudy for a lot more than pig's ears. "I do believe," Pamela had said in her gossipy way, "that the man's *connected.*"

"Do for me? Other than do me?" Rudy snickered meaningfully. "Nah. Thought I'd head into the bar for a pop, is all. The meeting we was all at's been postponed."

Quill opened the door to the Lounge and motioned him through ahead of her. She'd learned the hard way not to let a Grabber get behind you.

Rudy lunged into the room, then stopped short and gazed at the Lounge appreciatively. "Nice place," he approved. "First time I been in here in the daytime. Most bars don't show up as good in the daylight." He gave an approving whistle. "No crap on the floor, either."

"Excuse me, Mr. Baranga. I'd like to catch Mrs. Oberlie, if I can." Quill edged around him, and scanned the room for the pet psychic.

Rudy stepped aside, obligingly. "Great ambiance, too. Where'd you get them?" Rudy pointed a hairy thumb at the round tables arranged around the slate floor. The tops had been created out of wood from a gym floor Quill had scrounged when the old Hemlock Falls High School had been renovated. "Those tops are pretty damn great."

"I designed them," Quill admitted. "And we had a local finish carpenter make them up."

"Nice," Rudy said. "I like that bar top, too. Mahogany, innit?"

"Yes," Quill said in an abstracted way. "It

47

dates from the nineteen-twenties, when the Inn was a speakeasy."

Olivia herself wasn't at any of the tables. But there was a large, wildly flowered tote bag stashed under the table by the french doors leading to the outside terrace. A sequined fuchsia bolero wrap hung over the adjacent chair. There was no trace of the gin on the table, which didn't mean much; the waitstaff would have cleared away the dirty glasses almost before they met the tabletop. There was no trace of the dog, either. So perhaps Olivia had taken the animal outside for a short run. Its name, Quill recalled, was Little Bit.

"Buy you one?" Rudy offered, with a nod toward the long bar.

"Perhaps later," Quill said tactfully. "Although . . ." Rudy was not only a suspect, but a potential mine of information. She hesitated just long enough for Rudy to make up her mind for her.

"You should always make time for a pop!" He put his hand under her elbow and steered her toward the bar.

Nate had his back to them as he restocked the shelves on the back wall. Rudy settled himself onto a bar stool and pulled Quill down next to him. "Barkeep!" he said, and snapped his fingers. Finger-snappers came above Grabbers on the Horribles list, but not by much. Quill sighed. With luck, she could slide away as soon as Nate gave Rudy a drink.

Nate turned around and gave Quill a good-natured grin. No one at the Inn had a good idea what Nate actually looked like. Most of his face was concealed by a huge brown beard. He was almost as broad as he was wide; not fat, but solid.

"Hey, boss," he said.

"Hey, yourself."

His gaze flickered to Rudy. "Mr. Baranga? The Johnny Walker Blue?"

Rudy slapped his chubby thigh. "Hot damn. Only been in here the once before, and lookit that. He got it in one. I got a fin for guys like you." He slapped a five-dollar bill on the table. "Go ahead, sport. It's yours. And you can put the booze on my tab, like before." He beamed at Quill. "You got a classy place here, baby. Now what can I do you for?"

Quill looked at him assessingly. Ten years of inn keeping had taught her more about human beings than she sometimes wanted to know. But she'd bet the sum of the unpaid bills in her desk drawer that the man hadn't heard about Lila Longstreet's death. Not even the insensitive Rudy could be that oblivious, if only because Lila was someone he must have known well.

"Nothing for me right now, Mr. Baranga. I can't stay long. I was just looking for Mrs. Oberlie, actually. Have you seen her around?"

Rudy scowled. "That broad? This about replacing those chairs? You wanna get paid for those, you're right. You should be looking for her."

"Mrs. Oberlie smashed up the chairs?" Quill asked, startled. "My goodness. I thought that was Mr. Kittleburger."

"Nah. Good old Maxie pitched the chair at Bumbottle. Bumbottle threw it back at him and missed. That sucker lamed into the wall. Broke the chair. And the wall, too, come to think of it."

"Bum . . . ? Oh, you mean Mr. Kittleburger threw a chair at Mr. Barnstaple."

"But it was Livy stirred the whole hoo-ha up. She's the president, right? If we got a couple disagreements amongst us, like we do now and then, she's supposed to be casting oil all over the waters, like they say."

There were several things about this speech that bemused Quill. The first was Mr. Baranga's grammar, which was belied by his obstreperous manner. Nobody paid much attention to the proper use of "among" versus "between" anymore. The second was the reference to oil on the waters, which was quite biblical for a guy who was supposed to be Kittleburger's muscle. She studied him. Perhaps there was more to Rudy than met the critical innkeeper's eye.

"And she didn't? Calm things down, I mean?"

Rudy snorted. "Stirred 'em up, more like."

Quill accepted a club soda from Nate with a nod of thanks. "What broke the meeting up? Other than the chair-flinging, I mean."

"What breaks any meeting up?" Rudy said.

"Well," Quill said. "I'm the secretary of our local Chamber of Commerce, and all kinds of things break our meetings up. A few months ago we had a pretty significant women's rights issue over a . . . um . . . well, it was a nudie bar, to be perfectly frank."

Rudy waved the hand that wasn't holding his Johnny Walker Blue. "My question was, whaddayacallit? Rhetorical. What broke this morning's meeting up was what's been breaking the meetings up all week." He slapped his glass down on the bar top. Nate obligingly filled it up again.

"And that was what?" Quill asked, after a long moment.

"Huh?"

"What broke the meeting up?"

"Oh." Rudy sipped his drink in a ruminative way. "It's like this, see. I ship meat. All kinds of meat. Pork, beef, chicken, goat, whatever." He shrugged in a mildly defensive way. "And it's offal, right? The leftovers, if you get my drift. I mean, for pet food, whaddya want? Chicken feet gotta lot a protein. Just ask them Haitians. They make soup out of the feet, if you can believe it."

Quill ignored this.

"So Bumsteeple . . ."

"Mr. Barnstaple," Quill said, more for clarification than anything else. It was useless to try and sensitize the Rudy Barangas of this world.

"Right. See, he wants us to go vegetarian."

"Vegetarian? You mean he wants the members of the International Association of Pet Food Providers to manufacture vegetarian pet food?"

"You got it, cutie."

"But, can dogs and cats survive on a vegetarian diet?" Quill asked.

Rudy grunted. Quill didn't know if that was a yes or a no.

"But what's to prevent Mr. Barnstaple from going ahead and making vegetarian pet food all by himself?"

"He does already. He's owns that Vegan Vittles."

"Surely he doesn't want all of the members to drop what they're doing now?"

"Yep, he does," Rudy said. "Matter of principle, he says. Me, I think it's something else." He looked wise. "You know how people pay a bundle for this organic stuff? They'll pay a bundle for organic dog food, too, specially if it's vegan or whatever Millard calls it." Rudy sighed happily. "Thing is, in America, principles cost you, see?"

"But why should you all have to go along with it?"

Rudy swiveled around on his bar stool and pointed toward the french doors leading out to the terrace. "Her. That's why. Says meat's bad for our image. And you know what kind of clout she's got."

Olivia Oberlie.

The fuchsia bolero, which had been draped over the chair arm, was now draped across the shoulders of a large purple-haired woman in a resplendent purple caftan. Olivia sat at the table closest to the doors. Her strange and luminous eyes — pale turquoise, and in Quill's opinion, a large part of the reason for her mystique — stared unseeingly straight ahead. Rudy was right about Olivia's clout. Her TV show was incredibly popular. Her face appeared with regularity in *People* magazine as pet psychic to the stars. Everybody wanted Olivia to talk to their animals. And everybody would believe her if she claimed that dogs preferred highly priced carrots to eating their bovine friends.

Olivia's flowered tote bag now sat on the table in front of her. It was wriggling slightly. Quill hoped it was her dog, Little Bit, in the tote, and not a member of the pet psychic's more exotic fraternity of reptiles, flying mammals, and rodents.

Rudy swung back to the bar and thumped his glass on the bar top. Nate filled it up again. Rudy addressed him in a cozily confidential way, "Sport? You know that TV show she's got?"

"Mind Doesn't Matter," Nate said. "Sure. I've seen it."

"I've heard of it," Quill said.

"It ain't half bad," Rudy said thoughtfully.

"It's terrific." Nate put his elbows on the bar and leaned forward. "You know, there's got to be something to that psychic stuff."

Rudy hunched over the bar. "You're right about that, partner. You see that one show where the elephant told Olivia he had to get back to the savanna or he'd die of loneliness? Saddest thing I've ever seen in my life."

"Yuh," Nate said huskily. His eyes looked suspiciously moist.

"Choked me up," Rudy said. "Those elephants, they're great guys." He shook his head sadly. "It's a crime to put 'em in zoos, that's what it is."

Both men stared at their feet and sniffled.

Quill wondered briefly if she'd wandered into a bar on a planet not her own.

"Guys," she said. "I'm missing some information here. Are you telling me that Olivia supports the vegetarian pet food movement?"

Rudy wiped his eyes with a grubby handkerchief. "That'd be correct."

"And that she's going to pressure your group members to stop making meat-based pet food and grind up what — celery, lettuce, carrots?"

Rudy made a pretend gun of his thumb and forefinger and pointed at her. "You got it."

Quill tugged thoughtfully at the curl over her left ear. Vegetarian pet food seemed unlikely to provide a motive for murder. It was a squabble issue, not a smack-you-over-the-head-with-a-blunt-instrument issue. Certainly, Olivia Oberlie's support of the movement was logical; she made her living — a highly profitable one, if *People* magazine was right — by playing on her viewers' undiscriminating affection for the animal kingdom at large. But if she wanted the IAPFP to become a wholly vegan organization, there was nothing to stop meat-manufacturing members from forming an association of their own. She'd bet her best set of camel-hair paintbrushes that something else was going on. Something that was a motive for murder. And she had to discover what that something else was.

Olivia had settled into a stagily contemplative pose at her table. Out of the corner of her eye, Quill saw the newest member of the waitstaff, Cassie Winterborne, come through the archway leading from the Inn dining room to the Lounge. Cassie must have drawn the afternoon shift. Olivia gestured grandly to her, and the little waitress trotted to her table. Quill slid off the stool and headed over to Olivia's table herself. As she left, she heard Rudy ask Nate, "You see that episode where Olivia got the true story out of that tiger that half chomped his trainer's head off?"

"Pretty amazing," Nate agreed. "I say it's always a good thing to have the other guy's point of view. Myself, I didn't believe the trainer one bit. The tiger had the real story."

"You got that right. I'll have another Blue there, sport."

Quill arrived at the table and smiled at Cassie, whose cheeks were pink with star-struck excitement. "Miss Oberlie just wanted a bit of lunch, Quill," she said. "It's okay to bring food in here, isn't it?"

"Absolutely."

"Thank you *so* much, my dears." Olivia's voice was as much a part of her on-camera charisma as her turquoise eyes. It was warm and luxuriant, like the best sort of caramel. Her gaze drifted dreamily to the view of the falls from the french doors. "I walked outside this exquisite place, for, oh, I don't know how long. Eternity, perhaps. Or perhaps it was only a moment. The very air here is filled with peace."

"You're going to love the Quiche Quilliam," Cassie breathed. "It'll make you feel peaceful, too."

Olivia laughed kindly. "Bless you, my dear. We're quite famished after our walkies. Aren't we, Little Bit?"

The tote bag thrashed wildly.

"Does Little Bit want something besides the fresh carrots, Miss Oberlie?" Cassie asked anxiously.

"I'll ask." The psychic closed those astonishing eyes. In repose, her face was plain, with a heavy jaw and a thin-lipped mouth. Quill wondered if she wanted to paint her. It was the expressiveness of Olivia's face that lent it its charm. Getting that expressiveness into a portrait would be an interesting challenge.

Her eyes flew open. "Little Bit says, perhaps a few green beans?"

"Oh, wow," Cassie said. "For sure. I'll get her as many green beans as she wants. Can I *learn* to talk to animals, Miss Oberlie? I mean, I would just like, totally freak, if I could figure out what *my* dog Charley thinks about."

Olivia shook her head, regretfully. "I'm sorry, my dear. Truly sorry. If I could pass my Gift to the many, I would. But, alas, it seems that I alone have been Chosen. However, if you would care to bring your pet to see me, I'd be delighted to chat with Charley." She smiled with warm benevolence.

"Wow, sure. Well. I'll get right to that order, Miss Oberlie," Cassie said breathlessly. "Is there anything else?"

"There is, as a matter of fact," Quill intervened. "Would you check and see what happened to that coffee Meg was going to bring in?"

"Sure, Quill. And, Miss Oberlie?"

Olivia merely gazed at her warmly. "I see into your heart," the look said. "And I like what I see."

"I just love your show. I just love it."

Olivia smiled. "Thank you, Cassie, dear."

Quill waited until Cassie trotted off to the kitchen and then sat down.

"You were having quite a conversation with our Mr. Baranga?" Olivia said interrogatively, before Quill could speak.

"Uh, yes."

"I assume that you heard about our little *contretemps* in the conference room this morning." Those amazing eyes were sorrowful.

"Well, yes, but that's not . . ."

Olivia put a warm hand over Quill's. "Please accept my sincere apologies on behalf of our association. We're in the middle of a major policy change, and I'm afraid tempers fray." She sat back with a sigh. "If you would total up the bill for the breakage and see that it gets sent to the association headquarters, I'll see to it personally."

"Well, thank you," Quill said. "But there's no need for you to take the trouble."

"No trouble at all. We're short a secretary as you know, and I am happy to pitch in."

Short a secretary? Quill straightened hopefully. Perhaps Olivia *had* heard about the death.

"Of course, Lila won't be resuming her duties until late next week. It takes some time to get these things sorted out, I'm afraid. But she *will* be back."

For a horrible moment, Quill had a vision of a reanimated Lila at a computer keyboard, blood-stained fingers typing merrily away. "Her affairs?" Quill said, faintly.

"Her poor mother passed on quite suddenly, you know."

"Her mother?"

"You are aware she had to leave the conference on family business. That she checked out yesterday?"

Quill bit her lip.

"Such a shame, too," Olivia continued in orotund tones. "You and your sister have provided the most wonderful hotel experience for us all. I know Lila was enjoying it as much as I am. As a matter of fact, I've been making arrangements to shoot one of my *Mind* segments here, as you may know already."

"At the dog and puppy show," Quill said. She'd forgotten about that. The dog show was one of the Chamber of Commerce's newest fundraisers.

Olivia waved one arm in an imperial gesture. "The peace here is . . . ineffably peaceful. The channels of human mind to that of the Lesser Ones are well and truly open here. This is a place that may well bring me to the Peak of my Powers."

Quill decided that the only way she could be forced to watch *Mind Doesn't Matter* was if she was roped and hog-tied. She also decided that somebody else could give Olivia Oberlie the bad news about Lila. She couldn't stand to be talked to in capital letters. She made a move to get up. "Well. I have a few things to see to this morning. I'll just . . ."

From across the room, Rudy yelled in astonishment. "Ground into sausage? You gotta be kidding me!" He turned on the bar stool and shouted, "Livy! Come and get a load of this!"

Nate shot Quill a guilty glance. Quill sat down again. She took a deep breath, "Miss Oberlie?"

"My fans call me Olivia. I do hope that you will, too."

"Olivia, then. I'm afraid that your stay here may not be as pleasant as we could wish," Quill began.

Olivia Oberlie could swear like a trooper.

61

And at the news of Lila's death, she did. The cozily caramel voice turned brittle. The turquoise eyes glittered with rage. Olivia's highly valued peace of mind, in fact, deserted her completely.

"I'm truly sorry," Quill said, when the psychic at last ran down. "Cassie should be here with the coffee any minute."

Olivia lifted her lip in a snarl. "Coffee, hell. What I need is another gin."

Quill caught Nate's eye and gestured. He nodded and turned to the liquor bottles.

"Not," Olivia said, as Nate placed a tumbler of what appeared to be straight gin in front of her, "because I liked Lila. I hated the little witch. But I do like good gin." She took a gulp and smacked her lips. "And this is good gin." She set the glass back on the table with a thump. "Well, goddamit. What the hell am I gonna do now?" She looked up as Cassie placed a plate of Quiche Quilliam in front of her and her theatrical manner dropped on her like a cloak. "Marvelous," she said. "Just marvelous!"

"And I brought Little Bit some water along with the veggies," Cassie said. She edged the two bowls onto the floor. Olivia opened the tote bag and called, "Bit? Bitty? Din-din!"

A snow white Bichon Frise stuck its head

out of the tote and surveyed them with its button eyes. Olivia set the dog tenderly on the floor. The dog looked at the vegetables in some bewilderment, and then began to eat in a resigned sort of way. "She thanks you most sincerely, Cassie!" Olivia said.

"Oh, wow," Cassie breathed. Quill raised her eyebrows. Cassie needed another few days at waitress training. She cleared her throat. Loudly. Cassie cast an apologetic grimace Quill's way. "Sorry. Sorry. I'll be back to check on your meal in a bit, Olivia." She grimaced again. "I mean Miss Ober-lie."

Olivia chuckled as Cassie bounced back to the hallway leading to the Inn proper. "That kind of enthusiasm's really quite attractive, you know."

"It is," Quill agreed. "But our customers expect the more traditional mode of service. Unobtrusive. Mannerly. Not . . . bouncy. I don't know what's gotten into her."

Olivia shrugged in a deprecating way. "My fans," she said with a large gesture, "are frequently unrestrained. It's my Gift, you know. It draws them."

"I can see that," Quill said in a voice totally devoid of expression.

Olivia cast her a shrewd, assessing look, and relaxed into more human behavior. "It must be difficult to get staff up here," she said, after a bite of Quiche Quilliam. "Mmm. This is quite good. Quite good. Anyway." She made that imperial wave again. "This place is in the back of beyond. On a road to nowhere. You must be bored out of your skull here in the winter. Can't be much profit in a place like this."

So much for the ineffable peace of Hemlock Falls. "We have very few business problems here," Quill said in the politest tone she could manage. "The Inn has done very well for us."

"Business problems," Olivia echoed heavily. She stuck her fork in her quiche and knocked back another half inch of gin. "Oh, my god. Am I going to have business problems! Damn that Lila, anyway."

"Was she really that crucial to the association?" Quill asked in surprise.

"In the normal run of things? Hell, no. The problem's her voting stock."

"Oh?" Quill said alertly.

"Thank goodness I found you, Livy." Pamela Durbin settled into the chair next to Quill in a haze of lavender sachet and a swirl of full skirts. She carried a large lace-trimmed tote that contained a cross-looking Pekinese. "Hello, Quill. How are you?" Her thick Georgia accent slurred the phrase into "haaryew."

"I'm well, thank you," Quill said. "I hear the store is doing well, too."

"Money's rollin' in hand over fist," Pamela said cheerily. "Pookie here's jus' over the moon about it, and so am I." Pookie curled his upper lip over his eyeteeth and snarled at nothing in particular.

Pamela was a fleshy woman with loosely permed ash-blonde hair styled off her face. Quill had never seen her without a strand of pearls and diamond ear studs. "I'm just so glad I picked Hemlock Falls as the ideal place to open the Puppy Palace. D'ya know I had some customers all the way in from Syracuse this morning? Come all this way jus' to look at my Shiz Tsu." She smiled widely. A bit of her red lipstick had rubbed off on an eyetooth. "And you know it's me you have to thank for scheduling this convention here, Quill. I've been a loyal IAPFP-er for years and years, haven't I, Livy? I know what our members like."

"I do know that you talked Ms. Longstreet into booking the convention here at the Inn," Quill said. "And I certainly won't forget it."

"The whole *town's* got me to thank for the dog and puppy show this Saturday," Pamela added complacently.

65

Pookie barked.

"Did you hear that?" Pamela said delightedly. "Pookie said, 'Right,' didn't he, Olivia? I swear I can understand everything this dog says to me." She smiled sweetly at Olivia. "Maybe I'm getting psychic, too."

Olivia's eyes narrowed to slits. "I sincerely doubt that, Pamela. And was there something specific you wanted from me?"

Pamela leaned across the table, her substantial bosom flattened against the top. She dropped into a dramatic whisper. "You heard about Lila?"

Quill marveled at the speed with which Pamela had connected with the Hemlock Falls' gossip mill. She'd only been in town two months, but she was already at the center of the mill, doing more than her fair share to keep the rumors flowing.

Olivia didn't respond for a moment, but gazed distantly over Pamela's shoulder. Her eyes closed. She raised her hand, palm outward and said in a faraway voice: "I will address that in due course." She blinked. "Sorry. I felt — something coming through. No matter. And yes, Pamela, I had heard about Lila. But I will not discuss it now. We will wait for the others to join us."

"Is that what you See?" Pamela breathed. "That the others are going to join us soon?

What others?"

"Them." Olivia pointed. Quill turned around in her chair. Millard Barnstaple shambled in from the flagstone terrace. Tall, thin, and dressed as usual in baggy chinos and a denim work shirt, Millard's long graying hair was tied back in a ponytail. He gazed benignly at them though wire-rimmed glasses. His wife Priscilla followed him. Quill wondered again at the contrast between them. Priscilla was as neat and as well tailored as Millard was sloppy. The dissimilarities weren't limited to wardrobe. Priscilla was as precise as her neatly cropped hair. Millard, on the other hand mumbled, muttered, and blustered in all the wrong places.

"Well, well, well," Millard said in a reedy voice. He slouched into the chair next to Olivia. "And what are you three ladies up to?" He smiled, showing well cared for teeth. "Planning another murder? Ha ha."

"Don't be an ass, Millard," Priscilla snapped. Her face was white, and more than usually strained. "And find me a chair if you please."

Millard nodded agreeably, extended one long arm, and pulled over a chair from a neighboring table. There was a short yelp and Millard jumped. "*Damn* that dog," he said furiously. "He bit me."

"You knocked him with the chair leg. He saw that as an attack," Olivia said, "and so, I must say, did I." She picked Little Bit off the floor, settled him in her lap, and eyed the Barnstaples with imperious disdain. Pookie the Peke emerged from the depths of Pamela's tote and snarled. Little Bit, in his turn, snarled back.

Millard flung his hands up in a mock defense. "Sorry, sorry. It was old Millard's fault, no question. Don't want to start a dog fight, here."

"That Peke's in terrible shape, Pamela." Priscilla settled her horn-rimmed glasses more firmly on her nose. "You ought to exercise him more often. And stop feeding him crap. Do you both good to trim off the excess fat. There's not a ringmaster on the whole circuit that wouldn't throw him out of competition."

"That may be your opinion," Pamela said with sudden tears in her eyes. "For what your opinion is worth."

"I, at least, have a fundamental understanding of dogs. I don't think they're people in dog suits."

"You've got a nerve," Pamela said in dudgeon.

"Well, Priscilla! Pamela!" Quill interrupted brightly. "It sounds as if you both have a lot of experience with dog shows. Perhaps you could give the Chamber some advice about the dog and puppy show the town is hosting on Saturday, Priscilla. There's a Chamber meeting here in a little while. I'm sure we could all benefit from your advice."

Millard gave a shout of laughter, and then muttered, "Sorry." Priscilla flushed dark red. Olivia half-closed her eyes and smiled like a cat. Pamela fluttered, charm bracelets tinkling like wind chimes.

"Just forget it," Priscilla muttered.

So for whatever reason, Priscilla's dog expertise was a volatile topic for this group. Quill cast around for a safer topic of conversation. "I haven't been down to see the Puppy Palace yet, Pamela," Quill said, in desperation. "Have you finished painting?"

Priscilla snorted in loud contempt, "Pampered puppies, my foot. You're nothing more than a pet store."

"I love dogs," Pamela said earnestly. "And I believe in them and I take care of them. You save that 'pet store' snottiness for the kind of person who buys from puppy mills."

"You certainly have a lot of luxury goods at your place," Quill intervened. "Or so I hear."

Pamela dimpled. "Why, yes I have. And I'm jus' *dyin'* for your thoughts on my decoratin' scheme. Rumor says you're a famous artist, Quill. I just knew I should have asked you about what color to paint my walls."

Millard gave a shrill hoot of laugher. Priscilla smiled sourly. "She's not that kind of artist, Pam. You are *such* a fool."

Pamela's blue eyes filled with more tears. She placed a damp, plump hand over Quill's. "Did I say somethin' offensive? I'm so sorry."

"Certainly not. And I'd love to come and see your store." Quill snatched at that reliable diversion and asked, "Anyone for coffee?" just as she saw Meg approach the table, a laden tray in both hands.

"And a side of sausage?" Millard chortled.

This met with a disapproving silence. Millard slouched farther down in his chair and shrugged, "Just kidding, ladies. Millard's quite a kidder. So. You've all heard the news? About Lila being ground up into sausage?"

"Awful," Pamela said. "Just purely awful."

Priscilla's lips tightened. She stared fixedly at Millard.

"I'm afraid it was no surprise to me," Olivia said gravely.

Pamela opened her blue eyes as wide as

they would go. "It wasn't?"

Olivia shook her head, much as Julius Caesar must have done when he refused the emperor's laurel leaves the first time. "I believe I saw something. Last night. An omen."

"Olivia," Pamela's voice was hushed. "Do you mean . . . do you think? That is, your Gift . . ." she turned to Quill. "You know, of course, about Olivia's Gift?"

Quill nodded.

Pamela reached out and touched Olivia's purple-clad forearm. "Do you think it's growin'? So that you can read people?"

Olivia nodded gravely. "I *have* wondered about it. Yes. This past year, especially." Olivia brought her hand to her brow in a gesture that said she was infinitely weary. She dropped her hand suddenly. "But no. No," she said, decisively. She sat very upright in her chair, reminding Quill of nothing so much as a giant eggplant. "My Gift, such as it is, is directed solely to the lives and welfare of the Lesser Ones. Except." She went very still. "Except that I see another murder!"

CHAPTER 4

The noise in the Lounge was horrific.

"Olivia 'saw' another murder, huh?" Meg said furiously. "What she *saw* was the television crew from WKFC barging through the terrace doors. Just in time to catch the 'prophecy' on tape. Argh! Just *look* at those idiots!"

Quill stood between Nate and Meg behind the bar, watching the melee with bemusement. She wondered how much of a rat she'd be if she just slipped out the back way and went home. She'd moved into Myles' cobblestone house immediately after their marriage. It sat at the edge of a small, heavily treed ravine with a stream and a pool at the bottom. They owned the ten acres of woods surrounding the house. And it was quiet. So quiet that you could hear the bass splashing in the shallow pool at night. In marked contrast to the peace at her new home, the Inn was never truly quiet; a twenty-seven-room, two-hundred-year-old building at the edge of a thriving village was never quiet. It was rarely this noisy, either.

"Don't even think about it," Meg said.

Quill jumped guiltily. "About what?"

"You've got that look. Like you're planning on sneaking out the back door. Don't you *dare.* Besides. We've been through worse."

Quill didn't think so.

"And there's a Chamber of Commerce meeting in about half an hour, so you're stuck. Anyway," Meg added optimistically, "this crowd will clear out. Half the people in here are here for the Chamber meeting. The whole thing's a matter of bad timing."

The news of Channel 15's arrival — with popular anchor Angela Stoner at the head of the crew — had spread like Mazola on linoleum. Anyone within jogging distance of the Tavern Lounge had shown up to get in on the action. In a matter of minutes, the Lounge's teal-blue walls were lined with gawkers, and the empty tables filled with curiosity seekers.

And there was a lot to gawk at. Millard Barnstaple argued furiously with his wife. Robin Finnegan, the disbarred lawyer, sat with them, his legs crossed, his mouth sulky, and his indifferent eyes on the raging Priscilla, whose raised voice had the penetrating volume of a buzz saw. Her rant, Quill noted with interest, appeared to be about Millard's refusal to buy something. Since the phrase "less than twenty million, you idiot" appeared with regularity, Quill assumed the something in question was large.

In the opposite corner, Pamela had an ineffectual hold on Pookie the Peke, who was busy outyapping the smaller, shriller-voice Little Bit by a country mile. Most everyone's attention was on the activities in the middle of the room, where Olivia held court.

Olivia was in full professional spate. Angela Stoner leaned attentively toward her, microphone in hand. The Channel 15 Steadicam rolled tape. Victoria Finnegan, elegant and unmistakably a lawyer in her gray pinstriped suit and her Hermes briefcase, sat at Olivia's side. Occasionally, Victoria's attention was drawn to her husband Robin, who ignored Victoria and the battling Barnstaples with arrogant aloofness.

The Lounge itself was a mess. Bits of shattered coffee cups and the best part of a Sachertorte littered the wood floor. Doreen Muxworthy-Stoker, the Inn's septuagenarian housekeeper, wielded a mop in the middle of the detritus with a nice disregard for the newspeople's ankles. Her gray hair bristled around her sharp-nosed face. She looked like a cranky chicken. Once in a while, she looked up at Quill and winked. Quill always winked back. Doreen had been with the Inn almost from the outset, showing up at the kitchen door with her suitcase in one hand, and a bottle of floor polish in the other.

Cassie Winterborne wound her way through this chaos serving coffee and drinks and uttering an occasional "Wow!"

Rudy Baranga surveyed all of this from his bar stool with the foggy concentration of the truly swozzled.

"We should get her a hockey stick," Meg muttered.

"Who?"

"Doreen."

Doreen swung the mop with vigor. Angela Stoner gave a shriek, jumped hastily aside, and shouted, "Cut tape, dammit!"

"Score one for the home team!" Meg shouted. "Hit her again, Doreen!" She lobbed a handful of peanuts over the bar. Pookie the Peke shut up as soon as his beady black eyes fixed on the peanuts. He lunged off Pamela's lap and charged, knocking Angela Stoner off balance yet again.

Angela swung at the dog. The Peke snarled and lifted his leg. Angela turned the air blue with curses and swung her microphone in a lethal arc. Shrieking with dismay, Pamela dashed into the melee, grabbed the Peke by the scruff of the neck, and hoisted him into her arms. She scurried back to her table with a sob, while Pookie howled curses at Angela over Pam's shoulder.

"I suppose," Quill said after a long moment, "that we should do something."

Meg cupped her hand behind her ear. "What?"

Quill raised her voice. "I said we should do something!"

"Like what?"

"I don't know. Get up on a table and blow a trumpet. Call the cops. You suggest something."

They both looked at Nate, who had, on the rare occasions when rowdiness overcame the Lounge, served as bouncer. He shook his head regretfully. "Sorry, Quill. I don't take on females."

"There's men out there, too!" Meg said indignantly. "It's not just women!"

"But the women are making all the noise," Rudy said. He belched, and raised his finger for another shot of Johnny Walker Blue. Nate shook his head regretfully and raised the empty bottle.

Quill realized Rudy was right. If you included Pookie and Little Bit, the females were making all the noise. Although to be fair, the females outnumbered the males by a substantial margin. So statistically. . . . Quill started to count heads. Suddenly, she stiffened and cried out, "Oh, no!"

"Now what?" Meg broke off in mid-sentence as she followed Quill's pointing finger. "Oh, nuts. The cops. And not the good kind. Quick. Duck down behind the bar."

Quill dropped to the floor next to her sister.

Meg ran her hands though her hair, making it stick up in dark brown spikes all over her head. "Wait. I've got a better idea. We can't crouch down here until they leave. We'll get out of here altogether. We'll hide out at the Croh Bar and drink beer."

"Sounds good to me. What about the Chamber meeting?"

"You can forget the Chamber meeting."

Quill was secretary. She was terrible at it. "Great idea."

"But stay *down*. And follow me."

In the best covert style, they crouched, ran, and crouched again. They got as far as Rudy Baranga and the remains of his Johnny

Walker Blue before Nate leaned over the bar top and said, "Too late. He's seen ya."

They both rose to their feet under Rudy's bemused gaze.

"What are you two up to?" Rudy said.

"We just . . . see someone we'd rather avoid," Quill said.

Meg brushed peanut shells off her bare knees. "Like you'd rather avoid the avian flu," she said acidly.

"You mean those cops that just walked in?" Rudy squinted blearily at the three uniformed men filing through the terrace doors.

"Not all of them," Quill said glumly. "Just the one with a face like a ferret."

"It's the state police," Meg said unnecessarily, since the uniforms were unmistakable. "Not the cops. As such."

"Yeah?" Rudy swung his head around and looked at them with friendly interest. "You guys wanted for somethin'?"

"I thought Davy was handling Lila Longstreet's murder," Meg said crossly. "That wimp. One stupid little murder and he freaks out and calls in the state troopers. We could have handled this by ourselves."

"At least it's *quiet* in here," Quill said fervently. Which it was. The arrival of the state police had startled everyone into interested silence. Otherwise, there wasn't any positive side to this situation at all. State Police Lieutenant Anson Harker was one of the few sociopaths Quill had ever met. Come to think of it, he was probably the only true sociopath she'd ever met. Even the murderers that she and Meg had helped capture over the years had a conscience.

Harker had no conscience at all.

Harker had developed an unhealthy interest in Quill ever since a noted journalist had fallen dead at her feet years ago.

He smirked at her, crept up in his snide way, and touched the brim of his cap in a parody of politeness. He was a neatly made, compact man, with flat black eyes and a face almost totally devoid of expression. "If it isn't the Quilliam sisters," he said. "Again." His glance slid over Quill's figure like a pair of clammy hands. He barked, "Sarah Quilliam? I'm taking you in for questioning as a material witness in the murder of Lila Ann Longstreet."

"Me?" Quill said indignantly. "A material witness is someone who is involved some way with the crime. I haven't been anywhere near Lila Longstreet since she checked into the Inn three days ago!"

"So you say," Harker sneered dangerously. Quill looked around helplessly. Meg stepped in front of her and stood with her arms crossed defiantly. "You'll have to get through me before you get my sister."

"Just a moment, officer." Victoria Finnegan clicked crisply across the floor. Quill had met her when she'd checked in with her husband, but hadn't had much of a chance to get to know her. She was big-boned but very thin, the kind of slenderness that comes from rigorous dieting. She looked like a woman who denied herself as many of life's pleasures as possible. Olivia floated behind her like a large purple balloon. The TV people jostled behind Olivia. It was quite a procession.

"We'll get this on tape, guys." Angela Stoner and the Channel 15 crew elbowed their way through the rest of the curious crowd up to the bar itself. Angela stuck the microphone in Harker's face. He pushed it aside, drew his thin lips back in a grimace, and addressed Victoria with contemptuous courtesy. "And who're you?"

"I'm an attorney," she said flatly. She stepped in front of Quill and pushed her behind her back, for safety, Quill assumed. Grateful for the support, but a little bewildered by it, it took her several moments to realize that Victoria was positioning herself for the camera and didn't have Quill's safety in mind at all. You could drop a plumb line between the camera lens and her profile. If plumb lines were horizontal.

Victoria stuck out her pointed jaw, lifted her chin, and demanded, "And how do you figure that this woman is a material witness?"

"None of your business," Harker said.

Victoria addressed her questions to Quill over her shoulder to avoid losing the camera angle. "Did you see the murder, Quill?"

Quill peered over Victoria's shoulder and shook her head.

"Did you see anyone with any kind of weapon entering or leaving the scene of the crime?"

"No, of course not. If I had, I would have chased them."

Victoria opened her mouth to speak, then thought the better of it. She turned to Harker instead. "Have you established a time of death?"

"That's a police matter, counselor." The sneer in Harker's voice was palpable.

"She'd been dead several hours at least," Quill offered. "*Livor mortis* was quite marked."

Victoria accepted this with a nod. "There you are, Lieutenant. Miss Quilliam is not a material witness. She's a witness to finding

81

the body. Along with, as I understand it, about thirty grade-schoolers and a hog farmer. Officer? I demand that you let this woman go." She smiled into the cameras. "And if you need to find me officer, I'm Victoria Finnegan, attorney-at-law. You'll find my name and phone number on my website, Victoria at Finnegan.com."

"You planning on leaving my employ, Vicky?" Maxwell Kittleburger cut through the crowd like a shark in the middle of a herd of seals. Like Rudy Baranga, he had a dark fringe of hair around a balding scalp. And he was heavily built. But it was a thick, muscular stoutness that owed a lot to exercise equipment. And where Rudy exhibited a rather cheerful menace, Kittleburger's presence was both powerful and malign. His black eyes swept the crowd. "Am I missing something, here?" His voice was mild, but there was an iron-willed edge underneath. "Olivia, I thought we were reconvening the meeting at two." He looked at his watch, a diamond encrusted Rolex, and gave her a mocking smile. "It's after two. Quite a bit after two. When I didn't hear from you, I decided to come and see where the hell you all were. And here you all are. On television, no less. Are you announcing our parting of the ways?" The last part of this sentence was delivered with unmistakable malice.

"Great cut line," Angela Stoner breathed. "Stop tape."

Kittleburger looked at Rudy and gave him a nod. Rudy slid off the bar stool, hitched up his pants, and made a beeline for the Steadicam.

"Wait!" Olivia said dramatically. Her interjection was so abrupt that everyone in the room turned to look at her. She pressed the palms of both hands to her eyes. "There is something behind the curtain. Wait! I feel it coming through."

"Oh, stuff it, Olivia," Victoria said. "The camera's off."

"And I want to get through the rest of our agenda," Kittleburger said. He used his voice like a whip. "With Lila gone, I've got to get back to Iowa. So let's move it. Now."

Harker, who had watched Kittleburger with his arms folded and his face a mask, raised his voice. "You'll need to be available for police questioning, Mr. Kittleburger."

Kittleburger lifted one heavy eyebrow. "I gave my statement this morning. To your captain. You need any more information than that, you check with him. Barnstaple? Victoria? Get your asses in line."

"Y'all can meet down at my place," Pamela said breathlessly. "Y'all know the conference room isn't available this afternoon. I'm givin' a report to the Chamber on the puppy sh . . ."

Kittleburger glanced briefly at Pamela. "Shut up." He turned on his heel and walked out. Pamela subsided in a flutter of charm bracelets. Harker, his face a dull red, leaned against the bar in a posture of assumed indifference.

"Well, I'm out of here," Angela said. "I've got a deadline to meet."

"I want all of you are out of here except this witness," Harker said. He straightened up and swaggered toward Quill.

"He can't do that," Meg said indignantly. "Can he?"

Victoria shrugged. Angela and the TV crew went out the door. Olivia stalked off, presumably after Kittleburger. Pamela looked from the TV crew to Olivia and trotted after Olivia, both dogs at her heels. The rest of the people in the room, with the exception of Nate, Meg, and Quill herself, drifted out after them.

Meg squared her shoulders. She narrowed her eyes at Harker. "Nate and I are staying right here. And so is my sister. You heard Victoria Finnegan. Quill's not involved."

Harker gave Quill his reptilian half-smile.

"Your lawyer friend? She's wrong. I can pull in any witness I like for questioning. You're coming back to the barracks with me."

"Then I'm coming, too, Harker," Meg said belligerently.

Harker hiked a shoulder indifferently. "Follow along if you like. Only people on official business come along with me in the cruiser."

Harker made Quill feel her skin was crawling with spiders. He had always been careful not to say anything out of line, even more careful not to touch her; it was his sly and insinuating delivery that gave her the creeps. That and the implicit threat that if he ever found her alone . . . she shivered, inwardly. She hated the fact that by some cosmic accident, Harker had fixed on her for his unpleasant fantasies.

"There is absolutely no reason why I can't accompany Mrs. McHale in your squad car," Meg said stubbornly.

"Cruiser," Harker corrected, "and . . . who did you say?"

Meg raised one eyebrow. "You didn't know, did you? That my sister married Myles McHale two months ago? The one guy in the world who can get your ears knotted down around your socks . . ."

"Meg." Quill put a hand on her sister's

arm. She hadn't taken the time this morning to check out the color of Meg's own socks, a reliable indicator of her sister's erratic temper. She checked them out now. They were a fiery orange. Not a good omen. "Let's not blow this out of proportion. I'll be glad to give you another statement, Lieutenant. I'd appreciate it if we could do it here, though. I have a Chamber of Commerce meeting scheduled in about two minutes."

Harker scowled. "You're coming down to the barracks, with me. Your cooperation in this is a matter of law."

"She's already given the police a statement!" Meg shook Quill's hand off irritably and glared at Harker. With her hair sticking up, she looked like Medusa's younger, cuter sister.

"Is that right," Harker said flatly. But he looked uncertain.

"So she's cooperated just fine. You can use the statement Quill gave Davy Kiddermeister, Harker. She doesn't need to be interviewed again. Just like," she added with a hint of malice, "Mr. Kittleburger. You wouldn't want it to look like you were playing favorites, would you? So your little trip here to harass my sister was wasted." She glared at him. "And *please* don't let the door catch you on your way out."

"Fine." Harker blinked slowly, like a snake in the sun. "For now." He smiled, slowly. "But I'll be back. And that's a promise."

Meg watched Harker and his troopers saunter out the terrace door with her hands on her hips and her chin stuck out at a stubborn angle.

Quill eyed her sister narrowly. "Thanks. I guess. But don't you think you annoyed him just a little bit more than you needed to?"

"I'm your sister. I'll defend you to the death." She put her arm around Quill's waist and gave her a quick hug. "You're by yourself again tonight, right? Why don't I bring over some dinner around eight? And we can get comfortable with a few glasses of wine. In the meantime," she nodded toward the foyer, where Elmer Henry stood with Carol Anne Spinoza and two other Chamber of Commerce members, waiting for Quill to let them into the conference room, "our mayor awaits."

Quill looked at the group without enthusiasm. The mayor didn't drive her as buggy as Carol Ann Spinoza did, but she didn't relish the idea of spending the next hour or two in the company of either one. Carol Ann was town assessor in those years when the pro-Carol faction (those villagers vulnerable to blackmail) outnumbered the anti-Carol faction (everybody else). This was a pro-Carol year, primarily because she'd hired a detective to follow the Kiwanis Club on its annual overnight trip to Toronto, and she was able to blackmail practically every guy over forty in town.

Elmer was far less annoying than Carol, but he did have a tendency to maneuver Quill into situations she'd rather be well out of.

On the other hand, Miriam Doncaster, the town librarian, and Howie Murchison, village attorney, were two of her favorite people in Hemlock Falls.

She greeted them all with a smile.

"Conference room's locked," Elmer said. Elmer and his formidable wife Adela had emigrated from one of the Carolinas — Quill could never remember if it was North or South — so many years ago that they almost qualified as true Hemlockians in the eyes of old guard. Elmer's Southern accent had long since disappeared into the nasal vowels of upstate New York, although it re-appeared under stress. He was a little taller than short, somewhat tubby, and prone to attacks of perspiration.

"It is?" Quill felt in her pocket for the keys. "Housekeeping started cleaning up in there and didn't have time to finish. We may have to work through a bit of a mess."

"Ew," Carol Ann said. Everybody ignored this. Carol Ann's bouncy blond ponytail and pristine tennis shoes hid the soul of a germ-obsessed fascist.

"Sorry," Quill said blithely.

"I'm sure it's just fine," Miriam Doncaster said. Miriam had maintained a sort of middle-aged glamour into her fifties that was much envied by her peers. She blinked her big blue eyes at Quill and said in a low tone, "I hear *you* had a heck of a morning."

Quill rolled her eyes.

"Is this Lila Longstreet the same bottle blonde that showed up at the Croh Bar last night?"

Quill held up her hand in a "wait a sec-ond" gesture. Everyone followed Quill down the hall to the conference room, where eight or nine other Chamber members milled outside the locked door. Pamela milled among them, the dog in her arms.

"Are we gonna find another body in there?" somebody called from the back of the crowd.

Quill's answering smile was a bit strained. She opened the door, made a quick inspec-tion of the repairs she'd ordered, and then stepped back so that everyone could file past and take a seat at the long conference table that dominated the room. Miriam put herself at the end of the line and said, "Well?"

Quill said, "Did the Lila Longstreet that showed up at the Croh Bar have green eye shadow, long glittery nails, a silicone-enhanced bosom, and . . ."

Miriam's eyes rested on Howie Murchison. "An eye for other people's partners? Yep. That's the one."

"Then that's the one I found in the cooler at Hogg's," Quill said.

"Ugh. And she wasn't ground up into sausage?"

Quill rolled her eyes in exasperation.

"I should have known better," Miriam said.

"Y'all hush, now." Elmer banged the gavel on the long mahogany table. Esther West (West's Best Dress Shoppe) placed the gavel rest in front of the mayor with a disapproving click of her tongue.

"I call this Chamber meetin' to order," the mayor said. "Rev'rund? You want to lead us in prayer?"

The Very Reverend Dookie Shuttleworth rose and blessed the people, the village, the county, and the state of New York.

Quill settled next to Miriam and drew her

sketchpad from her pocket. It wasn't the one with last month's meeting notes on it. "Nuts."

Miriam raised an eyebrow.

"I left last month's notes somewhere."

"It doesn't matter. You can never read what you wrote anyhow."

This was true. Quill had an idiosyncratic shorthand that no one could read but herself. And if too long a time elapsed between the note-taking and use of the notes, she couldn't decipher them, either.

Elmer rapped the gavel, "Quill? You got last month's notes?"

Miriam raised her hand. "I move that we suspend the reading of the previous month's agenda."

"So moved," said Harland Peterson.

Quill gave him a grateful glance. The big farmer grinned back at her.

Elmer sighed. "S'okay. Well, last month's business is more ideas for Chamber fundraisers. Life's getting more expensive, people, and our funds are in low water. Esther, you were going to give us some ideas on that."

Esther, who believed that the best advertising for her store merchandise was to wear it herself, was dressed in an autumn-hued print with a Peter Pan collar and a string of pumpkin-colored beads. She wore matching button earrings. She smoothed her spit curls, and then waved a manila envelope in the air. "I have here the actual votes on the fundraiser. I did a mailing to all of the Chamber members two weeks ago and we had a sixty-two percent return."

Quill frowned and scribbled on her sketch-pad. There were twenty-four members of the Hemlock Falls Chamber of Commerce, including the newest recruit, Pamela, of Pamela's Pampered Puppy Palace. She looked at the figure she'd calculated (14.88), raised her hand, then lowered it when nobody else seem to wonder who counted as less than ninety percent of a person.

Esther withdrew a number-ten envelope from the larger one. "I have here the results of these votes." She opened the envelope, read the contents, frowned, and then balled the paper up.

"Las Vegas Night at the Resort?" someone asked hopefully.

Esther cleared her throat.

"Well, what the heck," Elmer said crossly. "You want *me* to read it?"

"It's Las Vegas Night?" Esther said, making it into a question.

The mayor grabbed the ball of paper,

smoothed it out, and said, "It is not. It's the sausage breakfast. What the heck's the matter with that?"

Profound silence greeted him.

He scratched his ear in puzzlement. "Y'all don't want the sausage breakfast? Then how come you voted for the sausage breakfast?"

"Where you *bin* all day, Elmer?" Harland Peterson said.

"Syracuse. With the wife. Why?"

"It's not even true," Quill said. "I found the body. I should know. She was perfectly . . . intact."

"Except for her head," Esther said helpfully.

"Whose head?" Elmer demanded. "Whose body? God bless America, Quill. You don't mean to say you found *another* body?"

"It wasn't just me," Quill said indignantly. "As a matter of fact . . ." She bit her lip. She couldn't believe that she was about to tell a roomful of parents that a six-year-old had seen the body first. "Bernie Hamm was with me," she concluded.

"And they say she was ground up in the sausage that Bernie and Thelma make," Esther added in hushed tones. "I always thought there was something funny about that sausage. When I asked Thelma for the recipe last year, it just wasn't the same as the stuff they sell. I swear to heaven she left out a couple ingredients and it looks like I was right."

"Oh, for Pete's sake, Esther," Miriam exploded. "You stop that right now. Lila Longstreet was done in with a blunt instrument and that's all there is to it."

"I don't b'lieve this," Elmer muttered. "Quill, you and Meg found who done it, yet?"

Quill admitted they had not.

"Well, get on it, why don't you?" Elmer whacked the gavel on the rest this time. "Fine. Whatever. Let's move on, folks. Everybody in favor of Las Vegas Night as our second fundraiser this fall?"

Dookie raised his hand. "Yes," he said mildly. "As long as there is no gambling."

"Oh, for *Pete's sake!*" Miriam shouted. "Sorry, Dookie, but we're going to be here all day if we start on that. I move we have a bake sale as a fundraiser."

"Second," Marge Schmidt said.

"So moved," Elmer said. "Next order of business is current business. Which is the Chamber-sponsored Pampered Puppy Palace Dog and Puppy Show. Ms. Durbin? You want to let the folks in on your committee's plans, here?"

Pamela rose in a flutter of charm bracelets,

perfume, and exuberance. Pookie the Peke glared at them all from the security of his tote, which Pamela had placed on the table. "Thank you, Mayor. And thank y'all for welcoming me and my little business to this lovely, lovely village. And thank you especially for your sponsorship of what I hope will be a lovely, lovely show."

"Here, here," Harland Peterson said. He clapped his big hands together. Everyone else applauded politely except, Quill noticed, Marge Schmidt. Marge, dressed as usual in chinos and a bowling jacket with her name embroidered over the pocket, had abandoned the sequined tee for her usual cotton Henley. She looked at Pamela with marked distaste. The eyeliner Quill had noticed earlier in the morning had smeared even more, giving her the look of a belligerent raccoon.

Harland Peterson, however, looked at Pamela with something more than mere approval.

Quill exchanged glances with Miriam. The librarian leaned over and whispered. "He came into the Croh Bar Monday for the fish fry."

"With Pamela?" Quill said. "In Marge's own place? Right in front of her?"

"Betty *does* make the best fish fry in

Tompkins County."

"Phew." Quill shook her head. Well, that explained the newly dyed hair and the blue eyeliner. She'd been sure the tough old farmer and the (fairly recently) widowed Marge were going to make a thing of it. Well, it was too bad, that was all.

Pamela went to the white board that occupied the wall at the head of the table and scribbled enthusiastically across the top: "Best Lap Dog/Best Children's Pet/Best Happy Puppy/Cutest Puppy/Dog with the Best Vocabulary."

"These categories," Pamela said, "are much, much fairer than in those breed shows we all watch on TV. What I'm looking for, what we all want to reward, are the dogs that make our lives the happiest."

It was hard to argue with that. Quill thought that her own dog Max (who would win Best in Show if there were ever a competition for Ugliest Dog) would score pretty well in the Dog with the Best Vocabulary category.

The gist of the committee's ideas, Quill gathered, was a dog and puppy show to be sponsored by the Chamber, but with prizes to be offered by those business owners in Hemlock Falls willing to donate them. "For example," Pamela said, "the Pampered

Puppy will offer a whole month of pet food from that very, very fine company, Pet Pro Protein."

"That Maxwell Kittleburger's company?" Marge demanded suddenly.

"Why, yes. Yes it is." Pamela paused politely. Marge didn't say anything more. But the scowl on her face was ferocious. "Well, um, so that's our ideas. The show will begin promptly at nine on the high school football field." Flustered, she sat down abruptly.

"Hooray," Harland said, and clapped again.

"I think these classes are a fine idea," Esther said earnestly. She had, Quill recalled, quite a handsome standard poodle. "And Pamela, I just think your shop is so sweet. I just love going in there. Love it. It's so nice having you right next door." She turned to the rest of the group. "Pam bounced these ideas off us a few days ago in our last committee meeting. The committee, as you know, is me, Pammie, and Harvey, here."

Harvey Bozzel, Hemlock Falls' best (and only) advertising executive, smoothed his gelled blond hair and smiled modestly.

"Harvey," Esther said breathlessly, "is going to tell you all about our fabulous new idea."

Harvey rose, smiled even more modestly, and said in a well-modulated voice: "Well. We have some wonderful news for you. You may all know that at the moment we have a World-Famous Celebrity right here in Hemlock Falls. We have asked her to judge a very special category in our wonderful dog show. And she has accepted!"

There was an encouraging silence.

Esther leaned forward. "We have created a class *where the dogs vote on each other!*"

"Hah?" Elmer said.

"All Olivia Oberlie has to do is ask them! And she's agreed to do it! Right on her show on cable TV." Esther sat back, flushed with triumph.

"That certainly will put us in the headlines," Miriam said dryly.

"It sure will," Elmer said in great excitement. "Why, everybody watches that show *Mind Doesn't Matter.* And us dog owners are going to be on it, too!"

"I meant the headlines that read 'Town Loses Collective Mind Entirely,' " Miriam snapped. She heaved a long sigh. "I've never heard anything so ridiculous in my life."

"This is a great opportunity!" Harvey shouted.

"We are going to look like a bunch of idiots!" Miriam shouted back.

Harvey sat down with a scowl. Pamela patted him on the arm in a consoling way, and then began to whisper earnestly in his ear. Harland, who was seated on the other side of Pam, gave Harvey a glare that would have curdled milk on a cold day in Alaska.

Quill tuned out the rest of the discussion, which rapidly turned acrimonious. She doodled a large Olivia Oberlie in a Roman toga with "We Who Are About to Die Salute You" scribbled underneath because she couldn't remember the Latin. Then she lettered in "Suspects" at the top of the page, and rapidly sketched a weedy Millard Barnstaple cringing under the heel of a cranky-looking Priscilla Barnstaple. She added the downtrodden Robin Finnegan, and a portrait of Victoria Finnegan in a general's helmet with a pair of pearl-handled pistols on her hips. She added Pamela in a Scarlett O'Hara ball gown, and then a glowering Rudy Baranga. Maxwell Kittleburger turned into Donald Trump with an Uzi. Finally, she lettered in the chart that she'd relied on for so many of her cases.

"Means," she muttered to herself. "Motive. Opportunity . . ."

Miriam nudged her. "Quill?"

Quill blinked. The conference room swam back into focus.

"Is it true?" Miriam asked. "Olivia Oberlie's predicted another murder?"

"Well, sort of," Quill admitted.

"What do you mean, 'sort of'?" Elmer demanded.

Quill closed her eyes in an effort to remember accurately. "She said 'I see another murder.' " She opened them. Everyone was staring at her.

"So there's no 'sort of' about it!" Elmer said.

"I don't think we should even think about planning a Chamber function with a murderer running around loose!" Esther said nervously.

Carol Ann Spinoza demanded the reformation of the (thankfully) defunct Hemlock Falls Volunteer Police Force. Marge told them all not to be a bunch of wusses, and anybody who believed in a middle-aged fart who talked to animals was an idiot. Dookie thumped the table gently and said that there was no place for so-called psychics in the Hemlock Falls Church of God. The volume of the discussion rose. From what Quill could tell, support for Olivia Oberlie's psychic abilities was running two to one, in favor.

Quill looked down at her sketchpad and created the silhouette of a sinister profile with a fedora. Then she penciled in an elaborate "X."

"The point is," Carol Ann Spinoza yelled, rising out of her seat, "that someone is going to get killed. These people are all at your Inn, Sarah Quilliam. And what are you and that stuck-up little sister of yours going to do about it?"

CHAPTER 5

"Stuck up?" Meg said. "Me?"

"Forget it." Quill curled herself up in the corner of her couch and took another sip of the Syrah. Meg had arrived at her house at eight that evening, as promised, and with a basket full of food, also as promised. She'd prepared a cassoulet; the evenings were getting cool as true autumn approached, and the hearty stew was perfect with the muscular red wine. Quill was indulging herself with a second glass after dinner.

"And they want us to do something about a murder that hasn't happened yet?" Meg shrieked.

"If we do something about the murder that *has* happened, maybe there won't be another one."

"Now you're doing it," Meg said accusingly. "Don't tell me you're buying this cosmic woo-woo stuff. If Olivia's accurately predicted another murder, it's because *she's* going to commit it."

"Cognitive dissonance," Quill mused. "No, I don't believe that Olivia's any more psychic than Max, here." Max, stretched out in front of the fireplace, thumped his tail lazily at the sound of his name. "But even the most reliable skeptics, like Marge, are convinced there will be another victim. I'm worried about it, too. So here I am, holding two opposing opinions at the same time. Olivia's a fraud, but someone's going to get killed. Go figure."

"We don't even know why there's a first victim," Quill continued. "We don't know what time she was killed, how she was killed, or even if she was killed somewhere else and moved to poor Bernie Hamm's place afterward. For that matter, why Bernie Hamm's hog farm? Why not the ravine, which is where a truly sensible murderer would dump the body?"

"Actually, I found out a lot of that stuff this afternoon," Meg said with just a touch of smugness.

"Good," Quill said. "That means I can fill out my chart."

"Yep. But there's something I want to talk to you about first. This marriage of yours . . ." Meg rose from the Eames chair that Quill had brought from her old quarters at the Inn and walked around the living room, tripping occasionally over an exposed nail in the flooring. "When *are* you getting around to fixing this floor?" she interrupted herself irritably. "And for that matter, the walls in here look like a disease. How can you stand it?"

"The remodeling is taking more time than I thought," Quill admitted.

Myles had bought the old cobblestone years ago. It'd been owned by a Peterson — which one of that fertile family Quill could never remember — but Petersons as a group weren't particularly interested in the interiors of their houses. Myles wasn't either. So when Quill had moved in, there'd been a lot to do. She'd stripped the indoor-outdoor carpeting out of the living room, first thing, and exposed wide-planked pine floors in need of serious repair. But the wallpaper — magnolias mixed with calla lilies — was too hideous to live with, and she had started removing that, too. The wallpaper had been pasted onto the walls with some fiendish variant of Superglue. It was far more unsettling to the eye than the splintery floor, so for the moment, Quill spent most of her spare time chipping away at the wallpaper with a steam iron and a caulk scraper. Meg was right. The walls looked infected, if not downright terminal.

Meg halted next to the fireplace. "You know something? This room is ghastly."

Quill followed her gaze, and said with amusement, "It's worse than ghastly. Remember the first year at the Inn, though? And the year we remodeled the Palette? Those jobs were just as awful to begin with. And look what we ended up with."

"You just love to remodel," Meg accused her. "You and Myles could have sold this place and built a nice new house."

Quill ignored this. "I'm thinking about a Frank Lloyd Wright–ish feel to this room." She gestured with the wine glass. "Some nice glass doors in the south wall, there, so we can walk out to a stone patio. And from there, steps down to the little pond."

Meg glanced at her, and then looked away. "So it's not the living conditions."

Quill went very still. "What isn't the living conditions?"

"Come on. I'm your sister. You think I don't know when you're okay and when you aren't? You aren't okay. So tell me about it. Unless . . ." Meg's eyes brightened. "You aren't, you know, pregnant?"

"As of this morning, nothing's changed. I'm not pregnant."

"So?" Meg dropped to the floor and

crossed her legs. "Do you want to tell me about it? How come you're depressed?"

"I thought we were going to start solving the murder of Lila Longstreet."

"No detective does her best work when she's depressed."

"Nonsense. All the best detectives do their best work when they're depressed. Look at Harry Bosch. Peter Wimsey. Phillip Marlowe. Sam Spade, Kinsey Milhone. I'd run out of air before I ran out of successful depressed detectives."

"So depression is good. Fine. The chances of solving this case have increased mightily. But just for the record, how come you're depressed?" She bit her lip, and then said diffidently, "Have you discovered you don't love Myles?"

Myles, who slept better if she was curled under his left shoulder. Who called at unexpected moments so he could hear her voice. Myles, who had been utterly transformed by marriage into a happy and contented man.

"Ha," Meg said. "What a happy look you've got, Quillie. So that's not it, thank god. You love Myles. Myles obviously loves you. You aren't fazed a bit by the truly gruesome condition of your current living arrangement. So what's up?"

Quill shook her head. "I don't know. I wish I did know. All I can tell you is that I feel too big for the room."

Meg drew her dark brows together. "Okay. You want to run that by me one more time?"

"I feel squashed. Constricted. Compressed." Quill curled her knees up to her chin and stared into the fire. "Like Alice, after she drank the stuff that made her grow too big for the room."

"There was that time a few years back when you took off to that artists' retreat? You came back from that feeling just fine. Maybe you should go there again?"

Quill shook her head. "That's not it." She sat up and stuck her hands in her hair. "I'm not sure what it is." She looked up, "Just tell me I'm not making *your* life miserable."

"Nah. I'm fine." She smiled impishly. "Finer than fine."

"And Jerry?"

Jerry Grimsby, master chef, rolling stone, and the man who'd seduced her sister away from marriage to the steady and reliable Andy Bishop.

"That jerk!" Meg flared. "You know we agreed to be absolutely, utterly open about how we rated each other's recipes."

"Hm." Quill had been dubious about this pledge from the start.

"And you remember how I agreed with him about my Duck Quilliam."

Quill suppressed a wince. Meg's response to Jerry's disdain for her Duck Quilliam had wrecked more than her usual quota of eight-inch sauté pans that month.

"I not only accepted his criticisms with grace . . . although he's always had a bee in his bonnet about black beans and mango salsa and absolutely utterly refuses to acknowledge the prejudice, so what does he know about duck anyway? Not much. But I knew that. So my duck was doomed from the outset. A bean-and-salsa-loving reviewer would have had a far different take on Duck Quilliam, believe me."

"Hm!" Quill repeated, with more cheerful emphasis.

"So, when he asked me to review his *chevon glacé,* I did so with the confidence that I would be extended the same courtesy that I extended him! Master chef to master chef. Each maintaining the highest level of professionalism in their critiques."

"And did he? Maintain the highest level of professionalism when you gave him your opinion about the glazed goat?"

"Did he, HA!" Meg shouted.

Quill hoped that Jerry had used his own kitchen's sauté pans and not the ones belonging to the Inn.

"So?"

"So I'm not speaking to him, of course."

"I thought the two of you had agreed to do the cooking demonstration for the Tompkins County Gourmet Society next week."

"I don't have to speak a word to that bonehead to do that, do I?" Meg said cheerfully. "I'll just cook like mad and ignore him. I'll cook *better* than he cooks and ignore him."

And they would have made up by then, anyway, Quill thought. *Phew!*

She had to admit that her relationship with her sister was a lot more restful since Jerry had come into her life. The two of them had a fine time yelling bloody blue blazes at one another, making up, and starting all over again the next week. The Inn kitchen was a lot more serene, too. So serene that under chef Bjarne Bjarnson had quit, claiming that he needed more stimulation than the job was currently providing to cook at his best.

"You and Myles never seem to get upset with each other," Meg said. "I don't know if that's a good thing or a bad thing."

"It's a good thing," Quill said. "A marriage should be like an ideal day at the Inn. Absolutely no crises."

"Well, I prefer days like we had today," Meg said innocently. (Her sister was a charter member of the school of the blindingly obvious.) "I mean — it's an awful thing to start the day with a murder, and of course I don't mean I'd prefer that all our days started with murder. By the way, Doreen said to tell you that she's going to have a cost overrun this week because she had to pay overtime to get the conference room and the Tavern Lounge cleaned up after all the hoo-rah, but Quill, hoo-rah is stimulating! And best of all," she clapped her hands together. "We have a case!"

"We don't have a case yet," Quill said. "We have a body and a list of questions." She'd deposited her sketchpad and pencil on the coffee table with her purse and a sheaf of bills she'd brought home to pay. "Here. I wrote some of them down. And I spent some time on the computer while I was waiting for you. There's a fair bit of information about IAPFP and its members. They've got a web page and it links to all the members' businesses. So. We have a lot of background information. Not that background information is going to do us much good."

Meg was scanning the list of questions. " 'Was the victim killed elsewhere and the body moved to Heavenly Hogg's?' Yes."

"Yes?"

"You betcha."

"And you know this, because?"

"Because while you were in the Chamber meeting, I spent the afternoon at the Croh Bar, just as you suggested I should."

"I didn't suggest that you spend the afternoon at the Croh Bar!" Quill said indignantly. "I suggested you spend the afternoon in the kitchen!"

Meg, her eyes on the list, waved her hand in "don't-worry-about-it" fashion. "Jerry covered for me." She lowered the sketchbook and grinned at Quill over the top edge. "He lost a bet."

"What bet . . . never mind. This is something I truly don't want to know."

" 'Estimated time of death?' " Meg read aloud. "About twelve hours before you and young Quincy discovered the body. Which would make it . . ." Meg counted silently, "about eight o'clock the previous evening."

"Monday night," Quill said. "Well. We can cross Pamela Durbin off our list of suspects right now."

"Yeah?"

"At the relevant time," Quill said, in mock prosecutorial style, "the suspect was eating fish fry with Harland Peterson in that very same Croh Bar."

Meg dropped the sketchbook in her lap. "Get out. He took another woman to Marge's own restaurant?"

Quill nodded. "Not only that, he thinks that the dog and puppy show is a great idea."

"What dog and puppy show?"

Quill explained, briefly. "And when Esther said that she and Pamela had come up with the dogs voting for the top dog idea, Harland clapped right along with the rest of them."

Meg shook her head as if to clear it.

"They want Olivia Oberlie to do the canvassing," Quill explained.

Meg's mouth formed a soundless O. "So the village is going to look as if it's populated by a bunch of crazies on national TV." Then she said, "What! Harland Peterson thought that was a good idea? The toughest dairy farmer in Tompkins County? The same guy that ran the PETA protestors off his property with a shotgun because he raises veal calves?"

"Yep."

"Poor Marge."

"Poor Marge. But lucky Pamela. She's out of the frame. So erase Pamela from the suspects list, Meg."

Meg flipped to the pages with the caricatures and shook her head. "I'm not about to erase a Quilliam. Do you know how valuable this sort of thing will be? Especially after you die. Think of Picasso and all those cocktail napkins."

Quill slid off the couch, grabbed the pad, and erased Pamela's image. "We've still got too many suspects."

"What were the rest of your questions? Maybe we can eliminate some more."

" 'What was the cause of death?' "

"This will turn your stomach." Meg said soberly. "But it seems she was unconscious when it happened. She was run over."

"You mean, somebody . . . ugh." Quill swallowed hard. "But Meg, this may not be a murder, as such. It could be an accident. That's manslaughter."

"Not when she was run over twice, it isn't," Meg said dryly. "And it wasn't as if the truck backed up in a panic, either. There were two separate sets of treads moving forward on her skull."

"Yikes."

"You said it." Meg got to her feet rather stiffly. "Oof. Are you planning on putting carpets on this floor, eventually?"

"Eventually," Quill said. "Where are you going?"

"I've been experimenting with pumpkin desserts. Pumpkin sorbet, pumpkin mousse, and pumpkin crème. I stuck them in your refrigerator. If you can call that thing in your kitchen a refrigerator. If you can call that room it's in a kit . . ."

"Just shut up," Quill said amiably.

The kitchen was directly through a doorway in the north wall of the living room. A hundred and fifty years ago, it had been a keeping room. Quill found the basic proportions very pleasing. Two large mullioned windows faced the backyard on the north side, and a large, long, brick fireplace took up the east wall. Either the Peterson Myles had bought the house from, or the Peterson before him, had walled off the fireplace with plasterboard. Unlike Sheetrock (of which Quill was very fond), plasterboard was thick, crumbly stuff that created an unholy mess going up and an even worse mess coming down. Quill and Myles had gotten about half of the fireplace uncovered before he'd left on his current trip.

The floor was Armstrong tile dating from the early sixties, if Quill was any judge. And the appliances dated from the sixties, too. There was a harvest-gold Tappan gas range (which actually worked fairly well, as long as you adjusted the oven temperature down

35 degrees when you baked) and an avocado-green Westinghouse refrigerator. A cheap oak table provided counter space, as did two squares of stainless steel mounted on cabinets on either side of the sink.

There was also a brand-new Meile dishwasher standing in glorious isolation against the west wall.

Meg put her hands over her eyes and said, "Bleah, bleah, bleah!" as she made her way to the refrigerator. She pulled out three large Tupperware bowls. Quill removed two clean plates and six spoons from the dishwasher, and sat down at the table.

"I've got a sauterne in here somewhere," Meg muttered from the depths of the Westinghouse. "Ah. Here. You must know that I completely abandoned any responsibility for the temperature of the wine when I stuck it in there."

She set the armful of food and wine on the table and settled down opposite Quill. "Next question."

"The murder weapon's a truck?"

"Yes." Meg squeezed her eyes shut. "I'm trying to think. I don't know anything about trucks. I don't even like trucks. It seems to me that the tires were Michelins. The kind that fit on a Dooley? Like in Tom Dooley?"

"A dually," Quill said briskly. "A double axle."

Meg stared at her. "You have absolutely no idea what that means."

"You are absolutely right. Except that it's a big truck. A domestic truck."

"What in heaven's name is a domestic truck?"

"You know, not a semi or anything. Like a big old pickup."

"The kind owned by half the guys at the Croh Bar. Terrific."

"True," Quill said. "But where would the IAPFP find a dually? None of them checked in with cars. No, wait. That's not true. Olivia has that whacking big Cadillac. And Rudy has a Cadillac, too. What is it with wealthy people and Cadillacs? Are you sure that the murder weapon was a truck?"

"That's what the police said."

"Then we should check with Henry Peterson. He does most of the car rentals around here now that George is gone."

"You know what, Quill? That was our first case."

"It was, wasn't it?" They were both silent, remembering.

"Well," Quill shook herself. "We have to be on the lookout for this truck."

"Along with half the state troopers in

Tompkins County," Meg said. "Maybe we should concentrate on leads with a little less scope. Next question."

"Okay. Who identified the body?"

Meg tugged at her lower lip. "I don't have the slightest idea. Why do you think that'd be important?"

"It probably isn't. Except that there may be someone close to Lila who isn't a member of the IAPFP."

"I'll go to my source tomorrow," Meg said. "First thing."

"As a matter of fact, who is this source?" Quill stuck her spoon into the pumpkin sherbet. "It's not Esther West, or Betty Hall, or the mayor? I mean, I hope it's someone more reliable." She took a bite of the pumpkin ice cream.

"What do you think?" Meg asked anxiously.

Quill, her mouth full, held up six fingers.

"Six!" Meg scowled. "Jerry gave it a seven. But then, he knows all too well how tricky iced squash can be. Oh, well." She got up and dumped the remainder of the ice cream into the sink. Quill quietly spit the stuff still in her mouth into her bowl and congratulated herself once again on the new rating system. It had been Jerry's idea actually. The old rating system was a simple "thumbs up/thumbs down" arrangement, and it sent Meg into really interesting temper tantrums. "If you go zero to ten, you avoid all of that rejection reaction," Jerry had said knowledgably. "Meg won't settle for less than a ten, but she figures your average master chef settles for six and above." If her sister had just swallowed a nice sedative, Quill thought, she would have given the pumpkin ice cream a screaming negative one hundred and forty-two.

"Here, I'll rinse this off, too." Meg picked up her bowl, looked at it, and gave Quill a suspicious glare. "Did you spit the rest of this out? Is it that bad? Never mind, I don't want to know."

"This information you have about Lila's death," Quill resumed. "It seems pretty specific."

"Straight from the horse's mouth. Davy was in the bar nursing the one beer he always allows himself and was he peeved about Harker."

"You mean Davy didn't call Harker in on the case?" Quill said. "That's odd. Who did?"

"You'll never guess."

"I don't want to guess," Quill said impatiently.

"I'll tell you in a minute. Here." She

spooned the pumpkin mousse onto a clean plate.

Quill took a tentative swallow. "Wow. And I mean 'wow.' This stuff is fabulous."

Meg blushed.

Quill took another, larger bite. "It's like the best pumpkin pie I've ever eaten."

Meg frowned.

"I mean, it's the essence of pumpkin," Quill said hastily. "It's diaphanous."

"Diaphanous?"

"It's wonderful," Quill said sincerely. "It's a triumph."

"Jerry thinks I ought to take it to the competition in Vegas."

"Jerry's absolutely right." Quill set her spoon down so she wouldn't gulp the rest of it. "Now. Who called in the Staties?"

"Maxwell Kittleburger."

"Really?" Quill took another bite of the mousse. "You have to call this mousse something unique and amazing. Quilliam Celeste. You know, I didn't see anything at all of him this afternoon, Kittleburger, I mean, after the Chamber meeting. He's such a," she stopped and searched for the right word, "violent man, Meg. I wonder where he was?"

"More important is where he was around eight o'clock Monday night."

Quill reached out to scoop more mousse onto her plate. "We're just going to have to find out. We're going to find out where all of them were. And after that — we're going to look for a motive. And I'm going to start with Maxwell Kittleburger himself."

CHAPTER 6

Quill woke at five o'clock in the morning to a silent house. Living with Myles had changed a lot of things. Before her marriage, in her rooms at the Inn, even in the dead of night the Inn was alive with purpose. The kitchens waited for the dawn arrival of the prep crew. The guest rooms were filled with somnolent bodies. And the sound of the falls outside was a constant music.

She lay in her comfortable bed, aware of Max asleep at her feet, the empty space beside her — which wasn't truly empty, since she carried Myles in her heart — and the quiet rustle of the trees outside. The world of her home with Myles was totally different. Her attention was directed inward, the demands of the Inn and all its residents eight miles and a universe away.

The outward demands seemed too heavy, at the moment. That why she felt squashed, pressed down, constricted.

The phone rang at six. Myles? His daily call earlier than usual?

"Hey," she said into the receiver.

"It's just me," Marge Schmidt said. "You up?"

"Sure."

"You want to stop by the Croh Bar for coffee in a while?"

Quill rubbed her eyes and yawned. "That would be nice." She sat up in bed. "Is anything wrong?"

"Maybe." Marge dropped the handset into the receiver.

Quill rose, let Max out, made coffee, let Max back in, then showered, wound her hair in a knot on the top of her head, and stared at the contents of her closet. The weatherman had called for a hard frost last night and the days were getting cooler, too.

"What should I wear today, Max?"

Max cocked his ridiculous ears. He'd wandered into her life six years ago, the year, Quill remembered now, of what she thought of as the Case of the Crafty Ladies. His coat was a chaotic mixture of brown, ochre, gray, and white. His vet, a crusty septuagenarian named Austin McKenzie, had recorded Max's breed as Lab/collie/giant schnauzer/? With the dominant breed being?

Quill pulled on a cream fisherman's knit sweater, a beige wool skirt, and a pair of soft boots. Long ago, she'd simplified her life considerably by investing in minimalist dressing: five wool skirts and ten heavy cotton sweaters for fall and winter; five silk skirts and ten silk shirts in spring and summer. All her clothes were in the colors that warmed her fair skin and hazel eyes, and that treated her carrot red hair with some consideration: sage, cream, bronze, and the whole palette of browns.

"What d'ya think, Max? Do I need a little blusher? Some mascara?"

Max cocked his head. There was no doubt in Quill's mind that if she entered her dog in the "Best Vocabulary" class of Pamela's dog and puppy show, that Max would win hands down. "You do realize I'm investigating the meanest man in Karnack Corners, Iowa, this morning. I have to look terrific." Max shook his head violently — either, Quill guessed, because he didn't like her particular color of lip gloss, or he had picked up another case of ear mites in his peregrinations around the village Dumpster. "I've come up with an extremely clever way to interview him. Want to guess what it is?"

Max scratched himself vigorously. Quill

shook her head. More had changed about her mornings than a new kind of peace and quiet. She was talking to her dog instead of to another human being. And she was doing it a lot. "You don't give a hoot, do you? But you'll do as someone to talk to until Myles comes home. Come on. Go-for-a-ride, Max."

This Max understood very well.

The road to the Inn took her directly through the village, so the Croh Bar was on the way. She pulled into the parking lot, wondering what Marge had to say.

For years, Marge and her partner Betty Hall had run the All-American Diner ("Fine Food! And Fast!"), and for years, it was the most popular place in town. But not, Marge was heard to grumble more than once, the most profitable. The most profitable place in town was the run-down, seedy joint known as the Croh Bar. And when Leonard Croh finally decided to retire and move to Florida, Marge and Betty bought it. Like the All-American Diner, the Croh Bar opened at six o'clock in the morning; unlike the diner, no one under eighteen could set foot in the place, so the patrons tended to be older, or single, or both.

It was a great place to get up-to-the-minute news of the goings-on in Hemlock Falls.

Quill glanced at the clock over the bar as she walked in. Just before seven, which meant that the truckers would have cleared out, but that those farmers who'd finished morning chores would be eating breakfast. She scanned the booths that lined both walls and found Marge alone at her usual spot in the back. Quill waved and joined her. "Hey, Marge."

" 'Lo, Quill."

"You're in here early this morning."

Marge raised one gingery eyebrow. "I'm always in here 'bout this time."

And usually with Harland Peterson, Quill thought. But she said aloud, "Shall I sit down?"

"Nobody else is planning to sit there, far as I know."

Quill slid onto the bench across from her. "You want coffee?"

Quill nodded.

"Bit of the special? Betty's cooking here today."

Quill nodded a little more vigorously. Betty Hall made the best diner food in upstate New York. Maybe the whole of New York. Meg claimed she could make a case for its being the best diner food on the continent, but noncompeting chefs tended to support each other with enthusiasm.

Marge leaned out into the aisle and hollered. A faint response came from the general direction of the kitchen. Marge settled back into her seat. "Be out in a minute. Heard from the sheriff lately?"

Quill knew Marge didn't mean Davy Kiddermeister. Whenever old Hemlockians referred to the sheriff, they meant Myles. After taking early retirement from the NYPD, he'd held the post for eight years.

"Last night," Quill said, "and briefly again this morning."

"When's he due back?"

Quill shook her head. "I wish I knew. I wish *he* knew. Soon, I hope."

"You tell him about this Lila Longstreet business?"

"Ah. Hm," Quill said noncommitally.

"Not too happy about it, was he? He kicks up something fierce when you and Meg stick your noses in."

He did, indeed. "You didn't say a word yesterday when Elmer demanded that we solve the case and solve it quickly," Quill protested.

Marge made a "what's-it-to-me?" face. "So you and Meg got any idea who killed her, yet?"

"No. But we have a list of suspects. We think the list is pretty sound. I mean, no one in town knew Lila from before, did they?"

Marge shook her head. "Not as far as I've heard. She's from some place out West, isn't she? Karnack Corners, Iowa. Where Kittleburger's plant is. Talked her up one night this week, before she got bashed over the head like that. This was her first time up East. She liked it here just fine. But she was really chomping at the bit to get to New York City. Said she'd dreamed about it since she was a kid."

"So my suspect list *is* pretty reliable," Quill said. She explained how she and Meg had decided whom to investigate. "And it doesn't look as if this was an accident. Or a random killing."

"Wasn't raped and she was run over twice, deliberately," Marge agreed. "I can see how you're thinking that the only people around here that would have a motive for her being dead are that bunch up at your place."

"Makes sense."

Marge nodded. Betty whipped down the aisle and placed a plate of scrambled eggs, hash browns, rye toast, and pancakes in front of Quill. She added a smaller plate of crisp Virginia-style bacon. "Juice?"

"No thanks, Betty."

"You and Meg find out who killed that Longstreet person?" Betty asked.

"Not yet."

"You can take your own sweet time about it, as far as I'm concerned." Betty wiped both hands on the front of her red-checked apron, gave an abrupt "so there" sort of nod, and whipped back to the kitchen.

Quill looked after her in mild surprise. Betty was taciturn to a fault. And as good-natured as she was taciturn. She turned to Marge.

"No use asking me," Marge said. "Not sure why Bet didn't take to Lila. But I didn't take to her myself. She was a real pain in the ass the night she dropped by here. She had the worst kind of big-city, snot-nosed attitude, thank you very much."

"She surely did," Quill said a little ruefully. Lila's preferred method of getting Quill's attention had been to snap her fingers. The snap was followed by a list of really stupid demands: there were too many pillows in her room; housekeeping had to be summoned instantly to remove them. The wine was corked. (As if! Their somme-lier Peter Hairston kept the finest cellar within a hundred miles. And that included the prestigious Finger Lakes wine region nearby.) The specious complaints had gone on and on. The entire staff had been heartily sick of Lila within hours of her arrival. "I was ready to whack her over the head with a blunt object myself."

"The men, now," Marge said darkly. "If I was about to investigate, I'd start right there with the men. You know that hair was straight out of the bottle. And those big purple eyes of hers? Contact lenses."

"Really?" Quill said. "Are you sure?"

"Lost one right here at the bar Monday afternoon," Marge said. "Found it myself. As for those boobs . . ." She snorted.

"Fake," Quill said succinctly.

"As a three-dollar bill," Marge said with satisfaction.

"So she was in here Monday afternoon?"

"That she was."

"Was she with anyone?"

Marge scowled. "That primped-up bit of sticky Southern swamp."

Quill took a moment to work this out. "You mean Pamela."

Marge's lips were a thin line of peevishness.

"Was she with anyone else? Lila, I mean," Quill added hastily. "Not Pamela. I know that Pamela was with . . ." she stopped herself in mid-sentence. "Could I have another cup of coffee, please?"

Marge glared at her and jerked her chin at the carafe.

"So that's when you had a chance to talk with her," Quill mused. "Did she talk to anyone else?"

"She bossed Betty around some, or tried to. Basically she and Her."

"Pamela," Quill supplied.

"Gabbed away on those two bar stools up front. Then She . . ."

"Pamela." The venom that Marge could put into a capital letter was pretty amazing.

". . . took off to get ready for a date, She said." Marge paused, sighed heavily and continued. "Then Lila knocked back the rest of her beer and left. Didn't leave a tip. Figures."

"Did Lila tell you what she did for the IAPFP, Marge?"

"Whined a lot about how bad the pay was. Trashed each one of the members, one by one. But she was secretary-treasurer of the association," Marge said. "And if it's incorporated . . ."

"It is. I checked."

"Then it'd be the standard stuff. All incorporated businesses have to have four elected positions: president, vice-president, secretary, treasurer. No one person can hold more than two positions, and the president can't be the vice-president. At least in the state of New York."

"IAPFP's incorporated in Iowa," Quill said through a mouthful of hash browns. "What *does* Betty put in these, Marge?"

Marge grinned. "If I tell ya, I have to kill ya. Anyway, most rules of incorporation are the same nationwide, more or less."

"So as secretary-treasurer, Lila signed off on the bookkeeping."

"Although she might not have actually done the bookkeeping, but, yeah."

"And kept the minutes, et cetera, et cetera," Quill said, just like the King of Siam. She was beginning to feel as baffled as that stage character, too. "I'll tell you, Marge, try as I might, I can't think of a motive linked to the IAPFP business to save my life. I mean, this is a professional association, but all they do is put out a newsletter and go to meetings once a year. They listed a lobbyist on their website, but what kind of huge political issues are you going to run into over pet food? They can't even have that much of a budget. The annual dues are pretty hefty, but we're not talking millions here. Just enough to pay an office worker and some modest overhead expenses."

Marge rubbed her chin reflectively. "If it

isn't money or power, it's gotta be sex."

"Sex," Quill said, "or something else that's up close and personal. Maybe she was blackmailing one of the others?"

Marge shrugged. "Who knows?"

"You said she trashed the members. Did she say anything that might be a lead?"

Marge frowned a little with the effort of recollection. "Victoria Finnegan's a shark."

"She's the IAPFP attorney of record."

"And she cut off her husband's balls a long time ago."

"Oh, dear." Quill tugged at the curl over her left ear. "Robin's been disbarred. Do you think I should find out about that?"

"Couldn't hurt. Anyway," Marge sighed, "let's see. She said Kittleburger's an old crook. Olivia Oberlie's a fraud. And the Barnstaples are idiots."

Quill had withdrawn her sketchbook from her pocket and was scribbling frantically. "All of this has a lot of potential, Marge. Crook. Fraud. Except the part about the Barnstaples being idiots."

"Well, now, maybe not. The reason the Barnstaples are idiots is that Millard is the one raising Cain about vegetarian pet food."

"That," Quill muttered as she scribbled some more, "is a reason for Rudy Baranga to knock off Millard Barnstaple, maybe. It'd cut into his meat business big time. But I'll put it down anyway. Right next to the argument Millard and Priscilla had yesterday."

"And that was about?"

"Buying something."

Marge grimaced. "Everybody's always buying something these days. You notice that? Nobody keeps anything. It's just grab, grab, grab."

Marge, although the richest woman in Tompkins County, was probably the cheapest. "This was about buying something worth less than twenty million."

"That so?" Marge considered this. "House, maybe?"

"Some house."

"Not if you're in Palm Beach or Marin County, California."

"Maybe," Quill said doubtfully. "Robin Finnegan was sitting right there and Priscilla kept pulling him into the conversation. Would you want a relative stranger's opinion on whether you should buy a house?"

"Thin, Quill. It's thin. But I suppose it all helps."

"It sure does," Quill slammed the sketchbook shut. "This is terrific, Marge. When I left the house this morning, I didn't have a really focused idea of where this investigation was heading. Now I've got a couple of great leads. Crook. Fraud. Although it'd be nice if we had some actual evidence."

"Evidence," Marge agreed with a fair degree of irony, "is a little hard for your basic amateur detective to come by." Then she said rhetorically, "So what have you got so far?" She drummed her fingers on the table. "Meg was in here late afternoon, yesterday, bending Davy's ear. My guess is you have at least some idea of how the murder was committed. He was so ticked off that Kittleburger called the troopers in, Davy was."

"We've got the time of the murder," Quill said with some pride.

"So you're going to check on where all your suspects were at the time? Just what *was* the time?"

"Eight-ish. Monday night."

Marge's face fell. "*She*'s out of it?"

There was no need to ask who She was.

"Um, yes." Quill said. "So that does let Pamela out of it."

"Well, blast it all to kingdom come anyway."

Quill was shocked. She thought about why, for a moment. Because Marge was making it personal, that was why. Oh, dear. "You didn't really think Pamela Durbin smacked Lila Longstreet over the head with

134

a blunt instrument, did you?"

"I was hopin'," Marge said bluntly.

"But you can't let cases like this become personal." Quill let it go. "This is so frustrating. We have some excellent leads. But they're all oriented to establishing motive."

"It'd help to have that forensics report," Marge suggested.

"You bet it would. I know that the scene of the crime guys were there. They must have taken a cast of the tire tracks. And I'll bet they went over the body with a fine-toothed comb. I'd give a lot for a copy of that forensics report."

"No go with Myles, huh? He won't get it for ya?"

Quill grinned reluctantly. "I didn't really come right out and ask, you know. I did hint. But he hates calling in favors. And he doesn't really . . ."

"Think you should be sticking your nose in," Marge said. "Well, what if we figured out how to get hold of that forensics report ourselves?"

"You and I?" Quill blinked at her. Marge had been drawn into a case they'd had several years ago. But she'd been a pretty reluctant partner. "That's why you invited me to breakfast?"

"Thought you would have figured that out

by now," Marge said very crossly. Her face was bright red.

"Oh," Quill said. "Well, I hadn't." And now that Pamela's in the clear, Marge didn't want anything to do with the case, being a basically law-abiding person. But if she backed out now, she'd look as if she only wanted to help hang Pamela Durbin. (Which she had.)

So Marge was stuck with giving them a hand.

Quill's first instincts were usually merciful. "Golly, Marge. Meg and I can handle this just fine ourselves. We have before."

"Huh," Marge said skeptically. "So you had a plan to get hold of the forensics report?"

"Not as such, no."

"Not at all," Marge said rudely, if accurately. "But I do."

"How would we do it?"

"Bound to be at the barracks, isn't it?"

Quill stared at her. "Break into the state trooper barracks? Are you kidding me?"

"Not break in, exactly." Marge rubbed her nose in a reflective way. "You see the ads about my new business yet?"

"No," Quill said apologetically. "I haven't. Another one, Marge? You're amazing. Meg and I have trouble enough with just one business. But you've got the realty company and the insurance company and all sorts of stuff. And now what?"

"Tech support."

"Tech support?"

"For computers. Computer systems, is what it is. For big users. Like the state troopers."

"You mean you can fix those big main-frame things?"

"There're no mainframes anymore," Marge said. As with Quincy, the word "stupid" hung in the air. "I don't do it myself. I got a couple kids on the payroll. And one of the accounts I landed was with New York state troopers."

"Holy crow."

Marge smiled. There was one thing at which she was brilliant and that was making money. "Anyway. I can fix it to make a service call on the barracks, if you want. And we can hack into the system and get a look at that report."

"Can we get a copy, do you think?"

"Nope. All that kind of stuff is tracked. And I'm not putting a business this lucra-tive on the line by screwing up. But if we do sort of accidentally see the report, well, we'll be a little further ahead on this case, won't we?"

"Clues!" Quill said. "We'd have clues! This is just terrific. But how are you going to get me in there?"

"Disguise," Marge said casually. "I've got that all worked out, too. But you'll have to put on a wig."

"I'll put a lampshade on my head and waltz down Main Street to get a look at that report. And when do we do it?"

"Davy says they've got to file a preliminary report within forty-eight hours. That puts us into tomorrow. If there's any weird stuff, the results won't be back by then of course, but we can always go back for another service call."

"Marge, you are brilliant." Quill reached over and shook her hand. "Brilliant."

Marge smiled in satisfaction. She also looked a lot happier than she had for a few days. Quill looked at her friend and sighed. Next to Pamela's luscious curves, Marge's solid frame looked workmanlike. And no makeup was going to make her fierce blue gaze anything but machine-gun-like. If Harland was going to swap all Marge's common sense, not to mention her intellect, for a soppy Southern belle who was convinced dogs could vote, he was a fool. "Men," Quill said, half aloud, "are idiots."

"You thinking of anyone in particular?"

"Um." Marge hated anyone interfering in her business. Especially her love life.

Quill's mind flew back to the Chamber meeting the day before. "Actually I was thinking about adding another suspect. Remember when you made that remark about Kittleburger at the Chamber meeting?"

"I didn't say he was an idiot."

"You didn't say anything at all. But you expressed contempt. Or something like it."

"I did?"

"You have a very expressive face, Marge."

"I do?"

"Yes," Quill said firmly. She believed that compliments, even if untrue, did everyone a lot of good. "What do you know about Kittleburger? I'm on my way to investigate him right now."

"You're going to investigate Maxwell Kittleburger?" Marge stared at her for a long moment, and then hooted with laugher.

"What's so funny about that?" Quill asked with dignity. "If you think I'm going to sit down and ask him where he was on the night of Monday the twenty-eighth at or around eight o'clock, you are much mistaken. I am far subtler than that."

"You'd better be. The guy's gonna chew

you up and spit you out if you're not careful." Marge considered for a moment. "He'd start by suing you for something and end by owning you lock, stock, and barrel. That's the kind of guy Maxwell Kittleburger is, unless you whack him a good one right off the bat. And you were going to be subtle around him how?"

"I was going to ask him about stock options."

Marge looked blank. Then she said, "What the billy blue blazes are you on about? Stock options? For one thing, Pet Pro's privately owned. So why would you be asking him about stock options? Not to mention the fact that the guy's a lot better at devaluing stock than recommending investments. One of his little side businesses is buying up healthy business. Then he . . ."

"Chews them up and spits them out," Quill said. "I get the picture. But when I Googled Pet Pro last night an article from the *Wall Street Journal* showed up. Apparently he's considering taking Pet Pro public."

"No kidding." Marge rubbed her chin thoughtfully.

"So I could just say I was reading the *Journal* the other day and I came across this article and did he think I should invest in his company if he goes public."

"It might work," Marge said shrewdly. "Guy like that likes to boast. No question. Look at that Donald Trump. So you get Kittleburger started on what a big muckety muck he is in business, you probably won't be able to shut him up. Thing is, you'd better have me with you."

"I should?"

"He's gonna lose you right about the time he starts talking discovery," Marge said. "Now me, he'll enjoy talking to. And we can slip in a couple of questions about where he was Monday night. And maybe some other things, too."

"But that still doesn't explain why you said, 'Maxwell Kittleburger' in that odd way at the Chamber meeting."

"It doesn't, does it?" Marge said with a sharklike smile.

"He must be at Harvey's," Dina said in response to Quill's inquiry. She and Marge had taken Quill's Honda to the Inn. Dina was at her post early this morning. She usually was early if she had spent the night in town with Davy. "At least, that's what I'm guessing. Harvey's pitching him." She sat behind the large mahogany reception desk and blinked at them through her large, red-rimmed glasses. Mike the groundskeeper had filled the oriental vases that stood on either side of the desk with late-blooming lilies, and their heavy scent permeated the air.

"Harvey Bozzel is pitching an advertising campaign to Maxwell Kittleburger?" Quill said. She and Marge exchanged glances that were in equal parts amazed and appalled. In the past, Harvey had been responsible for a nudie bar protest song, using the lyrics from "The Battle Hymn of the Republic," and the infamous Little Miss Hemlock Falls Beauty Contest. Everybody in Hemlock Falls loved Harvey — or at least tolerated him with a modicum of affection — but nobody could accuse him of even basic competency when it came to advertising and marketing ideas. He had organized a Civil War reenactment in which the town had *lost* the battle.

Marge, who thought tact was for wusses, said, "He's out of his mind. Kittleburger'll have him for breakfast. Come to think of it, how the heck did he convince Kittleburger to see him, anyway? The guy's an idiot."

Quill was pretty sure Marge was referring to Harvey. "Now, maybe Harvey actually came up with a great idea. You read about little ad companies that come up with million-dollar campaigns all the time. They absolutely slaughter the high-powered competition. The *Wall Street Journal*'s filled with stories like that."

"Since when do you read the *Wall Street Journal*?" Dina asked with interest.

"Since she started posing as a detective," Marge scoffed. "Dina's right. This doesn't make any sense."

"Hey," Quill protested. "You find real genius in unexpected places. Harvey's been trying for years to land a big client — and what could be bigger for someone like him than Pet Pro Protein?"

"How'd Harvey get Kittleburger over to his place, anyhow?"

"He left this for Mr. Kittleburger. Sort of a sample, to get his attention." Dina pulled out a large piece of tissue paper–covered cardboard from beneath the reception desk. A note attached to the board was headed: "Bozzel Advertising! Nothing But the Best! For the Best! H. Bozzel, Pres!" Below the head was a note in Harvey's spiky handwriting: "An idea for your new logo."

Quill flipped the tissue paper up.

Harvey was a pretty good illustrator. He'd sketched a can of cat food and designed a new label. The silhouette of a cat, ears up, whiskers at a rakish slant, stared out from the center. The lifeless body of a mouse dangled from its jaws. The header beneath read: "Mousee Morsels! Pet Food the Way Nature Intended!"

The three of them gazed at the drawing in silence.

"I think it's gross," Dina said. "Frankly."

"It *is* gross," Quill said. "The question is, why in the world did Mr. Kittleburger bite? So to speak."

"I don't know that," Dina said.

"I know *this*," Marge said. "It'd be a darned good idea to find out."

"It would?" Quill said. "But what does it have to do with the murder investigation?"

"Not a thing. But what d'ya think Kittleburger's gone over to Harvey's to do?"

Quill spread her hands out in a "search me" gesture.

"I'll tell you what he's going to do. Kittleburger's got a reputation worse than Disney."

It took Quill a second to work this out. "Oh. You mean about suing people that mess around with the Disney logo or the Disney image. But for heaven's sake, Marge, we're talking about pet food here."

"Far as Mad Max is concerned, Pet Pro Protein is the Holy Grail. And I'll tell you something." Marge's chin jutted out, in-

144

creasing her resemblance to George S. Patton. "He's not going to try his bully-boy tactics here in *my* town. You coming with me, Quill?"

"Wow," Dina said, "this is just like the movies."

Quill's personal preference was to avoid unnecessary trouble. Between Meg, murder investigations, and the hassles of running the Inn, she had enough upsets. "I should really stay here and settle down to paying some bills."

Marge grabbed her upper arm and began to pull her to the door. "You can take care of the bills later."

Quill hung back. It seemed rude to remove Marge's hand from her arm, so she said, merely, "I don't want to."

"You think I'm going to start punching old Max, or something? Nah. I'll be diplomatic like you wouldn't believe. We'll pry that sucker off of Harvey and take him back to the Croh Bar for lunch."

"It's too early for lunch."

"Coffee, then. Come *on.*"

The two of them returned to Quill's Honda and Quill drove back the short distance to the village.

The sun was at an angle that flooded the cobblestone storefronts on Main Street in golden mellow light. Yellow and white chrysanthemums filled the stone planters that were spaced at intervals down the sidewalks. The village looked far too peaceful for anything but cheerful conversation and contented idling.

There was an empty spot right in front of Harvey's office. Quill parallel parked quite neatly, and she and Marge got out of the car. Village ordinances banned any advertising signs more that eight inches high and three feet wide. So the dark green sign with the gold letters over Harvey's front door read BOZZEL FOR THE BEST! (ADVERTISING AT IT'S GREATEST) had a fairly tasteful appearance. Although, Quill noted, Harvey still hadn't deleted the annoying apostrophe from "it's." It just, he claimed, didn't look right without it.

Marge shoved the glass front door open with all the subtlety of a tank invasion. Corrine Peterson looked up from her phone conversation with a startled scream, said a hasty "No, it isn't him, thank god," into the handset, and hung up. Then she rose to her feet. "Hi, Mrs. Schmidt. Hi, Mrs. McHale. What's wrong *now?*" Her pretty round face was smudged with either toner ink or carbon. She looked worried.

"What was wrong before?" Marge demanded.

"Uh," Corrine said. She smiled brightly, if with noticeable effort. "Harvey, I mean, Mr. Bozzel is in production in another part of the building. How-may-I-help-you?"

Marge snorted. "Corrine. There *isn't* another part of this building where he could be in production. What part of this building would he be in except right here? The pet store? The hardware?"

"Actually," Corrine said, "he's out." She sank back into her chair. "That production stuff is what I'm supposed to say if he's not in."

Marge loomed over Corrine's desk. Corrine shrank back against the wall. "Was he in this morning?"

"Well, sure. The *Pennysaver* ads are due by ten sharp on Thursdays or Mr. Stoker goes absolutely bonkers. So Harvey was working on those."

"Did Harvey have a meeting this morning with a guy, pot belly, bald spot in the middle of a bunch of greasy hair, and a big fat cigar stuck in his puss?"

"Yes," Corrine said, "he did." She stared at Marge with all the fascination of a rabbit in front of a snake. "And it didn't go well."

"No?"

"Nope."

Marge took her knuckles off the edge of Corrine's desk. "What happened?"

"This man. The one you just said. He came slamming in here so hard I thought the glass was going to bust right out of the doorframe." Corrine took a deep, pleasurable breath; clearly, the love of drama was edging out her distress. "Well! He said, 'Where's this Bozzel.' Well! I said 'Do-you-have-an-appointment?' Well!"

"Corrine," Quill said. "If you could please just tell us what happened."

"The guy went into Harvey's office. The thing is, he didn't just bust in, he quieted down real fast and kind of rolled in, you know? Like a showdown. Anyhow, he was in there for about twenty minutes."

"You hear anything of what was said?" Marge demanded.

"Huh-uh. The door's too thick. Anyhow, he came out and left. And then Harvey came out and said he was going to be out of town for a while and to hold all calls." Corrine leaned forward and said in a whisper, "I think he was scared of this guy."

"You do, do you?" Marge said grimly. "And do you know where 'this guy' got to?"

"Nope. Sorry," Corrine shook her head. "He was some kind of mad, though."

Marge turned around without a good-bye,

and went back outside.

Quill said good-bye to Corrine, asked her to call the Inn when Harvey returned, and joined Marge on the pavement. "Harvey's been run out of town, Marge. Good grief. What do you suppose Kittleburger said to him?"

Marge shrugged. "The usual. 'I'll keep you tied up in court so long, there won't be enough left to bury you.' That kind of shit."

This sounded more like the voice of experience than mere opinion. "Have you . . ." Quill began.

"Have I what?" Marge peered up and down the street, as if Kittleburger might be hiding behind one of the lampposts.

"It just sounds as if you know more about him than the information you'd get from reading the *Wall Street Journal*."

"Maybe," Marge said. "Maybe not. Well, I'm not spending the rest of the morning chasing this guy. I'm going to stop at the office for a bit." She jerked her thumb in the direction of MARGE SCHMIDT REALTY, which was three doors down from Harvey's place, between Nickerson's Hardware and the loathed Puppy Palace. "Do me a favor. When you do track this bozo down, give me a call, will ya?"

"Sure," Quill said. She watched in a

bemused way as Marge stamped off.

"So *something*'s going on between them," she said to Meg when she returned to the Inn. She'd found her sister in the kitchen as usual. She sat down in the rocker by the cobblestone fireplace. The grate was still filled with summer's dried hydrangea. Another few weeks and it'd be time to light the fire.

"Weird," Meg agreed briefly, "but not relevant to the murder." She stood at the birch-topped prep table. She was chopping pumpkin into one-inch chunks.

At midmorning the Inn's kitchen was usually quiet. The furor of the breakfast service had passed, and the chaos of lunch wouldn't begin for another hour. Quill pushed the rocker into motion. She loved this kitchen. Bundles of dried herbs and flowers hung from the old oak beams. Meg's favorite copper-bottomed pans swayed above her head as she vigorously chopped squash.

"And it always *smells* good in here," she said aloud.

Meg raised her head and smiled. "It does, doesn't it? So. Kittleburger must have gotten the best of Marge in some business deal, or tried to, at least. I can't think of anything else that would make her madder. But I still can't see how this relates to poor Lila. Although," she paused, the chef's knife suspended in mid-air, "it says a lot about — what she'd call him? Mad Max? I'll tell you, Quill, from what we're hearing about this guy, it sounds as if he could be the number-one suspect based on his character alone."

"Wait'll you hear the rest of what she told me." Quill summarized her early morning discussion with Marge.

"And you're going to disguise yourself and sneak into the trooper barracks?" Meg rolled her eyes. "Good luck. Better have Howie Murchison on hand to bail you out of the clink."

"It's quite legal," Quill said. "All of it except taking a look at the forensics report."

"At least it'll give us some hard information." Meg dumped a few handfuls of brown sugar into a sauté pan, threw in a large spoonful of butter, and turned up the Aga. "At the moment, question number one is where is Maxwell Kittleburger?"

Dina shoved open the double doors that led to the dining room. Quill took one look at her face and jumped out of the rocking chair. "Dina! What's happened? Are you all right?"

"I'm okay," she said. "But Mr. Kittleburger isn't. He's upstairs in his room. And I don't think he's going to be coming down anytime soon. At least not on his own. Somebody's killed him."

CHAPTER 7

"Great Jumping Jesus," Doreen said. "I can't keep maids on staff for love nor money. And for why? 'Cause of the corpses. You do realize that this Kittle-whosis . . ."

"Kittleburger," Quill said glumly.

"Was in the same room where we found that Mavis person ten years ago?"

Meg scrubbed at her face with both fists. "Mavis wasn't found dead in her room. She was found dead outside her room. Somebody pushed her off the balcony and into the gorge."

"Well they mighta had the same consideration for Enid's nerves. Does it matter all that much to a murderer where the body's laying? Could'a pushed him over the balcony easy as pie instead of laying him out on the bed like that."

Meg put her head in her hands. They were sitting in the dining room. They'd been sitting in the dining room since eleven o'clock that morning, when what looked like the entire Tompkins County Sheriff's Department descended on the Inn after Quill had called first, the ambulance, and second, Davy Kiddermeister. It was now after three o'clock.

"At least Davy had his head screwed on right for once," Doreen grumbled. "Called the county before that trooper Harker could nose in." She shifted uncomfortably in the cushioned chair Quill had insisted on bringing in for her. Although she fiercely denied it, Doreen had a mean case of arthritis.

"I don't know about that," Meg said. "These guys closed the Inn. Harker at least didn't close us up."

"We weren't a scene of the crime at the time," Quill pointed out.

Meg got up and crossed the deep blue carpeting to the archway that led to the reception area and peered around the corner. "There's only one room up there that's the scene of the crime. So why close up the rest of the place?" She crossed back, swinging her arms restlessly.

"We're not closed, really. Just nobody new in and nobody old out. And the kitchen's open."

Meg sat down and stretched her legs in front of her. "So you think the person who killed Lila killed him?"

"I think it was poison. You saw it. The poor guy was blue. And he'd thrown up all over . . . never mind. Why don't you give Andy . . . never mind that, either." Andy Bishop, whom Meg had jilted the day of their wedding, was rapidly becoming the best-known pediatrician in upstate New York. He was pretty good at poisons, perhaps because little kids tended to stick things in their mouths they shouldn't. "Murderers mostly stick to the same MO, don't they? So I'm not sure of anything right now."

"I'd just like to know how we're going to get the forensics report on this crime," Meg said in a near whisper. "All the guys in the Tompkins County Sheriff's Department love Myles. Do you think . . ." There was the rustle of many people coming down the front stairs. Quill nudged her silent. "Whoa," Meg said. "Here they all come."

The remaining live members of the International Association of Pet Food Providers came into the room one by one.

Meg lit up with excitement. "Now that we've got all the suspects in the same room, maybe we can grill the guilty party into confessing. Just like Nero Wolfe."

Olivia Oberlie led the way. Her caftan

today was bright pink. "She's changed her tote, too," Meg hissed. Little Bit, her head hanging over the edge of another brightly striped tote, regarded them all with weary forbearance.

Olivia saw Quill and turned with the slow deliberation of a cruise ship headed into port. The rest trailed after her like so many tugs. One by one they settled at the tables around Meg and Quill: Robin and Victoria Finnegan, Millard and Priscilla Barnstaple, Pamela Durbin and Pookie the Peke, Rudy Baranga, and Olivia herself.

"We are much diminished in number," Olivia said, settling into the chair opposite Quill.

"I am truly sorry," Quill said sincerely. "This whole experience has been just awful for you."

"So I told the investigation officer. Lieutenant Provost. Simon, his name is. His headquarters are in Ithaca."

"The county seat," Quill said, "yes."

"Did he bug you with a lot of questions?" Meg asked innocently.

"He was, of course, interested in my Prophecy. He'd caught the eleven o'clock news last night." Olivia's turquoise eyes darkened a shade. "I believe he thought I may have had a hand in Max's death. I soon

156

set *him* straight,"

"You did? Well, that was lucky." Meg drummed her fingers on the table. "So how did you?"

"How did I what?"

"Set him straight?"

"We were all at a meeting at Pamela's at the time of the murder," Victoria Finnegan said. She looked at her husband with dislike. "Except for Robin. He says he was hiking down Hemlock Gorge."

"Which can absolutely be verified," Robin said. He ran one skinny, long-fingered hand through his hair, which was dirty blond and lank. "I told you. There was an informal search party out for a missing camper. I walked along with them for a while. There's at least six Cornell co-eds that will swear I was mucking around in that bloody stream at nine forty-five this morning."

"Nine forty-five?" Quill said, startled. "How in the world can the police be that accurate?"

"He was on his cell phone when he was stuck," Millard said, "he was always on his cell phone. I gave him article after article about the research they've done linking excessive cell phone use and brain tumors, but did he listen to me? No." He smirked, "Guess he doesn't have to worry about brain tumors now."

"Stuck with what?" Meg asked.

"They don't know what the poison is as of this moment," Priscilla said crisply. "But they know it was an injection because they discovered the syringe in the bedclothes. Whatever it was sent him into convulsions. It must have been quite unpleasant." She curled her lip. "And you, Millard, might at least make some effort to be civilized about this. The man is dead, after all."

"The man, as my dear wife so mincingly calls him, was a complete jerk." Millard tossed his head back. His ponytail curled like a snake over his left shoulder. "And any of you that pretends to grieve can shove it where the sun don't shine."

Pamela took a small lace handkerchief from her sleeve and began to sob gently into it. "Any death is horrible," she said somewhat indistinctly. "I don't believe that y'all are as tough as you're makin' out."

Meg regarded her unsympathetically. "Would you like some tea?"

"I surely would."

"I," Olivia said, "would like a gin. Neat."

"Wait a minute." Quill bit her lip. At 9:45 that morning, Maxwell Kittleburger had been harassing poor Harvey Bozzel. Hadn't he? Quill rubbed her neck. She was starting to get a headache.

A guy with a potbelly and a bald spot in the middle of greasy black hair and chomping a big cigar.

That described Kittleburger, all right.

It also described Rudy Baranga. She looked at him. He sat with his left ankle balanced on his right knee. He winked at her, waved his cigar, and said, "If the bar's open, Nate knows my usual."

"I'll go and tell Nate to send in that Cassie to take the orders," Doreen grumbled. "Maybe that nosy lieutenant will let me go home now. I already answered all of his questions."

"As far as I know, he wants us here all night," Millard whinnied. "Ha ha. Just kidding! But man, did you all look rattled for a second."

Doreen said, "t'uh" in disgust and stamped out of the room.

Meg said sunnily, "It was a good thing you were all in that meeting together this morning."

"Except for Robin," Priscilla said. Then, in response to his look of active dislike, "I like to be accurate."

"What sort of meeting was it?" Meg sat relaxed in her chair, ankles crossed, arms folded.

Pamela dabbed at her eyes, folded her handkerchief, and put it away. "I called the meeting," she said. "I was hopin' that the association would kick in more money to support the dog and puppy show."

"Hm." Meg accepted this with bright interest. "And what did you all decide?"

"It degenerated into a quarrel over the vegetarian movement, as it always does these days," Priscilla said with an expression of distaste.

"I jus' don't know *how* you people can eat anything with a face," Pamela said hotly. "And how you expect our poor dumb friends to do it either is just beyond me."

"They are not dumb," Olivia pronounced solemnly.

"I didn't mean dumb like stupid," Pamela protested. "I mean dumb as in they can't talk."

"They talk to me."

"Well, the Lesser Beings, then."

"Do you all support vegetarian pet food?" Quill asked.

Priscilla tilted her head in a considering way. "It's much healthier, you realize."

"Bullshit," Rudy said.

"I don't like to hear that language used in my presence, Rudy," Olivia said.

"Well, get used to it," he said rudely. He

jerked his chin at Quill. "You getting the drift of this, cookie?"

"No," Quill said. "I don't understand why it's such an issue."

"Some pet owners are concerned about contamination of the food chain," Victoria said. "Or at least, Pamela here's been trying to convince them of the dangers."

Pamela fluttered her false eyelashes against her cheek. "In my own small way . . ."

"In her own small way," Victoria said with a malicious smile, "Pamela's been writing her congressman, hiring a lobbyist, sending out articles, trying to get the state of New York to ban meat-based pet food. And of course with Olivia's TV show having such influence . . ."

"It is nothing less than cannibalism," Olivia pronounced.

Meg yawned, blinked, and said sorry.

"You two don't seem to get what's at stake here," Victoria said contemptuously. "Max had just contacted an investment banking firm, well, actually, I'd contacted it for him, to begin the process of going public."

"I get what's at stake here," Meg said. "I just don't care very much. Quill? I've got stuff to do in the kitchen."

Quill's attention was on Victoria and she barely acknowledged her sister's exit. She'd received an exhaustive lecture from Marge about the advantages of IPOs. Initial Public Offerings, that was it. "There's a lot of money in an IPO," she said intelligently. And a lot of money was the best possible motive for murder.

Victoria gave her a glance of qualified approval. "Under certain circumstances, yes, there is. But if the circumstances are that the second-highest populated state in the union is going to ban meat-based pet food, and your company is the third-largest provider of meat-based pet food in those same fifty states, the profit prospects go way, way down."

"Way down," Priscilla said with a pleased air.

Victoria smiled thinly. "And of course, Priscilla was supporting this, not out of conviction . . ."

"Vegan Vittles is committed to the healthy minds and the healthy bodies of our dogs and cats," Millard said angrily. "You can say what you like about Priscilla . . ."

"Thank you, Millard," she said dryly

". . . but my company is absolutely founded on vegetarian principles. Our furred and feathered friends can get adequate protein from many sources. It doesn't have to be meat."

"Of course, there is that lawsuit from the Great Dane owner creeping up on you," Robin said with a sly grin.

"Bullshit. Capitalist crap," Millard said heatedly. "If the damn dog starved to death it wasn't because of *my* food." He added viciously, "You know what we need to do here in this U.S. of A.? We need to disbar *more* of your kind."

"May I take your order, please?" Cassie said into the silence.

"Nate knows what I drink," Rudy said instantly.

"I'll have a martini," Victoria said. "Now, Quill, you're missing the most important piece of information here, because, of course, it's about money. It's always about the money."

"No, it isn't," Quill, said.

"I beg your pardon?" Victoria, startled out of her self-congratulatory rant, looked at Quill directly for the first time that day.

"I said it's not always about the money."

"Listen to the woman, Vic," Robin said meanly. "Might make a human being of you yet."

"Shut up, Robin," she said pleasantly. "At any rate, Priscilla here has been trying to buy Pet Pro for months, now."

"Two months," Priscilla said. "Vegan

163

Vittles needs Pet Pro's manufacturing capacity."

"And anything that keeps the price down is just fine with her." Victoria leaned over and scrabbled in her purse. "Can I smoke in here?"

"I'm afraid not," Quill said.

"He's got a cigar." She nodded at Rudy without looking at him.

"It ain't lit," Rudy said.

"Then I'm going outside for a minute. Can I go through the kitchen?"

"Sorry," Quill said, who didn't feel sorry at all. "New York State says no."

Victoria walked to the archway with quick, nervous strides, turned right, and disappeared.

"Was Pet Pro actually for sale?" Quill asked Priscilla. "Or were you making an unsolicited offer?"

"With Max it *was* all about the money. He was either going to take it public or sell it to me. If somebody hadn't killed him, I would have had an answer by the end of next week."

"Oh?"

"Those investment bankers Victoria hired begin discovery next Monday. Max makes dog food, sends it to the reseller, and makes more dog food again. It's not a very complicated business, and Max was a devil for simplicity anyway. Even with Lila gone, discovery's going to be a pretty straightforward process. You know about discovery?"

Quill looked wise and kept her mouth shut.

Priscilla smiled in a catty kind of way. "Right. Sure you do. All the accounting's checked for accuracy. The bank accounts are verified. That sort of thing."

"And Lila was important because?"

"Oh, she handled the books for Max, too. To be exact, she checked on what bookkeeping sent her. She didn't do much physical work herself. At least, not that kind of physical."

"Really," Quill said casually. "By the other kind of physical you mean . . ."

"Max, of course. Max was such a bastard I think Lila may have regretted getting involved with him. People just . . ." she stopped short and bit her lip.

"People?" Quill nudged gently.

"People didn't really understand Lila." Priscilla stared down at her clasped hands for a long moment. "But there you are." Her glance fell on her husband. Cassie had returned with the drinks and bowls of the handmade chip mix that usually sat at the bar. Millard was tossing the chips into the air and into his open mouth. He missed more frequently than he succeeded. At the table beyond him, Olivia sat with a tarot deck, apparently instructing Pamela in the tarot's mysteries.

"She owned stock," Quill said suddenly.

"Excuse me?" Priscilla set her glass of sauvignon blanc down squarely in the middle of the cocktail napkin.

"Lila owned stock, Olivia said. Stock in what?"

"I don't have the least idea."

"It wasn't in Pet Pro?"

"Pet Pro's privately held, as you very well know," she said testily. "And Max owned almost all of it. I think there's a bit that belongs to a son, and an even smaller bit that belongs to his mother. He could have given some to Lila, I suppose. But why that would make a difference to Olivia, I can't imagine."

"And Lila didn't own stock in your company?"

"Not a chance."

"Priscilla, what happens to Pet Pro now? Who inherits it?"

She picked up her wine and took a large sip. "The Kittleburger Trust. It's a philanthropic organization, if you can believe it." She gave Quill a thin-lipped smile. "At some level, Max knew he was going to hell when he died, and in my opinion the trust is a sop to the gods. As for my bid to buy the company? Forget that as a motive. Max died at a time of maximum inconvenience for me. Typical of him." She swallowed the rest of the wine and said, "I'll have more of this. Where's that waitress?"

"Cassie will be by shortly." Quill got up, a little stiff from sitting in one place for so long. "Will you excuse me?"

She slipped through the double doors into the kitchen. A smaller than usual dinner staff had arrived and preparations for the evening's dinner were well under way. Meg stood in front of the Sub-Zeros, a clipboard in her hand.

"Hey," Quill said.

"Hey, yourself. Hang on a second. Elizabeth?"

Elizabeth Chou, who had been promoted to part of Bjarne Bjarnson's responsibilities in the kitchen after the Finn had left for more contentious pastures, straightened up as if on military parade.

Meg spoke rapidly and to the point. "The dining room's open only to the suspects in this stupid murder. Which means six dinners, plus the dinners for the rest of us."

"And the policemen?" Elizabeth asked.

"Sandwiches," Meg said firmly. "I'm only going to offer the guests two entrees and these three sides. If the pet people don't like it, they can lump it." She handed the clipboard to Elizabeth and sat next to Quill at the prep counter. "So you've fled the scene?"

"I have never, in all my life, met such concentrated nastiness."

Meg shook her head. "I'm flat-out amazed that they haven't killed each other."

"Olivia and Pamela aren't so awful," Quill said, "although neither one is going to get penalized for having too many brains. I don't see either of them as killers. And they both have alibis."

"But that's just it," Meg said with exasperation. "All of them have alibis!"

"Not airtight, though," Quill said smugly. "Rudy Baranga can't have been at that meeting all that time. According to Corrine Peterson, at nine forty-five this morning he was busy harassing poor Harvey. I mean, I'm not one hundred percent certain, but who else could it have been?"

"Of course, that puts Rudy out of the running for the this morning's murder."

Quill could feel her face fall. "Nuts. So it does." She bit her lip and thought for a moment. "So what if they're all in it together?

You remember Georgia?"

"I remember Georgia," Meg said, a little sadly. "That was one of the toughest cases we've ever had."

"The trouble is that at least one of them is really annoyed that Mad Max is dead. This has bollixed up Priscilla's offer to buy Pet Pro. The rest of them are jumping for joy, though."

"Man," Meg said, "I hope that when I die, at least a couple of people will be sorry."

"I'll be devastated," Quill promised. "But Priscilla said any hope she had of buying Pet Pro has gone up in smoke. And I can't see her agreeing to alibi the murder. She looked mad enough to murder the murderer, if she catches him, as a matter of fact. So that leaves us with Victoria, Robin, and Rudy."

"And Pamela."

"I don't think so. I'm convinced that Max and Lila were murdered by the same person. And a ton of people saw Pamela with Harland Peterson the night of Lila's murder."

"And the two murders have to be connected because?"

"Lila and Max were in bed together, literally and figuratively. Just from a logical standpoint, it'd be absurd to suggest that there are two murders for two different reasons by two different perp . . ."

"Yeah, yeah, yeah. I get it."

"Meg?" Elizabeth Chou emerged from the refrigerator with a puzzled look on her face. "We are out of pork loin."

"We are not out of pork loin," Meg said flatly. "There's at least twenty pounds of it in there." She trotted over to the Sub-Zero, looked inside, and yelled, "Damn! What happened to the pork loin?"

"Meg?" Quill said.

"Did you give anybody twenty pounds of pork loin today?" Meg accused her.

"Of course not."

"Well, WHERE THE HECK IS IT!" She turned to the kitchen staff and demanded, "We have to search the place! That's a hundred dollars worth of meat."

Meg was definitely going to be distracted for the next few hours. Quill slipped off the stool and left the kitchen by the back door.

She stepped into the cool freshness of early evening. Autumn was closing in. The air was fragrant with the smoke of wood fires. Autumn light lifted Quill's heart. Its gold was rounder, heavier, and more melancholy than the light of spring and summer. "And winter's light is frozen white," she said aloud as Max the dog came dancing up to her. "And how has your day been?"

Max rolled over on his back and wriggled. The shaggy ends of his coat were fretted with burrs and twigs. "Down in the gorge again, I see." Quill pulled a few twigs free, bringing some of Max's coat with them. She rolled the silky hair between her fingers. "Want to go up to the old place, Maxie?"

"Ma'am?"

Quill jumped in alarm. Max, good old guard dog that he was, wagged his tail happily at the young policeman who approached her through the herb garden.

"You're not headed out anywhere, ma'am? The looey wants you all to stick around."

"I'm just going up the back stairs, officer." She looked up. Her former balcony was just above the kitchen door. "I'm feeling a bit nostalgic."

"Ma'am?"

"Never mind. How are things going?"

"Not too good, ma'am," he said seriously. He was young and a little pudgy. He made Quill feel quite maternal.

"I'm sorry to hear that."

"Well, the looey's not too happy either," he admitted. "And I think he wants to talk to you before he leaves."

"I'll be up in 340," Quill said. "And please tell him that there are sandwiches and coffee for the men in the kitchen. Just talk to my sister."

"Yes, ma'am. And thank you, ma'am. I'm so hungry my stomach thinks my throat is cut. How will I know her, ma'am?"

"She's the short cranky one throwing the pans around the kitchen."

She climbed up the fire escape, Max clicking along behind her. It'd been months since she'd taken this route. Months since she'd visited her old rooms. They'd decided to tear out her serviceable little kitchen and replace it with a wet bar, and an under-the-counter refrigerator. It would be ready for guests in a few weeks; Quill knew that Dina and Meg referred to it as the Sarah Suite behind her back.

She walked in, Max at her heels. Her comfortable leather couch had been replaced with a chintz love seat and chair in rose, greens, and cream. The old pine chest she'd used as a coffee table was in Myles' house. The biggest change was the carpeting. She'd put in a quiet beige Berber carpet when they'd first moved in more than ten years ago. It'd been replaced by a thick-piled rose.

But the view out the back was the same. She pulled the armchair over to the french doors that led to the balcony. It was almost full dark, now. Meg's herb garden was a dim stretch of humps and brush.

"Ms. Quilliam?"

She'd left the door open. She turned now and saw a middle-aged man with a bit of a belly and a tired face. He wore a rumpled tweed sports coat frayed at the elbows. His tie was loosened around his neck. "It's Mrs. McHale, now," she said, with that faint sense of surprise she still felt at the use of her new name. "You must be Lieutenant Provost?"

"Yes, ma'am." He shook hands. "So you're married to McHale?" He smiled warmly. "We could use his help right about now. Tompkins County lost a good man when he left for that security firm. If that's what it really is?"

Quill didn't say anything.

"Right. Well. May I sit down?"

Quill leaped to her feet. "Of course! I'm so sorry. And would you like coffee or sandwiches? I told your . . . sergeant?"

"Patrolman Guinness. Yes, he mentioned the food to me. I'll take advantage of that offer a little later, if you don't mind." He waited until Quill had resettled herself in the chair and then sat on the couch. "We've interviewed all of the staff that were here at the time of the murder."

"And you're sure the murder occurred at

nine forty-five?"

"Fairly sure, yes."

"Was Mr. Kittleburger actually on a call at the time?"

Provost sucked his bottom lip, and then eyed her in a thoughtful way. "Yes. He was. On his Minolta cell phone, to be precise."

"Did you punch the little 'last call' button on his cell phone? I mean, *who* he was actually talking to might be evidence, don't you th . . ." Quill faltered to a stop. Provost's gaze was not encouraging.

"With all due respect, Mrs. McHale . . ."

"Call me Quill, please."

"I've got one amateur detective on my hands already down in Summersville. To be perfectly candid . . . you don't mind if I'm perfectly candid?"

"No," Quill said in a small voice.

"Dr. McKenzie is a mighty pain in my backside. I sure don't look forward to having another."

"Of course you wouldn't," Quill said warmly.

"But I suppose there's no harm in telling you that he was talking to Mrs. Durbin."

"Pamela?" Quill said, startled. "Really? She didn't say a word about it."

"She seems unaware that the call was terminated because Kittleburger was — ah

174

— terminated. He was supposed to be at this general session of the International Association of what?"

"Pet Food Providers."

"And he wasn't. She said she called him to ask if he was going to be at the meeting. He said he wasn't. She said he grunted very rudely at her, and ended the call."

"And you think . . ."

"That someone ended the call for him, yes."

"But you can't actually prove it."

Lieutenant Provost looked very unhappy. "Yes, Mrs. McHale, we can. He received another phone call at ten to ten and the caller went straight to voice mail."

"And the phone was in his hand when we found him?" Quill said. "I see."

"I hope you can see that I'd appreciate it if you would limit your contributions to this case to answering my questions," Provost said testily. "I swear to god, mystery novelists have a lot to answer for. Why does everybody think he's a detective? If you want to be a detective, join the police force." He took a handkerchief from his chinos' pocket and wiped his forehead. "Sorry. Had to get that one off my chest. Now, I've got some questions about how you spent your morning."

Quill took him through her day, although she indulged in a little tactful editing when she recounted her conversation with Marge. Provost seemed uninterested in Rudy Baranga's visit to the hapless Harvey, merely remarking (as Meg had done) that it put paid to any suspicions about Rudy.

"And that," Provost said as he made a final entry in his notepad, "wraps it up for you, Mrs. McHale."

"So you've finished up here at the Inn?"

"You want to reopen? You can reopen."

Quill sighed. "I'd almost rather stay closed for another day or two. Maxwell Kittleburger was a pretty big deal in business. We're going to be besieged. It's incredibly disruptive." She looked at him hopefully. "Unless we can boot the suspects out?"

"I have asked the Barnstaples, the Finnegans, and Baranga for a second set of interviews," Provost said with care. "I've suggested that they stick around for them. Miss Oberlie isn't planning on going anywhere soon, apparently. She's involved with this dog show?"

"It's this Saturday," Quill said. "And, shoot, I just remembered that she's bringing her camera crew in to stay here for the weekend. She's going to feature the darn thing on *Mind Doesn't Matter*."

"Televised dog show, huh?" Provost said. "Pure breeds and such?"

"Pets and such." Quill glanced at Max, who lay belly-up on the floor, both paws over his eyes. "Actually, I was thinking of entering Max."

"Him?" Provost said with unflattering disbelief.

Quill's tones became frosty. "He's not beautiful. I do know that. But he's very intelligent."

"You're saying they have a smartest-dog class?"

"In a way. It's a class to test how many words your dog knows."

"That I'd like to see."

"You're welcome to come."

"I'd better get on home, or I won't be welcome there." Provost got to his feet with a groan. Quill and Max followed him out the door and she closed it behind her. "You're not locking it?"

Quill flushed. "I know, I know. But nobody locks up in Hemlock Falls."

"So that fire door," he gestured at the door to the fire escape, "it's not locked from the outside?"

"I'm afraid not."

"And at night? You don't lock up at night?"

"Well, no. But the guest rooms lock, of

course."

"But anyone could get in here, any time of day or night, and hide out in there, for example." He jerked his thumb at Quill's old suite. "You don't lock the rooms unless there's a guest in there. Jeez." He ran both hands over his face. "I ought to get forensics in every part of the heap. I don't have the budget for this." He rubbed the back of his neck. "You say the victim's pretty well known?"

"Quite well known, I should think." She added encouragingly, "But you must have some suspicions at this point?"

"Suspicions. Huh. Do you know what convicts perps nine times out of ten, Mrs. McHale?"

"Confessions?" Quill guessed. "I remember reading somewhere that most murderers actually end up admitting they did it."

"Most murders are spur-of-the-moment domestic or urban violence. And yeah, the combination of a good investigation and a good interrogator gets a confession. That's how your husband built his reputation. But with tricky little murders like these . . ."

"These. You just said 'these.' You think that Lila Longstreet's murder and this one are connected then?" Quill asked alertly.

Provost glared at her, but sailed on any-

178

way, ". . . it's forensics. Hard evidence. A hair in the carpet. A glob of spit where a glob of spit shouldn't be. Even a twig, a leaf, a splotch of water can bring the perp to his knees. So no, I don't have an idea of who killed Kittleburger or Lila Longstreet, but I'll have a much better one when the scene of the crime guys get the evidence back to me."

He turned and walked down the hall. Quill and Max trailed after him. "So you're going to investigate Lila's death, too?"

Provost stopped at the elevator — which Quill never used — and jabbed the down button with his thumb. "The one good part of my day was getting Harker off that case," he said with a good deal of satisfaction. "The guy's a menace. I got him shoved off looking for that missing hiker. He isn't going to have time to mess around with the Longstreet case. He'll be too busy chasing his own rear end through the woods."

The elevator doors hushed open. Provost stepped inside. He waved at her as the door hushed closed. "I'll be expecting to see *very little* of you in these next few days, Mrs. McHale."

"Very little," Quill grumbled to Meg after the police had finally gone. "You would

179

think, with all the budget problems, the police would be *glad* to have some help."

Meg yawned. "Doesn't make much sense to me. Are you going home, or do you want to stay here for the night?" She looked around her apartment. "We've got an Aero bed in here, somewhere." Her rooms were across the hall from Quill's former home. Just as Quill needed quiet colors and minimal clutter, Meg required colors that shouted amid chaos. Her carpeting was bright red. The couch was lemon yellow. Cookbooks, plants, and purple and green throw pillows tumbled around the floor. Meg sat in the middle of all this in a nightshirt that read "Yo, Mama" and a pair of striped socks.

"I think I'll head out, now," Quill said. "I'm going to stop at the Puppy Palace in the morning, and then Marge and I are going out to the trooper barracks. So I won't see you until dinnertime."

Meg grinned up at her. "If you and Marge aren't locked up in the clink."

"You could come, too," Quill said. "I'm keeping the Inn closed tomorrow, too, so we can avoid any skulking media types. Elizabeth seemed to handle herself pretty well today, didn't she? She can handle things on her own."

"She did quite well," Meg said. "As for going along with you guys — are you crazy? Somebody has to stay on the outside to post bail, if nothing else."

"Ha ha," Quill said. But she stopped on her way out the door and looked over her shoulder. "You will bail us out if anything happens, won't you?"

"Sure. But it'll cost you that Coach bag you bought in Syracuse last month."

"Opportunist," Quill said. "C'mon, Max. We're going home."

CHAPTER 8

Pamela's Pampered Puppy Palace occupied a small store on Main Street between Marge's Casualty and Realty and Esther West's Best Dress Shoppe. It was one of those retail spaces that never seemed to attract a permanent owner, despite its excellent location. It had been, at various times, Blue Man Computing, a yarn shop, an antiques emporium (the stock a jumble of odds and ends from various garage sales), and a women's gym called Fit After Forty.

It was a pretty spot; like its neighbors, the store was built from cobblestone. One of the ornate Victorian lampposts that lined Main Street was right in front of the store. A pink cloth flag was attached to the base of the cage that held the lightbulb. A sequined poodle leaped around the store name, which was figured in silver thread.

Quill parked the Honda on the street and put a quarter in the newly installed parking meters (a revenue-generating tactic by the town supervisors, who were desperate to avoid raising taxes).

Pamela had painted the mullions in the large picture window that fronted her store a bright pink. She opened her door as Quill approached and cried, "Well, I never! You came and visited after all!" She embraced Quill with cries of joy; the scent of her perfume was so strong that Quill had to hold back a sneeze.

She linked arms with Quill, pulled her to the edge of the sidewalk, and looked at her window. "I want you to take a look at this. I jus' finished painting those little stripes of wood. What are they called?"

"Mullions."

"It brightens the whole place up, don't you think?" She let Quill's arm go and looked up and down Main Street. "I'm hopin' to start a trend," she whispered. "All the other little strips of wood . . ."

"Mullions."

"Are white! Isn't that just the most boring thing?"

"Well, it's the most legal thing," Quill said apologetically. "The white's mandated by town code."

Pamela blinked at her uncomprehendingly.

"All the storesfronts are supposed to look alike. There's a town law that says so."

Pamela's rather watery blue eyes darkened. "If that isn't the stupidest thing. It's a free country, isn't it?" She frowned at the window. "It'd be a real pain in the ass to have to repaint that." She clapped her hand over her mouth in a girlish gesture. "Will you listen to the mouth on me? Sorry!"

"Maybe no one will notice the pink," Quill said diplomatically. "May I come in?"

"You are surely welcome. I'm jus' *so* anxious to get your opinion on the way I've decorated my little store."

The contents shrieked at Quill. Not the puppies and kittens, who were relatively quiet in their clean nests of shredded paper, but the pink walls, the pink-painted floor, and the red glittery balls hanging from the ceiling.

"Pink's such a happy color," Pamela said. "And of course, it starts with P."

"Starts with P?" Quill repeated.

"P's my lucky letter. Now." She rustled over to a wire cage that held a chubby golden retriever puppy. "This little darlin' could be just the dog for you, Quill."

"Gosh," Quill said. "We have a dog, you know." She tickled the pup's nose with one finger. The puppy scrambled to its feet and yipped enthusiastically. "Oh my," she said. "He is really cute."

"She," Pamela corrected her. She picked the puppy up and cuddled it under her chin. The puppy wriggled, caught sight of Quill, and barked. "You little darlin'," Pamela said. She dropped the puppy back into the cage. "I was just about to give them brekkies. You don't mind if I keep on working?"

"Not at all." A small desk jutted at right angles to the back wall. There was a chair behind it. Quill sat down rather tentatively.

"That's right," Pamela caroled, "you just sit right there and take a good look around." A large plastic bin had been wedged between two of the larger cages. Pamela scooped a pail full of kibble from it and began doling out the food.

"They're awfully quiet," Quill said.

"Priscilla says I overfeed them." Pamela tossed the remaining kibble back in the bin and began to fill the water cups from a two-gallon jug. "But I want them all to grow up big and strong." She stopped to pick up a small white kitten. "Like this fellow here. Look at those eyes, Quill. Have you every seen a brighter green?"

"A Persian?"

"Purebred. This little lovey comes with papers. She's worth every penny of the three hundred I'm askin' for her. All my dogs and cats come from the finest breeders in the world. If I had the time, I spend all of it shuttin' down those awful puppy mills." She gave Quill a sharp glance. "So don't you pay any mind to Priscilla Barnstaple's mouthy talk."

"Hm," Quill said. She had found this response quite useful when she hadn't a clue as to what the conversation was actually about.

"That *is* what she was talkin' to you about yesterday, wasn't it? How piss-poor my little stock of purebreds is. Golly. There goes my mouth again. But that Priscilla thinks she knows so much."

"Hm," Quill said.

" 'Course, the AKC didn't think much of her at all, did they?" Pamela dropped the kitten unceremoniously back into its nest. It ignored the kibble, curled up, and went to sleep.

"The AKC," Quill said. "Hm."

"Kicked her off the circuit. Took away her judge's certification. Serves her right, she thinks she knows so much."

"Took away her certification? My goodness. Why?"

"Well." Pamela settled her rather large backside against a cage of Jack Russell terriers. "*She* says it's because Max blamed her for his collie not even placing at the Virginia show last year. She says he blamed her for the fact that none of his dogs ever placed in the ribbons. Not so's you'd notice, at least. I mean, he took some. But nothing like he wanted to."

"And so Max had her credentials revoked?"

"She says he set her up." Pamela smiled. "Have to say I wouldn't put it past him."

"I'm surprised you even wanted him at the meeting yesterday." Quill felt extremely clever at the adroit way she'd introduced the case into the conversation.

"Oh, Max wasn't at the meeting," Pamela said. "He was busy getting killed. And since we wanted to buy his company, we put up with him."

"We?" Quill said, startled.

"Well, sure. Priscilla and me. And Millard, too. I own a good part of Vegan Vittles, you know."

"I didn't know."

Pamela shook her finger playfully in Quill's face. "Had to do something with all that money Daddy left me, didn't I?"

"So you must have been one of the last people to speak to Max before he died?"

"I guess I *was*," Pamela said with a kind

of mild delight. "I mean, who knew? Robin says the police think he was talkin' to me when he died. I mean, the man was killed talking right into my ear!"

"He didn't say anything about anyone being in the room with him?"

"He was goin' on about Lila." Pamela's smile faded. "Said the hick police here in this hick part of the country didn't have a clue. Said he was going to bring in a detective himself." She shrugged. "He'd been sayin' that from the git-go, though. He didn't treat her very well when she was alive, oh no. But as soon as she passes on . . ." She trailed off. "That's men for you."

The doorbell jangled. Pamela's smile broke over her face like a rising sun. "Now, and look who's here!"

"Hi, Harland," Quill said.

" 'Lo, Quill." Harland Peterson was a man of few — very few — words. The largest dairy farmer in the country, he was a big man; not especially tall, but built like one of his Galloway bulls. He'd been a widower for a long time, after a close and happy marriage to his hardworking wife. He'd begun to come out of his prolonged and silent mourning after a few supper dates with Marge Schmidt. The once-a-week Sunday dinners had become every-morning breakfasts at the Croh Bar and everyone in town was pleased to see it.

And here was Pamela, ten years younger, flirtatious to the bone, fluttering those fake eyelashes at Harland like a heifer in heat. (Except that she, Quill, hadn't a clue as to how a heifer in heat actually behaved.) She berated herself silently for snottiness, got up from the desk, and said, "I guess I'll leave you, Pamela. I have a few errands to run."

"Thank you so much for droppin' in, Quill. And I didn't even get a chance to talk about a little business I want to throw your way." There was that playful finger again. "Now, now, now. Harland here's told me how shy you are about your artist's career."

Harland's face was the texture of old saddle leather. Currently, it was the texture of red old saddle leather.

"But I want to hire you to paint a puppy mural on this far wall here." She waved at the back wall, which was currently filled with shelves of dog leashes, rhinestone collars, cat toys, rubber balls, and grooming aids. "I've got to soundproof this wall, anyway. That awful Marge Schmidt keeps complaining that she can hear the dogs. It's not *my* fault she can hear the dogs. It's the fault of whoever put these cheap partitions in. Anyhow, I'm thinking about expanding to the space upstairs. I can put all this stuff up there. And then the first thing customers would see when they walked in was pictures of puppies!"

"You don't live upstairs?" Quill said. Part of this store space, she knew, consisted of a one-bedroom apartment directly overhead.

"Goodness, no, I have a nice little place in the country, which, I hope, Mr. Harland here is going to see pretty soon." She brushed Harland's cheek with a playful hand. "Oh! You goin' so soon, Quill?"

Quill, who hadn't moved a muscle, said in a startled way, "Yes, of course."

"And you do like my little shop?"

"You've done such a good job on this shop, Pamela," Quill said earnestly, and escaped to the sidewalk outside.

"You been in there long enough," said a voice from behind her Honda.

"Marge?"

Marge emerged from behind Quill's car, a truly horrible scowl on her face. "Don't just stand there," she hissed, "keep walking."

"But don't we want to go on to the trooper barracks?"

Marge held her firmly by the upper arm. Quill had to follow her determined march down the sidewalk or rudely pull her arm free. She chose to march.

"And you said our appointment's at one-thirty, so we don't have to leave for another three hours — ouch, Marge. I'll come along. Just let me go, please."

Marge cast a harried look back at Pamela's Pampered Puppy Palace. Pamela came out, one arm linked with Harland's. Marge gave Quill a sharp poke in the side. "Go on. Look natural."

"I hadn't thought I looked unnatural," Quill protested. But she swung into a saunter. Then she said out of the side of her mouth, "Where are we going?"

"Croh Bar," Marge said briefly. "Got some more information for you."

"Good. I've got some for you, too."

"Ha!" Marge's voice was sudden and loud, "How's about those rhinos?"

"Rhinos?" Quill said a little wildly, "Rhinoceros?" Then crossly, "If you poke me one more time, Marge Schmidt . . ."

"Hel-loo-oh," Pamela caroled. She waved gaily at them from the passenger side of Harland's Cadillac Seville. "See you tonight at the Croh Bar, Marge? (Slow down a little, Harland, honey — that's it.) It's startin' to be one of my favorite places. That and the Inn at Hemlock Falls. Coeee!"

Harland, perhaps catching sight of the look on Marge's face, sped up suddenly and squealed around the corner and out of sight.

"Oh, the *Rhinos*," Quill said in sudden enlightenment, "the Rochester hockey team."

"Soccer," Marge corrected her, huskily.

Quill dug into her purse and handed Marge a Kleenex. "Men can be such *jerks*. I'll tell you what, Marge. That good old Southern girl act is going to get pretty old pretty fast. And can you see Harland putting up with that Pekinese dog for very long? The guys at the Elks catch Harland with a lap dog and they'll laugh him out of the order. He'd *hate* that."

"They might," Marge said.

"There's no 'might' about it. That's for sure. Now, what is it that you wanted to tell me? I picked up some pretty good information myself. Although Pamela was too dumb to notice it. Which is to say, have you noticed that men don't really form lasting relationships with dumb women? The smart men, that is. Smart men want a smart woman to talk to."

"You might be right," Marge said. She dabbed ferociously at her nose with the tissue.

"I am quite right about these things," Quill said firmly. Then feeling a change of subject was in order, she asked, "So what have you learned about the case?"

"I didn't learn anything yet. But we have an appointment." They had arrived at the door to the Croh Bar. Marge gestured Quill inside.

Midmorning at the bar was usually very quiet. The breakfast crowd had left to go about its business, and the lunch crowd hadn't yet started trickling in. But to Quill's surprise, Rudy Baranga sat at the counter, nursing a beer.

" 'Lo, there, ladies." Rudy tipped his cigar at them in a jaunty salute.

Marge gave him a not-too-friendly jab in the arm. "Right on time, Baranga."

"Would of come here for lunch anyway. Had such a good time here last night, I came back for a little more." His button-black eyes slid toward Quill. "No offense, cookie, but that place of yours is a little high-hat for me. And the company's not so hot, either. You and your baby sis excepted, of course."

"Of course," Quill murmured.

"So I'll give you lunch after you spill what you have to spill," Marge grunted. "Follow me, Rudy." Without looking to see if he would (he did), Marge stomped down the aisle to her usual booth in the back. Quill brought up the rear.

"Sit," Marge said.

They sat.

"Rudy here has an idea who might of killed Kittleburger," Marge said with her arms folded. Her face was expressionless.

"Really?" Quill said. "Have you told the police?"

"The cops and I . . ." Rudy sucked air through his teeth. "We don't get along so good."

"Oh." Quill debated with herself for a moment. "And why is that?"

"Yeah," Marge echoed. "Why is that, Rudy?"

He smirked and held up his hand, as if taking an oath.

Marge tapped the tabletop with one finger. Slowly. "Rudy's a meat wholesaler."

"Yes," Quill said. "You supply Pet Pro."

"There's a coupla other things he does for Pet Pro," Marge said. "This isn't the first time I've met Rudy. Is it?"

Rudy chuckled. "No, ma'am."

"We crossed swords, like the saying says. A coupla months ago. Kittleburger took an interest in one of the businesses I got down in Pennsylvania."

"Feed lot," Rudy said. "Goats."

"Goats?" Quill said. She was bewildered.

"It's a place where they sell goats to the

slaughter houses in New York City. Now," Marge said in great exasperation, "don't look like that at me, Quill. This is a very nice place."

"On account of it's halal," Rudy interjected.

"Halal? The Muslim way of slaughtering livestock?" Halal was indeed humane (if there was anything at all humane about a slaughterhouse. Quill had her doubts). Halal forbids the raising of animals on concrete. Animals are not to be uncomfortably confined. Any artificial supplement of any kind is forbidden. And the butcher asks the animal's forgiveness before its throat is quickly and painlessly sliced. That much she knew about halal.

"So you own this . . . place, Marge?"

"Yup. And Rudy here came to talk to me about selling it. To Kittleburger."

"And you didn't want to sell?"

"Nope. But Kittleburger figured to persuade me. Through Rudy, here." Marge's glare could have melted a good-sized igloo in ten seconds flat. "Now," Marge raised her right hand in a STOP! "We aren't here to talk about how I convinced Rudy to convince Kittleburger to back off."

"We aren't?" Quill said. She would dearly love to know.

"No. We're here because Rudy figures he owes me one. Right?"

Rudy ducked his head. "I do, Ms. Schmidt. I do."

"And so he says he's going to let us in on who did it." Marge explored a molar with the tip of her tongue. "I'm bound to say that I trust Rudy about as far as I can throw him." She leaned forward and grabbed him by his nice white tie. "Come to think of it, I can pitch a little squirt like you into the next county. So let's just say I don't trust him one damn inch." She released his tie. Rudy sat back and smoothed it lovingly against his maroon dress shirt. "So cough it up."

Rudy looked from side to side, in classic crook style. There was no one in the Croh Bar except the three of them and Betty Hall, who was polishing pilsner glasses up front. He leaned across the table and whispered, "Robin Finnegan."

"Victoria Finnegan's husband?"

"The one that got the old heave-ho from the bar association," Rudy said.

"He says he was out hiking at the time the Kittleburger murder occurred," Quill said doubtfully. "And he also says he has an alibi. Six Cornell University co-eds."

"They can account for all that time he was in the gorge? Do they know exactly where he was at nine forty-five?"

"And he offed Kittleburger because . . ." Marge made a "gimme" gesture with both hands. "I'm waiting on motive, here."

"Kittleburger's the one that got him kicked out of the law business, isn't he?" Rudy said.

"Kittleburger was responsible for Robin Finnegan's losing his license to practice law?" Quill tugged at the curl over her left ear. "Well. I suppose that's a motive."

"He and his wife had it pretty cushy, from all accounts." Rudy examined his cigar with a thoughtful air. "Then there was some problem with the money he was supposed to be holding for somebody?"

"A trust account for a client, yeah," Marge said. "And?"

"And the K turned him in to the cops. Bang goes the fancy boat in West Palm Beach. Bang goes the Porsche. And Bang! Bang! Bang! goes our Robbie's career. And Mrs. Robbie's, too."

"Victoria lost her job over something Robin did?" Quill said indignantly. "That is absolutely not fair."

"Yeah, well, that white shoe firm the both of them worked for didn't want either one of them around anymore. The K's one of their bigger customers, see."

"Clients, bonehead," Marge said. "Not customers."

"Right, clients. And what the K said goes. So they both got canned. Finnegan got probation and Mrs. Finnegan got a job with Mr. K at a salary that wouldn't keep a dog very happy, much less a highflier like our Vicki." Rudy leaned back with an air of satisfaction. "So there's your murderer."

"What about Lila Longstreet?" Quill said.

"Hah?"

"The two murders are linked, Rudy."

"Who says so?"

"I say so," Quill said crossly. "And actually, Simon Provost agrees with me."

"What kind of motive would Finnegan have to kill Lila?" Marge demanded.

Rudy shrugged. "Beats me."

"You're just guessing that he did it," Marge said in disgust. "You're a sneak, Baranga."

"That I ain't," Rudy said. "Take a look at this." He stuck two fingers in the breast pocket of his sports jacket and withdrew a piece of paper encased in a plastic baggie.

"Look, he has a note," Marge said. "Let me see that."

Quill read over her shoulder:

"My Room. 9:30. Keep It Quiet."

"This is Kittleburger's handwriting. No

question." He snatched the note back. "And the fingerprints are preserved, so no touching. Guess where this baby was found? Finnegan's trouser pocket, that's where."

"Who in the world found it there?" Quill said.

Rudy grinned unattractively, "Searchee la fam."

Quill had to process this. Then she said, "You don't mean Victoria did? His wife?"

"Wouldn't feel too bad if that one was put away, would she? Then again, maybe she would."

"So what do you want us to do about it?" Marge's jaw was at a belligerent angle.

"I figure you're upstanding citizens of this town," Rudy said. "You tell the cops you found this note. With the fingerprints of Robin on it, no less, and Kittleburger's handwriting and there you are. What you call strong circumstantial evidence."

"Why does this sound like a frame?" Quill said.

"Because it stinks," Marge said flatly. "Listen, bud. How did *you* get ahold of this note?"

"Well, now. If I told you that, I'd have to tell you a lie. Let's just say Miss Vicky's going to be some kind of pissed off when she goes to look for it and it's missing."

Marge leaned over and stuck her face close to his. "I asked you and I want an answer."

"Okay. Okay. You aren't going to believe it. But I got a phone call."

"A phone call," Quill said. "From whom?"

"Beats me."

Quill rubbed her forehead. She was getting another headache. "Why didn't this anonymous caller call the cops?"

"Huh!" Rudy said. " 'Cause those bastards trace phone calls, don't they? I'm telling you, it's getting harder and harder to get a little good work done these days." He fell silent, perhaps mourning the increased technological capability of the police force. "Well, what's past is past. So what's the deal here, Margie?"

"Don't call me Margie. Let's say we take this to the cops. The cops ask us where we got it. We say we got it from you. They come after you, anyway." Marge made a sound like "pshaw!"

"And I say, 'what the hell?' " Rudy smirked. "It's your word against mine, ladies. And without what they call corroborating evidence, the whole thing's up the pipe." He tucked the cigar into his shirt pocket. "Now, if you excuse me, I've gotta see a man about a horse." He shoved himself away from the table and ambled toward the door. Before Quill could think of a reason to call him back, he was gone.

Marge turned the plastic baggie over in her fingers. "So what do we do with this?"

"Give it to the police," Quill said instantly. "There's nothing else we can do. But this is just plain weird."

"Yeah, well. I say it's baloney." She took the note, ripped it up, and dropped it in the ashtray. "That shark's trying to frame her husband. I'm not havin' a thing to do with it."

"Yikes." Quill looked at the torn-up pieces of paper in dismay.

Marge shoved herself away from the table and stood up. "Right now, we're going to put you into one heck of a disguise."

CHAPTER 9

"I'm not so sure I like this," Quill said an hour and a half later. There was a full-length mirror on the back door to the back room of Marge's office. She stared at herself in dismay.

"Whatever," said the chubby kid. The chubby kid was Marge's resident computer technical support genius. He was tall, with a round, cherubic face and bright blue eyes. He had the longest eyelashes Quill had ever seen. He wore a t-shirt that snarled: "If It's Too Loud You're Too Damn Old." He sat in a swivel chair in front of a bank of brand-new computer equipment. The equipment lined one wall, almost filling the room. Empty potato chip bags littered the floor, crushed candy wrappers were strewn across the consoles, and three Big Gulp Styrofoam cups stood at attention around the chubby kid's swivel chair.

"That'd outfit scare the heck out of my

mother, god bless her," Marge said admiringly.

"Isn't she the Triple X World Wide Wrestling fan?" Quill asked.

Marge nodded. "Never misses a match, if she can help it. Got to hand it to you, Quill. No one would guess that you're how old? Thirty-six? I got all this from one trip to Wal-Mart," she added. "Didn't spend more than thirty bucks. Fact."

The reflection from the mirror would have scared Quill's own mother to death. She wore a glitter-ridden t-shirt cropped to just above her belly button. And she really didn't want to know — so she didn't ask — the provenance of the grungy black jeans she wore slung low on her hips. Marge had plastered a rose tattoo on her left bicep and a black circle tattoo on her right cheek. She swore the ink was temporary. Quill didn't trust the smirk on Marge's face as she said it.

Quill bent forward and carefully rimmed her eyes with kohl-black eyeliner.

"Now this." Marge thrust a tangled mass of hair at her. A bleached blonde mass of hair gelled into spikes.

"No," Quill said. "I hate wigs. They give me a headache."

"You've got to wear it," Marge said flatly.

"Anybody'd identify your own hair a mile off. That red is definitely different from any other hair in Tompkins County. More like carrots than tomatoes," she added ruminatively. "Never seen anything like it."

Quill sighed, tucked her hair up with hairpins, and tugged the repellent wig over her head. She stared glumly into the mirror. "It looks like I've got a dead rat on my head."

"Cool," said the chubby kid, whose name was actually Devon. "Like, very cool." He shoved one sneakered foot against the floor and then pushed the swivel chair around in a circle as he popped Doritos into his mouth.

The stranger in the mirror could have been any one of a hundred teenage girls slouching through the Galleria Mall on Saturday night. Marge handed her a tube of purple lip gloss. "In for a penny."

Quill sighed and applied it with a liberal hand.

"Now, that's a disguise," Marge said admiringly.

"No disguise is going to disguise the fact that I have no idea what I'm doing," Quill said. "How am I supposed to fake being a computer consultant?"

Devon snorted contemptuously. "The

cops don't know any more than you do. I'm just going to sit you in front of a terminal and pull up an ordinary word processing document. Then you just key in a series of ones and zeros. Like this." He swung around to his own screen, tapped at the keyboard and a blank screen came up. Then he banged away at the keys: 10010100010. "See? Just keep your eyes on the screen. Don't look down. Say 'shit' once in a while. You can hit the backspace key a coupla times and then start whamming away at the ones and the zeros again." He deleted his own handiwork with a few keystrokes and spun around to face them. "Now, about this report you guys want me to hack . . ."

"Not hack, precisely," Quill said a little nervously. "I mean, hacking's illegal. We just want you to find the forensics report on Lila Longstreet. When you do, I need to see it."

"So I'll just give you a signal when it's up on your screen. And if you're stuck for something to say, just throw out something like, 'I don't have enough RAM,' or 'This code's corrupted.' Got it?"

Quill bit her lip. The purple lip gloss tasted like grape Kool-aid. "Sure." If she got arrested, poor Myles would have a fit.

Devon swallowed another handful of Doritos and looked up at Marge. "That about it, Mrs. Schmidt? Are we good to go?"

"The duty sergeant's expecting you. I told him it'd take a couple hours to service the system, maybe more. Tell you what, though. You find that report and come back as soon as Quill's read it. I don't want her hanging around there in that getup for very long. We'll reschedule the actual service for another time. Got it?"

Devon nodded and opened a tube of Pringles.

"Now. One other thing. You get arrested, I don't know you from Adam," Marge said flatly.

"Ha ha," Devon said. "You mean no bail, right?"

Quill nudged him. "I don't think she was kidding."

"No sweat." Devon thrust the open Pringles can in her direction. "Have a chip."

Devon drove to the police barracks in his 2006 Porsche, complete with a Bose sound system and a CD player that blasted the most cacophonous music Quill had ever heard. She endured several minutes of the noise before she reached over to the dashboard and turned it off. "I'm sorry," she said. "It's your car. You have the right to play whatever you want to play. But, seriously, Devon, if I hear any more of that, I'll get sick to my stomach."

He widened his eyes, which were very blue and innocent. "No shit?"

"No shit. And you absolutely would not want me to throw up in this very expensive car."

"Hey. I'm cool with it." But he reached over, slid the CDs out of the player, and tucked them away in a carrying case.

"Thanks." Quill tugged her t-shirt down over the top of her jeans. It was a futile effort. Her stomach still stuck out. "Have you been out to the barracks before?"

"Couple of times. We installed a new server for them in June. It's taking them a while to get the hang of it. So, simple stuff goes wrong, and they call me out to fix it. One of these years they'll figure it out. Not too soon, though. I got my eye on a nice little speedboat."

The route to the trooper barracks took them along County Road 355, which Devon took at a surprisingly sedate pace. Quill resisted the urge to scratch at her wig, which was fiercely itchy, and at her tattoos, which weren't really itchy but felt as though they should be. Devon hummed to himself, tapped his fingers on the steering wheel, and shoved Pringles into his mouth in an absentminded way.

"So," he said eventually, his voice lowered to a conspiratorial tone. "How long have you been working undercover, Quill?"

"Excuse me?"

He glanced at her sidelong. "Mrs. Schmidt let me in on it. And you can trust me. No shit. Is it, like, pretty cool working for the Feds?"

"Pretty cool?" Quill repeated. Marge had told this kid she was with the FBI?

"I've been reading a lot about the FBI. You used to have to be either a lawyer or an accountant to join up, you know that?" He draped one arm over the passenger seat and steered one-handed. "Nowadays, basically, they want you to speak Farsi or be some kind of genius with computers."

"And are you some kind of genius with computers?"

"Mrs. Schmidt wouldn't have hired me if I wasn't. Thing is, I've been thinking about talking to a recruiter myself. Not to join up, but from what I hear, they could use a consultant with my computer skills. And it'd be pretty cool to get in on the espionage stuff." He beamed at her. His round cheeks were dusted with potato chip crumbs. "So what d'ya think? About hooking me up with some insiders?"

"I think we'd better forget we had this

conversation," Quill said sternly. She glanced out the window. "Especially since we're so close to the barracks."

Devon looked cautiously from side to side as he pulled into a parking space at some distance from the New York State Police Barracks 442 ENTER sign. "I've heard those listening devices can pick up conversations, like, miles away," he said. "Awesome. But I'm cool with this. I say zippo from here on in." He tossed the Pringles can into the backseat, where it joined another untidy pile of gum wrappers, empty candy bags, and crushed Styrofoam cups.

The barracks were located on about fifty acres of scrubby meadow on the north side of Route 15. A ten-foot-high chain-link fence surrounded the area. The barracks themselves were one story and cheaply pan-eled in T-11 siding. Several cruisers were parked at random around the large parking lot in front of the main entrance. The breeze scuffed across the asphalt in a desultory way. There was no one in sight.

Quill got out of the Porsche and waited until Devon grabbed his metal-sided brief-case, shrugged on his black leather jacket, and locked the car with a click of his remote. He headed straight to the main and — as far as Quill could tell only entrance.

She followed a few steps behind him, teetering on her four-inch clogs.

Devon checked in with the duty sergeant, who eyed Devon with indifference and Quill with concupiscence. She was momentarily stymied about where to clip her ID badge on her skimpy t-shirt. She copied Devon's example and clipped it to the front pocket of her jeans, where it dug into her thigh in an irritating way when she walked. Her undercover name, she noticed, was Alpha Lancaster.

The duty sergeant — who kept catching Quill's eye and smirking — led them to a large office equipped with several computer terminals. The windows looked out on the back of the building. The meadow had been cleared of brush and trees a hundred yards in either direction from the building. The sight of all that asphalt was depressing.

"We're going to need about thirty minutes when it'd be better if you didn't log on at all, sarge," Devon said. He threw himself into the chair in front of the screen next to a large CPU. "I'll let you know when it's okay to log back on."

"We shouldn't be off-line too long," the sergeant said. He pulled up a chair next to Devon.

Devon pulled a bag of red licorice whips

from his jacket pocket, stuck one in his mouth, and said, "Whatd'ya think you're doing there, dude?"

"Captain says it'd be good to learn more about this stuff." The sergeant's badge said "Trooper Brookes." "I'm supposed to sit in and figure out what's going on."

"Suit yourself," Devon shrugged. "But I'm sure you're going to be bored out of your skull." Without turning around he said, "Yo, Alpha."

Quill wished she had a piece of gum to snap. Instead, she cocked one hip and said through her nose, "Yo, Dev."

"You gonna run that systems check?"

"Sure, Dev."

"Over there." He nodded at the other station. Quill sat down. The computer hummed ominously at her. She took a deep breath, and clicked on the "enter" button.

"Checking code, Alpha?" Devon said. "Key F1/shift/control."

"Who, me?" Quill said. "I mean, yo, Dev." Sequences like that, she recalled, usually required that the user hold down all three keys at once. She did so, with a flourish. A little hourglass spun wildly on her blank screen.

"Checking code," Quill responded. "Roger."

Devon clicked madly away at his keyboard. Quill glanced carefully at his screen. A little hourglass icon spun there, too. The hourglass spun. And spun. And spun. Minutes crawled by. Devon chewed licorice whips. Quill sat with her hands poised on the keyboard and tried to look both alert and bored at the same time.

"Hey," Trooper Brookes said, after an excruciating ten minutes. "Is this thing broke, or what?"

"Told you you'd be bored out of your skull," Devon said indifferently. "Alpha. Key F2 /alt /insert."

"Roger," Quill said quickly. She clicked away. It seemed to make no difference at all. The little hourglass continued to spin.

"Shee-et," Trooper Brookes said after several more long minutes. "I'm gonna get me some coffee." He stood up and went out the door.

"Press 'enter,' " Devon said. "She's up."

"Okay, dude."

There was a short, heavily laden silence. Quill looked over at Devon, who regarded her unwinkingly. "Do not," he said, "call me dude."

"Why?" Quill said indignantly. "You called Trooper Brookes dude."

"Guys call each other 'dude.' You're not a

guy. Did you press 'enter'?"

Quill pressed 'enter.' The screen sprang to life. "Well, hotcha," she said softly.

New York State Medical Examiners Office
Forensics Division
STATUS REPORT: LONGSTREET, LILA
ANN

Quill grabbed a pen and piece of paper from a pile beside the keyboard and began to take notes as rapidly as she could.

"I'll stake out the hall." Devon got out of his chair and strolled toward the open door. He slouched against the doorframe and stared casually down the corridor.

"Houston," Quill whispered after interminable, frantic scribbling minutes. "We've got a problem."

"Yeah?"

"I've got it all down. But I don't have any place to put it!" She looked down at her skintight jeans, and too-skimpy-shirt in dudgeon.

"Red alert!" Devon hissed. He strolled casually back to his station and sat down. Quill balled her notes as tightly as possible and stuck them down the back of her jeans just as Trooper Brookes came back into the room carrying a cup of sludgy coffee.

"Delete and keystroke code, Alpha," Devon said casually. Quill deleted the screen and typed 1010001010 until her heart rate slowed to merely spooked instead of totally panicked.

By the time Devon explained to the befuddled Brookes that they'd have to come back next week, Quill felt calm enough to stroll back to the Porsche in an insolently laconic manner. Which she did. But as Devon leaned across the shift console to open the door for her, a cruiser wheeled into the parking lot, braked momentarily, swerved dangerously close to the Porsche, and came to an abrupt halt. Anson Harker leaned out the driver's window like a cobra snaking its head out of a basket. "What the hell are you up to?" he demanded. He shoved the cruiser into park and jumped onto the pavement. "I want to see some ID."

Quill froze.

"Get out of the way, Alpha, so I can talk to the lieutenant," Devon said indifferently. "I'm getting out of the car, Lieutenant. I've got our ID right here."

Harker turned his head and spit. The glob just missed Quill's high-heeled clogs. Keeping her face totally expressionless, she slid into the passenger seat. Harker stared at her for a long, fearful moment. He spat again, and then walked around the hood to face Devon.

"So it's you, Brewster," he said flatly. "It's about time that boss of yours got you out here. For what we're paying you guys a month, you should freakin' live here. And who the hell is the scrag with you?"

"She's a trainee," Devon said. "And not long for the program, if you ask me. 'Course that's up to Ms. Schmidt. But one of the reasons we're leaving is that Alpha forgot the software I need to update your server."

Harker's face loomed at Quill through the driver's window. Quill kept her eyes on her hands. "Yeah?" he said. His face disappeared and Quill heard him say, "You tell that fat slob of a boss she'd better not charge for this visit."

"I'll do that, Lieutenant."

"Right." Harker slapped the quarter panel and stepped back. "Get your ass out of here, then."

Devon slipped into the driver's seat. The Porsche started with a well-tuned roar. He drove out onto Route 15 at the same sedate pace he'd left it. Quill sank against the leather seat with a long sigh of relief.

"Thanks," she said.

"Figured he must be one of the ones you Feds are after, right?"

"After?" Quill said. "Oh, yeah. Right. I wish," she added in an undertone. She had a brief, glorious vision: Harker in handcuffs in front of a grand jury.

"The lieutenant's a known slime bucket," Devon said cheerfully. "Hope you nail his gnarly ass to the wall."

"Slime bucket doesn't begin to cover it," Meg said after Quill had swallowed an inch of ice-cold Grey Goose vodka, showered, and collapsed on the couch in her living room that evening. "You sure you're okay?"

"I'm sure."

Meg cocked her head. "Did you forget to wash off the tattoos?"

Quill, her freshly washed hair wrapped in a towel, the rest of her in a cotton bathrobe, sprang to the mirror that hung over her fireplace and shrieked in dismay. "She said they'd wash off!"

"Who did?"

"Marge, darn it!" Quill licked her forefinger and scrubbed at the dots on her cheek. "Phooey."

Meg's dark head appeared next to hers in the mirror. "If you pierced your tongue and spiked your hair, it wouldn't look all that obvious."

Quill threw herself back onto the couch.

Meg sat down next to her. "At least you got a look at the forensics work. Are you calm enough to tell me what you found out?"

"I have been totally calm throughout this whole thing," Quill said, her voice rising. "Who says I haven't been calm?"

Meg patted her arm. "You should be used to breaking and entering by now. Remember the paint factory? The tractor trailer? The Ro-Cor construction office?"

"This wasn't breaking and entering," Quill said. "This was impersonating a computer expert. And, I might add, you break and enter at night. When there's a chance to slip quietly and sneakily away. There was absolutely *no* way to slip quietly out of that parking lot."

Meg patted her kindly on the back. "Well, you're safe now."

"I am *not* safe now. What about this dumb tattoo? All that miserable Harker has to do is catch sight of me and how long do you think it'll be before he puts two and two together?"

"Yikes," Meg said. "I didn't think of that."

"Well, I did."

Meg squinted at her. "They've faded quite a bit. I'll bet the whole thing will disappear after another couple of washings. In the meantime what about makeup? Nope, I've got it. Band-Aids."

"Band-Aids?" Quill got up and looked in the mirror. "Brilliant, Meg. I mean, really. I could just tell people I fell into some poison ivy."

"If you tell people you fell into poison ivy you should have Band-Aids all over. In the interests of verisimilitude. If you don't have enough Band-Aids on hand, I can pick up some from the Rite Aide."

"How many Band-Aids do you think I'll need?"

"A couple on your hands and arms. And we'll dab some of that twenty-four-hour gel rouge on your nose and neck. That'll add to the . . ."

"Verisimilitude," Quill finished for her. "Terrific. I'll look demented." She flopped back on the couch and stared at the ceiling. "This case is taking some very unfortunate turns."

"At least we've *got* a case. I completed my half of the mission today, too. And the news isn't good."

"Uh-oh. What's wrong?"

"Basically, everybody has an alibi, *except*," Meg held one finger up, "Rudy Baranga." She tucked her feet under her and began to tick the points off on her fingers.

"First murder — Lila Longstreet. I

checked the whereabouts of all of our suspects on Monday night between seven and ten o'clock, since the autopsy hasn't pinned down the time any closer than that, according to Davy. Pamela was with Harland Peterson." Meg interrupted herself, "And you know, Quill, the big goof's absolutely gone on that woman. I swear she's put something in his beer. Anyhow, Robin and Victoria Peterson were in the Tavern Lounge, drinking and fighting. Nate says so. Half the waitstaff says so. Robin stomped out for about half an hour sometime after eight, according to Nate, but he stomped back in again by quarter to nine. Nate remembers that time because he was watching *American Idol* on the bar TV and somebody got kicked off the stage. Whatever. Anyhow, Priscilla Barnstaple read and watched TV in her room all night. She called down to room service twice. Millard Barnstaple drove to Syracuse and back in the Inn van . . ."

"Oh my god," Quill said. "Do we have Michelin tires?"

"Who knows? Who cares?" Meg said bitterly, "Because Millard got both a parking ticket and an airtight alibi. The ticket was on the windshield when he got back. He told Mike he wasn't going to pay it because the tickets follow the vehicle and not the driver, if that makes any sense. Anyhow, the time on the ticket was nine-thirty p.m. The address was outside the Marriott. And Millard was at a Vice-Free Vegans meeting there. Before you ask, I talked to the conference organizer, and there is no doubt that our passive-aggressive pal was there from seven-thirty on. It wasn't a ringer." Meg contemplated her toes; her socks were a depressed gray. She perked up a bit. "Nobody knew where Rudy was, though. Nobody had a clue."

"But why Rudy? He had everything to lose with both Lila and Kittleburger dead. Pet Pro was Rudy's largest customer."

"Motive," Meg said sternly, "is trumped by good hard evidence, every time."

"True," Quill admitted. "Okay. So nobody killed Lila Longstreet. Except somebody *did* kill Lila Longstreet. No one knows where Rudy was?"

Meg shook her head.

"I'll ask him." She scribbled on her sketchpad. "There. I've made a note to myself."

Meg looked skeptical. "You're just going to waltz up and ask him?"

"Not directly, no. But he drinks a lot of Johnny Walker Blue . . ."

"At fifty dollars a shot?" Meg exclaimed.

"Is he good for his bar bill?"

"I hope so. Anyhow, after three or four of those, it should be easy to find out where he was Monday night. Now, about Maxwell Kittleburger . . ."

"Nobody killed Maxwell Kittleburger, either," Meg said a little glumly. "That nine forty-five time of death is a real monkey wrench in the machinery."

"Then the time of death has got to be wrong," Quill said positively. "I know that most of the IAPFP members were at Pamela's. Who supplied the alibi for the time of Kittleburger's murder?"

"Esther."

"Esther?"

"You know West's Best is right next door. It appears she stopped into Pamela's Pampered Pooch's twice Wednesday morning. She had some new ideas for the puppy show. A costume class, I think she said. Anyhow, she saw everyone through the plate-glass window, 'waving their arms and yelling fit to bust' except for . . .

"Rudy?" Quill said hopefully.

"And Robin."

"Robin," Quill said. "Ah-ha."

"No ah-ha. I asked Dina to check on Robin's alibi, and yes, two co-eds ran across him when he was hiking in the gorge. She knows one of the women pretty well and says she's reliable."

"Hm," Quill said. "But the gorge isn't all that far from the Inn. There's a bare possibility Robin could have whipped up the fire escape stairs and clobbered poor Mr. Kittleburger, isn't there?"

"Only if the police are wrong about the exact time of death," Meg said. "One of the students says it was about nine-thirty when Robin joined them."

"Kittleburger's murder absolutely hinges on the supposedly exact time of death," Quill mused. "If the time of death is wrong, both Rudy or Robin could be in the frame. Now, Harker's not the brightest bulb in the chandelier. There has to be a way to rethink that nine forty-five target." She made another note to herself. "As for Rudy?"

Meg flung her hands out, palms up. "Nobody seems to know."

"Ah-ha."

"Maybe. But we still haven't discovered a logical motive for him. So right now, it looks as if those suspects who had a reason to kill Kittleburger couldn't have done it, and the guy who has no reason could have done it."

Both of them mulled this over. There was a crack in the plastered ceiling that Quill hadn't noticed before. She swung her feet up on the couch and stared at it. Suddenly, she was very tired. "Why don't we just leave this to the police? If we just left this to the police, I could get back to making this place livable. And I wouldn't have to walk around looking like the kind of fool that doesn't know enough to stay out of a patch of poison ivy."

"The quicker we solve this case, the quicker Harker will slither back to his place under the rocks. And the quicker we'll be rid of the poisonous pet people."

"True." Quill sat up. The ceiling could wait. "My day was a little more successful, if a lot scarier. It was worth it, Meg. Devon not only hacked into the forensics stuff on Lila Longstreet, he pulled up the autopsy report on Kittleburger. And a sort of 'to do' list that Harker had to write in response from a pile of questions from Simon Provost."

"Hot diggety." Meg curled in the corner of the couch and prepared to listen.

Quill smoothed out the crumpled sheet of paper she'd sneaked out of the trooper barracks. "As for Lila, the body was moved. So she wasn't actually killed at Bernie Hamm's. Which will make him feel a lot better. The lab found traces of dog hair, animal feces, and sawdust all mixed up together in Lila's clothes. None of it matched the area around the Hamms' place."

"Sawdust? Dog hair?"

"That, and some leaf mold." Quill shook her head, wonderingly. "It's absolutely amazing, Meg. They've pinpointed this particular kind of leaf mold. They checked with the horticultural lab at Cornell, and it comes from a spot three miles west of Route 353 near the Horndean Gorge, which, I need not remind you, is a ten-minute walk from our gorge."

"Holy crow." Meg sat up, her eyes alight. "So maybe Robin *could* have had time to meet Lila and get back to resume fighting with Victoria. And he might have had time to knock off Kittleburger, too."

"Maybe. Maybe not. We've got to work on the time of Kittleburger's death. That's crucial."

Meg drew her knees to her chin. "What about the murder weapons?"

"Lila was run over. Let's hope they find the truck. Let's hope they can find it and prove that it was somewhere near the Inn with the keys in it so Robin could steal it."

"Possible. But not probable."

"At any rate, the lab ran some tests on the carpet fiber they found on Lila's right sleeve, right hip, and right cheek. It's the same kind of carpet that's found in late-model Dodge double-axle trucks. Unfortunately, like the tires, there's approximately forty thousand vehicles with this kind of carpet in the backseat."

"I thought we were going to forget about pinning down which of forty thousand trucks they put the body in."

"But we can check out the spot where Lila's murder may have actually occurred."

"Why?"

"Why? Clues, that's why."

"Phuut!" Meg said rudely. "The police will have picked up anything important. You can just hack into the files again."

"I think we should check it out."

"That whole area's full of scratchy brush. You're not going to find me romping around in there. And I don't think you should, either."

This was very unlike her adventuresome sister. Quill regarded her for a long moment. "Okay. I know why you think I should be home with my feet up. You want me to be pregnant. Is there any reason why you should be home with your feet up?"

Meg smiled mysteriously. "Maybe. Maybe not."

"What does that mean?"

Meg started to hum an off-key version of

"Sit Down, You're Rockin' the Boat," which Quill took (correctly) to mean "butt out."

"Are you and Jerry thinking of . . . um . . . anything in particular?"

"Such as?" Meg demanded with a scowl.

"Such as nothing," Quill said hastily. "But I still think we should case the joint."

"The joint being six acres of underbrush, rocks, and various pitfalls. No way."

Stubbornly, Quill made another note to herself and continued, "Now the autopsy report just had the 'body of a well-nourished white female between the ages of twenty-four and thirty-four' sort of thing. Pamela identified the body, by the way. So that puts the kibosh on Suspect X."

"Suspect . . . oh. You mean the guy nobody knew existed coming out of the bushes to commit the murders. Like in a Patricia Cornwell novel."

"Right. At any rate, I didn't take the time to write all the autopsy results down — just the anomalies. There wasn't anything interesting. Her hair had been freshly dyed. Things of that sort."

"That color blonde is hard to keep up," Meg observed.

"It's also really hard to do with an at-home kit. So let's check out Nadine Peterson's hair salon. That'd be the most logical place for Lila to go — the nearest salon is in Ithaca. And people tell their hairdressers the oddest things."

"You never know," Meg agreed.

Quill made a third note to herself. The investigation was shaping up nicely. "The scene of the crime report listed her clothes, the contents of her purse, her shoes, et cetera, et cetera, et cetera. They listed everything. Keys, makeup kit, Nokia cell phone, wallet, the lot. By the way, Lieutenant Provost wrote a really sarcastic note to the fingerprint lab. None of the fingerprints on the purse matched the fingerprints on the body. The impression I got from reading the request Provost sent to them for more information was that Harker's work is notoriously sloppy. And that Provost wasn't about to put up with much more of it."

Meg looked pleased.

"Last note in the file was absolutely something we can do ourselves. Provost wanted someone to check out Lila's banking arrangements."

Meg nodded in agreement. "Now there's a really good idea. But does that mean we have to hack into the state troopers computer system again? Because I'll tell you right now — there's no way I'm dressing up in a wig and tattoos."

"We have Devon the hopeful FBI consultant," Quill said, a little smugly.

"Hm." Meg said, "Okay. So we trick Devon into thinking he's working way undercover for the Feds and he finds out all this financial stuff how?"

"Lila used a credit card to register, didn't she?"

Meg's eyebrows shot up and she nodded approvingly. "Okay. Good one."

Quill tucked the paper in the back of her sketchpad.

"Now. Kittleburger. The autopsy hasn't been done yet. But it looks as if he was injected in the back of the neck with some kind of powerful anesthetic. The scene of the crime people took carpet samples, et cetera. Thank goodness the room had been cleaned that morning. And you know how obsessive Doreen is about the housekeeping help. So they lifted very few fingerprints, which is good for elimination, and routine samples from his clothes." She sighed, "Nothing's really back, yet. I hope Simon Provost will be more helpful than that creep Harker. Although Myles might not mind giving us a hand."

"As if," Meg said.

"At the very least, he can give Provost a hand." Quill took one last glance at her notes. "And that's about it. The list of stuff Kittleburger had on him was the usual. Briefcase, cell phone, no signed notes from the murderer. So that's about it. But we've got some pretty good leads. And there's one more lead that Harker didn't list. Although Provost might have thought of it already." She paused dramatically. "Is Lila's mother really dead?"

Meg ran her hands through her hair. "Huh?"

"Lila left the conference early because her mother died. That's what she told Olivia. So, is her mother really dead? Or was it a trumped-up excuse? And if her mom's alive and well — where was Lila really headed, and why?"

"It's Thursday," Meg said. "We want these guys out of the Inn by the weekend, right? Well, we'd better hop to it." She raised her fist in the air. "Rudy or Robin?"

"Maybe both?"

"Forward, Caldecott."

"After you, Carstairs."

CHAPTER 10

"Lila's mother is in Niagara Falls?" Olivia said. "I don't understand you."

"It is a little confusing," Quill said kindly. "Would you like a little more coffee?"

Olivia frowned at her cup. Then she frowned at Quill. Olivia was having a late breakfast. It was well after ten Friday morning and the dining room was nearly empty. It was a glorious fall day. Outside the floor-to-ceiling windows that overlooked the falls, the sun shone in a brilliantly blue sky. The trees had turned color seemingly overnight, and the canopy of leaves surrounding the Inn was a riot of crimson, gold, and orange. Best of all, Quill had discovered that Windex removed all of the telltale tattoos, and she didn't have to walk around like the deer with a target birthmark on its chest in the Gary Larsen cartoon, waiting for Harker the Hunter to haul her into custody.

Olivia looked cross. "Is there a funeral

home in Niagara Falls that the body's been shipped to?"

"Mrs. Longstreet isn't dead, Olivia," Quill said, hoping that she was combining tact and directness in equal measure. "Lila lied about why she left the conference early."

"Oh." Olivia took a large bite of cranberry strudel and shrugged. "In that case, it was probably some man."

"What man would that be?" Quill spoke without thinking, "Mr. Kittleburger was already here."

"Lila didn't confine herself to one man at a time. Here's Pamela. She can tell you more about Lila's love life than I can."

"Hello, Quill. I was hoping to find you here." Pamela walked up to the table without the usual advance warning of jangling charm bracelets and heavy perfume. She was dressed in chinos that were a size too small for her ample hips, and a sweater covered with dog hair. "Sorry to drop in like this, y'all. But I had an early drive to Syracuse this morning." She smiled. "Picking up more of those precious puppies from that wonderful breeder near Covert. I dropped by to see you, Quill, about the program for the dog show tomorrow." She sat down in the empty chair directly across from Quill. "And now that I'm here, I'm just famished. Whatever you're having looks just wonderful, Livy. And what was it you were saying about Lila?"

Quill looked up and nodded to Kathleen Kiddermeister, their head waitress. She waited while Kathleen took Pamela's order, and then said casually. "I'd just asked Olivia about Lila Longstreet's reasons for leaving the conference early, Pam."

"Her mother isn't dead," Olivia said disapprovingly. "Did she mention anything to you about the real reason why she left?"

Pam shrugged. "Except for these annual meetings, I hardly knew the woman. There wouldn't be any reason for her to tell me anything different from what she told y'all."

"But you were the one who identified the body," Quill said. "I assumed that you knew her better than the others."

Olivia smiled meanly, "Not as well as Robin."

"Now, Livy," Pam said. "Poor Victoria. She has *such* a lot to deal with. But that Robin is no gentleman, if you ask me."

"Robin Finnegan was having an affair with Lila, too?" Quill said.

"Lila," Pamela said succinctly, "would have screwed a good-lookin' tree. Not that Robin's all *that* good looking. And after the scandal, what nice woman would want to have anything to do with him anyway? Well, I take that back. Priscilla was interested." She smiled the way that people do when they want you to know alternate lifestyle choices don't bother *them.*

"Good grief," Quill said. "Lila sure . . ." She faltered to a stop.

"Got around?" Olivia said dryly. "That she did."

"And the scandal?" Quill prompted.

Kathleen set a plate of Eggs Quilliam in front of Pamela, who purred like one of her kittens. "Will you just look at this? Now, what's all in it?"

"Spinach, hollandaise, Smithfield ham, eggs poached in a seasoned broth. And we bake our own scone-muffins. That was," she added in a burst of inspiration, "quite a scandal Robin created, wasn't it?"

"Did it make the papers here? It made all the papers in Karnack Corners." Pamela took a large bite of her eggs. "Darlin', this is just fantastic."

"Why do you suppose he did it?" If Pamela didn't give her a direct answer this time, Quill thought, she'd take the eggs and dump them on Pamela's fuzzy head.

"All those toys," Olivia said disapprovingly. "That's why he did it. That house was costing him a bundle. Plus the cars. Plus the weekend trips to Costa Brava."

"And the money came from . . ." Quill prompted.

"Why, Maxwell Kittleburger, of course." Despite her casual attire, Pamela hadn't neglected her makeup. She fluttered heavily mascaraed lashes. "You did know that both Victoria and Robin were partners in the firm that represents Pet Pro." She leaned across the table, breathing egg and spinach into Quill's face. "Well, when Robin was caught with his hand in the Kittleburger kitty, the firm fired him, of course, and then they were going to fire Victoria, too. But they made some kind of deal with Max, and Victoria ended up representing him practically for *free,* if what Lila said was true." She gulped some orange juice and smacked her lips. "Anyhow, the firm demoted Victoria, didn't press charges against Robin, and Victoria's working for pennies. Just pennies. So, naturally, that big old house is gone, the fancy cars are gone, and the weekend trips are to Wal-Mart instead of Bermuda. Ha ha." Pamela shook her head sorrowfully and finished off her egg in two large bites.

"Who," Quill said carefully, "actually discovered Robin's umm . . ."

"Defalcations?" said a voice in her ear.

Pamela looked up, momentarily discomfited. "You shouldn't creep up on people like that, Robin."

Quill rose from her chair, embarrassed. "Mr. Finnegan. I'm sorry. I didn't realize you were there."

There were heavy shadows under his eyes. Quill remembered quite clearly that he had worn a grubby blue shirt and striped tie the day before. Today he was dressed in a white shirt with a solid red tie. This shirt didn't look clean, either. He was in need of both a haircut and, Quill noted with slight distaste, a good shampoo.

"Did you come in for breakfast?" she asked. "If you'd like to sit down, I'll be happy to see what the kitchen can come up with. It's after ten thirty, so the kitchen's closed down, but we have coffee and scones."

"I'll get my breakfast in the bar, thanks." He rubbed his hand across his chin. "Actually, they sent me to get you."

"They?"

He grinned a little maliciously. "There's a small riot going on in the conference room. That little receptionist?"

"Dina," Quill said. "And she's not a little anything. She's a doctoral candidate at Cornell. And," she added doubtfully, "there can't be a riot going on in the conference room."

"Right. Well, you'd better go and see, hadn't you?"

Quill proceeded down the hall to the conference room at a slightly faster pace than usual. As she neared the open door, she could hear the rise and fall of the mayor's voice, interrupted by shouts of "you betcha!" and "hang 'em high!"

Robin was right. There was a small riot in her conference room. And the mayor seemed to be inciting it.

Quill would have lost a large lump of cash if anyone had bet her that Elmer Henry would be at the head of a vigilante committee in Hemlock Falls.

"I think we should run that sneaky son of a gun right out of this town," Elmer shouted.

"Who are we planning on running out of town?" Quill walked into the conference room with her head up, her arms swinging, and her stride confident. A recent management class she'd taken from the Cornell University Extension had called this the "power pose," and guaranteed its success in moments of management crisis. Quill figured it couldn't hurt to try it on those members of the Chamber of Commerce who currently sat at the conference table ready to smack somebody up the side of the head. There were four: Esther West, the mayor, Harland Peterson, and Carol Ann Spinoza. Dina sat at the far end of the table, in an interested posture. Quill sat down next to Dina. "And why are we going to run this person off?"

"It's because of Harvey," Harland Peterson said. "When Esther opened up her shop this morning, that Corrine came running in to tell her Harve'd emptied his desk out overnight and left two weeks severance pay on her desk."

"Not only that, Harvey left a call at Marge's office that he wanted her to put his house up for sale," Esther said. Her cheeks were pink with indignation, and her mild brown eyes glittered fiercely.

"And I say, we should run the guy out of town that run Harvey out of town." Elmer's face was pink with fury. "I can't b'lieve this Rudy guy. This jerk." He pounded his fist on the table. "What'd Harvey ever do to him? I say we find this guy and give him what for!"

"Yeah!" Esther shouted.

"Go to it," Harland said.

"This is your fault, Quill," Carol Ann said in her sticky sweet voice. "I am shocked out of my mind at the caliber of guests you have here these days."

Harland got to his feet. He was a big man, solidly built. The conference table was thirty feet long and solid mahogany, and it shifted as he leaned on it. "So where is the bum?"

Dina raised her hand and waved it in the air. "He's checked out."

"Checked out?" Elmer roared. "Well, where'd the son of a bee go?"

"You're kidding," Quill said in dismay. There went her chances of a cozy, drink-laden interview with their chief suspect.

"He went home, I expect," Dina said. "He lives in Syracuse. Right near his rendering plant. I can give you the address, if you want."

"Let's drive over there and give him what for!" Elmer shouted.

"Dina," Quill said. "For Pete's sake."

"Well, why shouldn't I give them Mr. Baranga's address? I think it's really rotten that he ran poor Mr. Bozzel out of town."

"This is *so* your fault, Quill." Carol Ann sat back with her hands folded primly over the purse in her lap.

"Guys," Quill ran her hands through her hair. "Just what are you planning on doing when you catch up with Mr. Baranga?"

"Punch his lights out," Carol Ann said

promptly. She stared at the mayor. "You can take him."

Harland cracked his knuckles. "I have to say she's right." (People very rarely referred to Carol Ann by name.) "The guy could use a little attitude readjustment."

"I think that's a very bad idea," Quill said firmly. "For one thing, are you absolutely sure that Harvey's left town because of this?"

"That Corrine said Harvey told her it was worth her life to tell Rudy Baranga where he'd gone," Esther said dramatically. "Who else could it be?"

"But, why?" Quill said, bewildered. "It just doesn't make sense." She rubbed her forehead. Harvey must have seen something that would tie Rudy to the murder. That was the only possible explanation for Harvey's precipitate behavior. And what was it that had caused Rudy to go charging over there? It was absurd to think it might be the logo for Mousee Morsels. Rudy had a lot of explaining to do. To the police, if not to her and Meg. "Dina, do you remember exactly what was in the note attached to that art board Harvey left for Mr. Kittleburger?"

Dina closed her eyes. " 'Dear Mr. Kittleburger, Attached please find a great new idea for Pet Pro. If you don't care for this, give me a call and we can discuss something that will be more to your advantage.' "

The first thing that occurred to Quill was blackmail. The second was that it was ridiculous to suspect Harvey of any such thing. The third was that it would be just like Harvey to get himself embroiled in a mess where Kittleburger's goon Rudy would think it *was* a threat to blackmail him.

"Somebody needs to talk to Harvey and find out what really went on," Quill said firmly. "And I think you guys should think twice about accosting Mr. Baranga. It's my impression that he's a dangerous man."

"You and Meg figure out who killed those two outsiders, yet?" Elmer demanded.

"Not yet," Quill said cautiously.

"You think this Rudy might be a murderer?"

Quill, loath to implicate anyone in murder, no matter how badly they may have scared Hemlock Falls' best (and only) advertising executive, shook her head, but in a very meaningful way.

"What I got to say is this," Elmer said nervously. "This Baranga might be the reason Harvey left town, and he might not. Maybe we need a little bit more information before we go raring off to Syracuse half cocked."

"If Rudy Baranga ran over that Lila Long-street's head and stuck Mr. Kittleburger full of some horrible drug," Esther said, "you bet we need a little bit more information."

"We don't know that he did do those things, Esther," Quill said patiently. "But Meg and I intend to find out."

"So the two of you are going to Syracuse and find out what's what with this character?" the mayor said. "I'm proud of you, Quill. The whole Chamber thanks you. You fix this," he hesitated, and then beamed, "we just might give you two a medal."

Quill stood up. "I am going to find my sister."

Meg was in the kitchen with Jerry.

"Rudy Baranga's connected?" Jerry Grimsby said.

"Are you asking us or telling us?" Meg slammed a leg of lamb onto the prep table and began to butterfly it.

"If nothing else, he is, or rather was, the muscle for Maxwell Kittleburger," Quill said. "And he's the only viable suspect we have at this point. The only person without a reasonable alibi."

"A *seemingly* reasonable alibi," Meg reminded her.

Jerry shoved his hand through his thick

hair and scratched his head. He was a big, bluff, comfortable-looking man with a hearty face and a warmhearted smile. He was also the only master chef whose opinion Meg respected, with the possible exception of the late Banion O'Flaherty. "From what you two have told me, he's not somebody to screw around with. You really think you want to mix it up with this guy?" He started forward. "Hey! Meg. You're not close enough to the bone, there."

"Butt out," Meg said.

"Really, kiddo. You should let me do this."

Meg's head was lowered in concentration. She didn't raise it, but rolled her eyes up so that she was glaring at Jerry like the possessed little kid in *The Exorcist*. At this juncture, Quill would have beaten a prudent retreat. Jerry merely said amiably, "Fine. No one's going to notice that you've left half the usable meat on the bone."

"That's right, Jer."

"On the other hand, you and I will know." He gently withdrew the boning knife from Meg's grasp. Meg gave a great sigh of exasperation and stepped back. Jerry flipped the leg of lamb over and began to carve with an elegant turn of his wrist.

"Fine. Go ahead. I'd just like to know how you're going to stuff the thing when it's three feet thick. And I'd also like to know how I'm going to make stock with a bone that's totally denuded of meat."

"Watch me."

"I am watching you."

Quill suppressed a laugh. Jerry winked at her. Then he and Meg exchanged sappy grins. Quill shifted on the kitchen stool and cleared her throat. She felt funny. She felt, she suddenly realized, like a fifth wheel. The kitchen was in full swing. She was clearly in the way. The lunch prep was even more chaotic than usual. News of Maxwell Kittleburger's murder had spread rapidly, and they were fully booked with gawkers and sensation seekers. Meg had called Jerry for backup. Which was a good thing. As long as Meg kept her mind on the job. "So I suppose," Quill said rather loudly, "that I should try and find Harvey to discover just what did go on in his office Wednesday morning. Right now, we don't have enough information to know what we're looking for when we go see Rudy. And why," she muttered to herself, since Meg and Jerry obviously weren't listening to her, "did Simon Provost let him leave town anyway?"

"So are you going to Syracuse, sis?" Meg asked.

"Maybe. First, I'm going to see if I can

track down Harvey."

"And you're going to talk to Dangerous Devon about hacking into Lila's financial records."

"Right," Quill said.

Jerry looked from one to the other. "Is this stuff you two are on to legal?"

"Yes," Meg said firmly. She scrabbled busily in her apron pocket. "I copied down her AmEx credit card number. Here you go."

"Are you sure . . . ?" Jerry began.

"Jer. Shut up and carve." She nudged him with her shoulder. She looked very small next to him. He wrapped one long arm around her and kissed the top of her head. "Did you track down that lost pork shipment, by the way? I could swear that it was in the big freezer in back. I'll tell you what, Meg. If you want to play detective, you should check that out. Leave this other stuff to the cops."

"Okay. Okay. So I won't go traipsing off to Syracuse. Hand me that pot of mint."

Quill slipped out the back door. Max sat patiently at the head of the herb garden. As soon as he saw her, he got up and danced toward her, tail wagging frantically, ears flattened in joy. "Well, you're glad to see me, at least."

Max barked.

"You think I've lost my Watson to a slightly chubby chef?"

Max barked again.

"She's not only my Watson, you know. She's my sister."

Mac crouched and whined sorrowfully.

"Well, I feel quite sorrowful, too." Quill felt a sudden rush of tears. Which was ridiculous. Her sister wasn't going anywhere. And she was fully committed to solving this case. "Would you like to go for a ride? Go-for-a-ride, Max?"

Max would. Quill drove the short distance to the village marveling at the beauty of the autumn. The air was crisp. The scent of dried leaves was exhilarating. The village itself seem to drowse benevolently in the sunshine. She'd have to be a true bozo to be sad in the middle of all this glory.

Quill was brought up short when she drove past Bozzel! Advertising! "That Corrine," or somebody, had hung a large red CLOSED sign on the front door. So the mayor and Esther hadn't been engaging in wild surmise after all.

The silver Porsche parked outside Marge's office on Main was evidence that Devon was in. And Quill noticed that a third sign now dangled from the Schmidt Realty, Schmidt

Casualty and Surety Company signs: SCHMIDT COMPUTER CONSULTANTS. Quill parked, remembered that Marge was indifferent to large animals in her office space, and invited Max to come with her. Marge's assistant, Ruthie, greeted her with a cheery wave, and offered Max a cookie.

"I'm looking for Devon," Quill said. "I'm hoping that Marge won't mind if he does a small job for me."

Ruthie was a prototypical, nice, middle-aged Hemlockian. Her short brown hair was neatly styled. She wore a spic-and-span pantsuit from West's Best Dress Shoppe in a properly autumnal brown. Her spectacles were encased in the pair of frames she'd purchased twenty years ago. And she was dead set on following the rules. "I'm afraid you'll have to fill out a request form, Quill."

"Um." Quill rubbed her nose reflectively. "It's not exactly the sort of request I can put into so many words."

"Hm." Ruthie looked at her disapprovingly over her spectacles. "You aren't trying that Internet dating anymore, are you? You're a married woman now."

"No, no, no. Nothing like that," Quill said hastily. "This has more to do with Mr. Kittleburger's unfortunate demise."

"Ah, *hm,*" Ruthie said, for variation. "Then you'll have to fill out a time and materials form."

"Just let the lady in, Ruthie," Devon said from the back doorway. "I'll take care of Mrs. Schmidt." He'd changed shirts. This one had a Munch-like reproduction of a screaming face with the legend: "Entropy Is Winning."

Quill followed him into the familiar crammed space.

Devon craned his neck to look out the open doorway. Then he whispered, "So. Did yesterday's gig help the case at all?"

"We need a little more information," Quill admitted. "On two different people, come to think of it. I need to take a look at this person's financial records. All I've got is an American Express credit card number. Can you do that?"

He took the slip of paper. Meg had included Lila's full name, home address, and email and phone numbers. "Maybe. Should be a piece of cake. But you never know. AmEx has got pretty tight security nowadays. No chance you have her social security number?"

Quill shook her head.

"Well, we'll see. Where the heck is Karnack Corners, Iowa? Well, that'll help. Can't be that many Lila Ann Longstreets around there. Next?"

"Is there any way you can help me find Harvey Bozzel?"

"Who?"

Quill explained.

"Do you have an email address for him?"

"Yes, as a matter of fact. It's Harvey@harveybozzel.com."

"Did you email him?"

Quill bit her lip. "Um. No. I didn't try that."

Devon gestured grandly at a second computer station in the corner of the room. "Be my guest. In the meantime, I'll see what I can run on this perp for you."

"She's not a . . . never mind."

Quill sat down at the computer, went online, and brought up her own email system.

Send to: Harvey@harveybozzel.com
Subject: Help!
Message: Harvey, where are you? Please call. It's urgent. Warm regards, Sarah Quilliam

She hit the "send" button, and then scrolled through her own messages. One from Myles that made her smile. She hit the "save" button. One from Golden Pillars

Travel agency, inquiring about reservations over Thanksgiving. And one from harvey@harveybozzel.com.

She opened the email.

Send to: Quill@HemlockFalls.com
Subject: Why should I?
Message: Leave me alone!

There was an Instant Messaging function. Quill hit it. Harvey *was* online, the bozo. She input:

Harvey, please. This is urgent. What happened with Rudy Baranga?

There was a long pause. Behind her, Quill heard Devon, merrily tapping away. Finally, it seemed reluctantly, there was a reply:

None of your business.
Did he threaten you?

No answer.

Harvey, do you know anything about the murders?

This time the answer was swift:

I know somebody offed Lila Longstreet.

Was there another murder?

Harvey, if you know ANYTHING about what happened to Lila, you MUST come back and help us.

Quill sat back and thought for a long moment.

It's your civic duty!

I don't know anything, I swear to god!

Harvey, Quill recalled wryly, was good at panic.

Then why did you leave town? When are you coming back? We miss you!

Another long pause. Then:

When he's in jail.

And Harvey signed off.
"It's Rudy Baranga."
"Huh?"
Quill hadn't realized that she'd spoken aloud. "Devon, how do I find a person's business address in Syracuse?"
"Google him. Or try People Finder. D'uh."

People Finder was better than the phone book. Quill found Rudy's home address, business address, and various phone numbers. Then she Googled him. She wished she hadn't. Rudy had made the news more than once. Assault with a meat hook. Illegal transportation of animals for slaughter. Various fines issued by the USDA for sanitation infractions. Rudy and the law were no stranger to one another. What in the world could she accomplish by accosting this man?

On the other hand, he'd seemed quite approachable in the Tavern Lounge. At the slightest hint of belligerent behavior, she could back off and run home like the prudent coward she was.

Max wandered into the room and shoved his nose into her hand. "Maybe I should take you with me, Max. Can you guard, Maxie? Guard?"

Max rolled over and presented his tummy for a rub. Quill obliged. She also decided to leave him at home.

"I think I may have to go to Syracuse this afternoon." She got up and looked over Devon's shoulder. "How are we doing?"

"Not too bad." The pride in Devon's voice was noticeable. "This Lila Longstreet was loaded. Look here."

"Holy crow." Quill leaned forward and

peered into the screen. "There's five hundred thousand dollars in that account."

"That's right."

"And it was deposited when?"

"Monday morning."

"The morning she checked out of the Inn." Quill sat down, thinking hard. "Can you tell where the money came from?"

"That'll take a while."

"Okay. Could you try to find out?" Quill got up and slung her purse over her shoulder. "In the meantime, I'm off to Syracuse. And Devon? This is where I'm headed." She scribbled the warehouse address on a piece of paper and said flippantly, "If I'm not back by six tonight, call out the National Guard."

"Seriously? I thought you guys have backup."

"We do, we do. But just in case my backup's shopping, or whatever, let my sister know where I am, okay?"

"Your backup's your sister?"

"Ask yourself," Quill said mysteriously, "is she really my sister?"

Max, perhaps sensing that the next car ride was going to terminate at home, where he would be stuck inside all day, took off down Main Street as soon as Quill opened the outside door. She called after him, gave it up, and got in the Honda for the hour-long drive to Syracuse.

Rudy's plant and its warehouses were in a northern suburb off Interstate 80, a location that provided easy access for trucks. Quill found it quickly enough. The main warehouse was visible from the interstate. The building was huge. Faded red letters marched across the long wall facing the road: BARANGA'S WHOLESALE MEATS. Quill pulled into the graveled yard and parked at the south end of the building near the main-door, marked OFFICE. The yard itself was empty, except for the back half of a semi–tractor trailer sitting near a pair of huge overhead doors. Weeds grew around the tires.

Quill knocked briskly on the door, and then rattled the handle. Locked. She trudged around the building to a pair of east-facing overhead doors. A large sign to the left of the doors read: HONK TO ENTER. There was a main door, here, as well. Quill turned the handle. It opened into a dark concrete corridor that seemed to run the length of the entire building. The air was artificially cold, and there was a faint smell of congealed blood. The only illumination was from the Plexiglas soffits under the eaves.

The north end of the corridor, she realized, probably ended at the office. The door to her left must lead to the open warehouse space. The door directly ahead of her led where? It was unlocked. She opened it and peered into total darkness. She fumbled on the wall to her right, found a switch, and flicked it on. The overhead lights were fluorescent. They sputtered briefly, and then shone a steady light on a series of huge coolers. He traded in offal, Rudy had said. Which was probably in those same coolers. Yuck.

The bellow of a huge air horn nearly shocked her out of her shoes. She jumped back into the corridor. She cracked the door to the warehouse space and peered out. The overhead doors began to rise with a slow, ominous rumble, like a portcullis rising at the entrance to a castle. Daylight flooded into an enormous room at least two hundred feet long. She saw the tail end of a huge tractor trailer, and heard voices. Rudy leaped out of the passenger side of the cab and stomped into the space. "Move it up," he shouted. "Move it up!" His back to Quill, he directed the semi backward until it was completely inside. It was a tricky operation, moving a vehicle that massive into a space that barely accommodated it, and Quill waited until the vehicle had rumbled to a complete stop to let Rudy know she was there.

Rudy stomped to the cab just as Quill emerged from the door, and shouted to the driver, "You sure nobody saw ya?"

The response was an indistinct mumble.

"You better be goddam sure," Rudy said. "I get any visitors from the Feds, you're gonna be communing with the fish in Lake Ontario. Hahahaha."

Quill drew back into the hall and let the door ease shut. There was a confused stomping and muttering, then the door handle turned. Quill whipped into the space with the offal-filled freezers, and left the door open a crack. There were three men in the hall, Rudy, the driver, and a familiar gray ponytail. The voice was unmistakable.

Millard Barnstaple.

Quill suppressed a shout of surprise.

"You think I should pay you for this job until I make sure you got out of Manhattan without anyone tracking you down?" Rudy said jovially.

"You did promise to pay, Mr. B," a voice said humbly. Not Millard, then. The driver.

"Here you go. And here's a little extra for your trouble. Next shipment won't be ready to go until I hear from Pest Control some-time next week."

"Monday night, like this week?"

"His wife thinks he's bowling," Rudy chuckled. "I'll give ya a call, Miguel, 'kay? Now, you go get those babies unloaded. And I don't want to see your face again until I ask to see it. Hahahaha."

A door opened and shut.

"You sure you can trust him?" Millard. A very nervous Millard.

"I got his green card, Bumbottle. He ain't saying spit without I tell him to. So, you got some cash for me?"

"Well, yes. In a way."

"In a way?" Rudy's voice was deceptively mild. "It'd better be my way."

"This deal with Kittleburger's all screwed up."

" 'Cause he's dead, you mean."

"Right, brainiac. Because he's dead. I forked over the last five hundred grand to Kittleburger Monday. The sale was supposed to be final Tuesday. Then we get these murders. Not," he added humorously, "that some of us will miss old Lila all that much . . ."

"We had a sort of a thing going," Rudy said.

Quill bit back an exclamation. She wondered if Lila'd ever had time to actually work.

"So you speak of her with a little respect. You got me?" Rudy blew his nose loudly. "Get on with on why you don't have any money."

"But now both of the people that could have given us control of Pet Pro have gone to meet their maker, so to speak . . ."

"Ain't any 'so to speak' about it," Rudy said glumly. "So, you're telling me what?"

"You can process this load, but I can't accept delivery. I don't have anywhere to put it. The Pet Pro sale's up in the air. Lila and Max always told me where to store it at Pet Pro. And they're both dead. All I need is a little time until we figure out who owns what, here." There was a definite whine in Millard's voice.

"The way I see it, you place the order for these babies with me, I deliver, you accept. It's no skin off my nose where you put 'em. You got room at Vegan Vittles. Put 'em there."

"I can't do that!" Millard said, "As you damn well know."

"Scared of little wifey?"

"I just . . . need some time. This is not a load you can just store anywhere. Kittleburger knew that. There has to be a certain amount of . . . discretion."

"Yeah, well, whoever offed Kittleburger

didn't do us no favors, that's for sure. Discretion. I say screw discretion and give me my check."

"You don't want this to get public anymore than I do," Millard said, sounding, for the first time, as though he actually had some backbone. "You scared the bejesus out of that little fairy in Hemlock Falls 'cause you thought he was on to this. So don't you tell me to screw discretion."

There was a prolonged silence, broken only by the sound of Rudy rasping his hand over his jaw. "Shit," Rudy said finally. "Okay. Look. I got some space in the coolers in this room here. Not much. The last delivery was larger than I thought it'd be and there's an overflow. So I'll stuff what I can in there. If I can't get all those little bastards in there, though, I'm dumping 'em into the lake. But you're payin' me for the whole load, Bumbottle."

"I'll pay you when you can tell me how much I'm actually going to get."

The discussion veered into an acrimonious debate over price. Quill, completely baffled, pulled out the small penlight she kept in her purse and fumbled quietly through the dark until she found a cooler. What kind of offal had to be handled with discretion? She eased the cooler open, switched on the penlight, peered inside, and stuffed her hand in her mouth so she wouldn't scream.

Rats.

Thousands of dead rats.

Thousands of dead, frozen rats.

Quill ran the penlight over the neatly stacked bodies. She switched it off. She waited until her breathing slowed to more or less normal.

A bribed official from New York City's Pest Control Office.

Harvey's logo of a cat with a mouse in its jaws.

Vegan Vittles. Guaranteed to be free of beef, lamb, chicken, pork, and goat.

But not of *rattus rattus.*

Rudy's markup was pretty good, indeed. Quill bet that he was getting paid at both ends: to dispose of the New York City rats, and to provide rat meal to the pet food people.

Poor Harvey. Rudy had seen that logo and leaped to the totally wrong conclusion.

There was a sound of a door hastily pulled open, and a shout, "Mr. B!"

"What?" Rudy demanded.

"You see that other car out front by the office?"

"What car?"

"Somebody's here?" Millard's voice rose to a squeak. "I've got to get out of here, Baranga. My reputation's at stake. Anybody finds out about this . . ."

"Cool it, Bumbottle," Rudy said. "What kind of car is it, Miguel?"

"Honda?" Miguel said.

"Honda," Rudy said. "Shit. Silver Honda?"

"Silver, yes."

"Goddamit. That good looking broadie's too much of a snoop for her own good."

"Who are you talking about?" Millard stuttered. "Do you know who's here? Is it the USDA?"

"Get inside the warehouse, you two, and check everything in the place. You're looking for a tall redhead. Good figure. Her eyes are sort of tea-colored."

"You're talking about Sarah Quilliam?" Millard's voice spiraled from anxious to panic. "She's married to that investigator McHale. The one that used to be a cop. She's a famous artist. Priscilla bought one of her paintings for twenty thousand dollars."

From where? Quill thought indignantly. How come she never saw that kind of money for her paintings? It all went to the galleries, that was why.

"We don't want her on our tails, Rudy. You've got to do something."

The doors slammed. Cautiously, Quill stuck her head out the door of the cooler room. The hall was empty. She raced down the corridor as if all the bats of hell were at her heels. If she was wrong about the office being at the end of the hall . . .

She wasn't. Who would have thought she'd want to kiss a door that had an OFFICE sign on it? There was a small waiting area around the corner that faced the outside door. There was a chair in it. Quill sat down, took two deep breaths, leaped up, unlocked the outside door, and was sitting with one leg crossed over the other when Rudy and Millard dashed in.

"Well, there you are, Rudy," she said pleasantly. "I thought I heard voices. I was just about to come and check. And Mr. Barnstaple, I didn't expect to find you here."

"This door was supposed to be locked," Rudy said suspiciously.

"Was it?" Quill blinked innocently at him. "It was open when I got here."

Rudy explored a molar with his tongue, sucked his teeth, and said, "You want something?"

She was in a quandary. She now knew Rudy was bribing the pest control officer

Monday night, and not driving over Lila Longstreet. And since his whereabouts that evening had to do with the load of sewer rats in his coolers, any questions about an alibi for the murder were going to inflame Rudy's suspicions. "You left the Inn without paying your bill, Rudy. I'm sure it was an oversight. But I'm here to collect."

"You drove all the way to Syracuse to collect on a bill I already paid?"

"I had a few other errands to run here," Quill said carelessly, "but it's a substantial charge. The bill for the Johnny Walker Blue alone is several hundred dollars."

"I didn't know you were a skip artist, Baranga," Millard snickered.

Rudy's flat little eyes never left her face. "Bullshit. All that little receptionist of yours had to do was process my credit card. You already had the number."

"It was rejected," Quill improvised. "And she's not my little receptionist. She's a . . ."

"Bullshit." Rudy jingled the change in his pockets. "You were maybe looking for my checkbook in my cooler?"

"I beg your pardon," Quill said frostily. "I know nothing at all about your so-called cooler."

"She knows, doesn't she?" Millard blurted suddenly. "She's found out about us."

"Shut up," Rudy said. He extended one forefinger and touched Quill's sleeve. She was wearing her usual combination of long wool skirt and fisherman's knit sweater, the latter in a warm bronze. "So where'd this come from?" He uncurled his fingers. Quill shrieked.

"That's a bit of rat tail, isn't it, Rudy?" Millard said anxiously.

"I really ought to be going." Quill half rose from her chair. Rudy pushed her back down. "I have *no* idea where that came from." Quill half rose again. Rudy's response was firm and immediate, "Siddown or I'll make sure you don't get up again."

Quill sat down.

"She's going to rat us out, Rudy," Millard tittered.

Rudy whirled. "One more word out of you, sport, and you'll wish you'd never been born." He rubbed his chin thoughtfully, and then sighed. "It's a darn shame, that's what it is."

"Look," Quill said steadily, "I know this is a cliché, but everyone knows where I am."

"Is that so?"

Quill nodded vigorously.

"I'll tell ya something, sweetcakes, you got no body, you got no case. We're going to have to feed you to the kitties. Sorry."

The thing was, Quill thought, he really did look sorry, an emotion that fled as quickly as it had come when all three heard the shouts outside.

CHAPTER 11

"I'm sorry, Quill," Howie Murchison said patiently. "Intent to inflict bodily harm does not carry the same penalty as actually *inflicting* bodily harm. Neither does menacing."

"Well, that's what he did to my sister," Meg said indignantly. "He menaced her with grinding her up into kitty chow!"

"I don't think he'd actually have done it," Quill said uncomfortably. She moved the cloisonné bowl on her desk from one side to the other and back again. "On the other hand . . ."

"On the other hand, if Jerry and I hadn't pulled into that parking lot when we did, you very well could have been divided into forty-four cans of Mousee Morsels. Just like that time in Palm Beach." Meg bounced off the couch and glared horribly at Howie, who was slouched in the guest chair, "I asked you to come over here so those jerks would get arrested!"

Howie, the least litigious lawyer of Quill's acquaintance, was also the village justice. He looked at Meg over his clear-rimmed spectacles and said mildly, "They have been arrested. Or rather, they will be. There's an APB out for both of them. They won't get far, Meg. Our law enforcement has gotten pretty efficient about fugitives these past few years."

"Yeah, but is there a huge priority on capturing crooks who've mislabeled cat chow?" she scoffed. "I don't think so."

Howie coughed. He got to his feet. He pulled on his ancient sports coat and smiled at Quill. "I'm glad nothing worse happened today. When the time comes to take your statement, give me a call if you feel the need."

"Thanks, Howie. And thanks for dropping by. Meg didn't need to wig out, but she did."

"Any time." He nodded amiably at them both. "You'll both be glad to know that Harvey's back."

Quill's eyebrows rose. "Already?"

"He was staying at that little Motel 6 over on Route 353. Soon as the word went out over the police scanner, he drove back into town and took down the FOR SALE sign on his house. He'll be open for business as usual tomorrow morning."

"Well, that's one good thing to come out of this anyway," Meg grumbled. She re-settled herself on the couch.

Howie paused on his way out the door. "I suppose it's too much to ask of you two — but can you at least try stay out of trouble?"

"We always try," Meg said. "Bring Miriam in for dinner sometime next week, Howie. I'll create something fabulous."

"You always do."

Howie left a small silence in his wake.

"So," Meg said. "Do you need another inch of Grey Goose vodka?"

"Nah. I was menaced, not actually bumped off." She looked at her sister with deep affection. "But I've never been so glad to see anyone in my life."

"We were the cavalry, weren't we?" Meg said with a pleased air. "I don't know why you decided to go to Syracuse by yourself, Quill. It doesn't show a whole lot of common sense."

"I wasn't a complete idiot," Quill said. "At least I left the address with Devon."

"Devon?"

"Didn't Devon call you and tell you where I was? I was going to do it myself, on the cell phone, but I figured you'd come dashing after me, and that would," she hesitated, and then went on a little dryly, "get you in hot water with Jerry."

"What do you mean get me in hot water with Jerry?" Meg said indignantly. "I make my own decisions, here."

"He didn't want you to hare off to Syracuse."

"So?" Meg said belligerently. "I would have gone with you if I'd wanted to."

"Right. So if Devon didn't tell you where I was, who did?"

Meg flushed. "Olivia."

"Olivia Oberlie?"

"The one and the same."

"But how?"

"She started prophesying away in the dining room. Cassie Winterborne ran and got me out of the kitchen. And you should have seen her, Quill. It was actually quite eerie. She was in this sort of trance . . ."

"That's hooey." Quill drummed her fingers on her desk. "The woman is no more psychic than I am."

"True," Meg admitted. "But she scared me enough that I grabbed Jerry and came after you. And you should be glad I did."

"People like Olivia have a very sophisticated way of gathering information they aren't supposed to have." Quill mulled this over for a minute. "Did she know exactly where I was?"

"She said she saw rats. Thousands of rats. And she saw Rudy and he was chasing you down a long concrete hallway. She convinced me that you really were in danger, and, of course, I knew immediately that you'd gone to Syracuse."

"How did you get the address of the warehouse?"

"It was on Rudy's bill."

Quill smacked the desktop decisively. "We need to find out just how Olivia got this information."

"Why? It couldn't have been all that hard to guess where you were. Elmer's been walking around the village telling people he promised to give you a medal if you accosted Rudy and lambasted him for running Harvey out of town. Half the people in Hemlock Falls could have prophesied that you were in Syracuse."

"It's not that. It's the rats."

Meg's face changed in sudden enlightenment. "Of course! How did Olivia know about the rats? That wasn't something that either Rudy or Millard wanted made public, was it?"

"It's also a pretty good motive for knocking Lila and Kittleburger off. What if Kittleburger threatened to expose the racket? What if Lila found out about it and was blackmailing Rudy?"

"I thought you said Kittleburger knew about the rats?"

"That's what I inferred from what Millard said," Quill said. "I could be wrong. We could find out."

"How? The two of them took off and headed for timber."

"According to Howie, it won't be long before the two of them are in custody. We can find out then." Quill leaned back in her chair. The ceiling in her office, unlike the ceiling in Myles' house, was a fine example of cast tin squares. She could spend hours looking at the intricate detail.

"This is not the time to contemplate that ceiling," Meg said sternly. "You still haven't told me everything you learned before Rudy nabbed you."

"I was so sure that Rudy was behind the killings," Quill sighed. "But his alibi for Monday night seems pretty solid. There's no way he could have driven round-trip to New York from Hemlock Falls in anything less than six hours. And he said that he met this pest control guy at nine. And the time of Lila's death . . ."

"Yeah, yeah," Meg grumbled. "Could he have hired somebody?"

"Maybe. He'd have the connections, if

anyone would." Quill felt quite encouraged. A hired hit man was going to solve all the niggling problems about time. Except that it was notoriously difficult to catch hired hit men, even for the police. She and Meg didn't have a chance. "We've never actually failed to solve a case before, have we?"

"Not so far." Meg sighed. "Doesn't mean it can't happen, though."

"I'm not ready to give up yet. There's too many leads to follow. The Barnstaples were the source of the five hundred thousand dollars that showed up in Lila's bank account on Monday, by the way. Priscilla wasn't quite honest with us, was she? According to Millard, they'd already made the deal to buy Pet Pro. That payment was the last of the earnest money."

"Why do you suppose Priscilla would lie about that?"

Quill shrugged. "Why do people lie about anything? But I think we should find out. Maybe someone *didn't* want the sale of Pet Pro to go through as planned. Maybe that's why Priscilla lied about it. Do you know where she is?"

"Half the Chamber of Commerce is over at the high school getting ready for the puppy show tomorrow. My guess is that she's there." Meg looked at her narrowly.

"You sure you don't need a nap or anything?"

"We investigators are tough. And if Olivia's over there, too, I'll have a chance to find out how she knew about the rats."

"Good luck on prying anything out of her," Meg said glumly. "I think she actually believes that she's psychic."

"Maybe. And maybe we've been looking at this case all wrong, and we should be after Olivia after all." Quill got to her feet with an effort. In the melee that occurred after Meg and Jerry had burst into the warehouse office, Quill had thrown her share of punches.

"And you're sure you don't mind that I'll be over at Jerry's tonight?"

Since Jerry's arrival in her life, Meg had been taking Friday nights off to give Jerry a hand at his restaurant in Ithaca.

"I'll be fine. Just give him an extra hug for me."

"He's pretty bummed that Rudy punched him out."

"Rudy's a professional thug. And Jerry didn't do so badly in that particular scuffle. Rudy's going to have one heck of a black eye tomorrow. Wherever he is."

Meg left with a cheery wave. Quill looked at her watch, surprised to see that it was only three thirty. It felt as if several days had passed since her foray into Rudy's warehouse. Suddenly, she wanted nothing more than to curl up under an afghan and sleep for the next three days.

There was a scratching at the door, and Max nosed in, looking hopeful. "Where were you when I needed you?"

He grinned at her, tongue lolling.

"Does it bother you in the least that I narrowly escaped being ground up into pet food?"

Max whined and cocked his head.

"You do understand practically everything I say," Quill marveled. "Which reminds me. We're going to enter the Best Canine Vocabulary class in this dog and puppy show tomorrow. So we'd better get over there and sign you up."

The Hemlock Falls High School had started out as a fine cobblestone building in the mid-nineteenth century, grown to a sprawling complex of not-so-fine brick buildings at the height of the baby boom in the sixties, and shrunk again to three buildings as the resident population of upstate New York fled south to more tax-friendly climes. It lay about two miles southwest of the Inn, adjacent to Peterson Park. It was a brisk afternoon. Quill decided to blow the fatigue out of her system by walking to the pet show instead of taking the Honda. This entailed putting Max on a leash, which, when he was in an agreeable mood, gave Quill the pleasant sense of being in a Ralph Lauren ad in which well-dressed, carefree women walked their handsome golden retrievers in a beautiful autumnal setting. Although agreeable, Max was in a mood to investigate everything in his path, so their progress was slow. By the time dog and mistress reached the athletic field, Quill had strolled herself into a serene and untroubled frame of mind.

The Hemlock Falls High School football team was called the "Hounds of Heck." The team logo was an orange mastiff on a red background. A large pink flag, announcing Pamela's Pampered Puppy Palace's First Annual Dog and Puppy Show, had replaced the banner that normally flew over the field during the football season. The show ring was marked off by the kind of fiberglass stakes used in fencing sheep; instead of the usual electrified tape, pink ribbons were strung between the posts. A fair portion of the twenty-four members of the Chamber of Commerce milled about the field, most with dogs at their sides. Esther West paraded proudly with her handsome standard-bred poodle, Fabio. Marge and her partner Betty Hall strolled with Betty's English bulldog, Cousin Itt. Adela Henry, the mayor's wife, glided like a frigate under full sail, their apricot Airedale mincing along with her. Adela's apricot pantsuit matched the dog's coat perfectly.

Quill viewed all of this with a sense of pleasure.

"You aren't serious about entering that dog in this show?" a sticky-sweet voice said in her ear.

Quill recoiled, much as she did when she unexpectedly ran across a snake in her path. "Hello, Carol Ann," she said warily. She cast around for a topic of conversation that would preclude Carol Ann's opinions on tax rates, felonious activities at the Inn, or the Quilliams' love life. "Quite a few people here today. I'm surprised at the turnout. The show doesn't start till tomorrow."

Carol Ann pouted prettily. It was always hard for newcomers to Hemlock Falls to believe that her blonde hair, baby blue eyes, and bouncy ponytail disguised a twenty-first-century Attila the Hun. "The high school isn't zoned for this."

"A dog show?"

"School-related activities only," she said. "You tell me how a dog show is related to school activities. It isn't. I was going to bring that up at the town council meeting yesterday."

"And did you?"

Carol Ann's white-blonde eyebrows drew together in a scowl. "Somebody forgot to tell me that the meeting'd been switched to the Elks club. I think it was Cletus Richardson."

And there goes his house assessment to sky high levels, Quill thought. "Are you going to sign your dog up for a class?"

"I don't have a dog," Carol Ann said flatly. "Worms. Fleas. Dog hair. It's disgusting."

"Then you're here because . . ."

"I'm here because I want to find out who is going to clean this mess up after all these animals leave." She tilted her head. "And why are *you* here? Somebody told me you were dead."

"I'm not," Quill said, startled. "Who told you I was dead?"

Carol Ann pointed. "Olivia Oberlie. She was prophesizing like anything a few minutes ago."

Olivia was holding court in front of the bleachers. Her white hair was swept up in an elaborate french twist. She wore a turquoise caftan and a baroque necklace, heavily worked in gold. A large knot of people surrounded her. Priscilla Barnstaple, dressed in khaki trousers and a twin set, stood with both Finnegans. Robin looked bored. Victoria was bent over Priscilla, talking earnestly. Pamela stood a little distance from them, her eyes fixed worshipfully on Olivia. Harland Peterson stood behind Pamela. His eyes, Quill was glad to see, were not fixed on Pamela with any kind of expression other than acute discomfort. He had Pookie the Peke on a rhinestone leash.

Quill wound her way through the crowd, pulling a reluctant Max.

"Thank god!" Olivia boomed. "Have I said it before? I will say it again! Character is destiny. Destiny is character! She was not doomed to die!" She swept through the crowd like Moses commanding the sea to part. "I had such visions." She clutched Quill by the back of the neck and drew her head down to her bosom, which was scented with gardenia. Quill sneezed. Olivia released her with a dramatic sigh. "So your sister was in time. Thank god!" she repeated.

"Olivia saw it all," Pamela said in great excitement. "She said Rudy Baranga had put you in mortal peril. And she called on your sister and told her to find you right away!"

"She did find me right away." Quill turned

to Olivia. "Thank you."

Olivia smiled that I-see-all-that-you-are smile. "There was no need to come here to thank me," she said huskily. "No need."

"Actually, I came here to sign Max up for the dog with the best vocabulary class," Quill said. "I talked to Meg. She said that you actually *saw* the rats?"

"I gave Meg a most urgent message." Olivia passed her hand over her brow. "When I am in a trance, however, I frequently don't know what I actually said. Pamela, my dear. You were there. Did I mention rats?"

"You did," Pamela breathed. "Thousands of rats, you said. And Rudy's warehouse."

Quill stood stock still. Pamela's Puppy Palace was right between Harvey Bozzel's advertising agency and Marge Schmidt's office.

"Quill? You're starin' at me." Pamela gave an uncomfortable laugh. "Do I have some spinach in my teeth, or what?" She turned to Harland and postured prettily. "You see anything, darlin'?"

"I have no memory of rats," Olivia boomed. "None at all."

"Rats," Quill said, "are notorious for gnawing holes in all kinds of places. In the walls between two offices, for example." She held Pamela's eyes with hers.

"Is that right?" Pamela said feebly. "Well. Ah. Harland, I think we ought to be trottin' along now."

"Why don't you trot right over here and talk to me for a moment?" Quill said.

Pamela looked at her reproachfully. "She saved your life, Quill, from all accounts."

"I *do* appreciate it. But . . ."

"But nothing," Pamela said airily. "If a person happens to overhear certain conversations by accident, there's no law against that, is there?"

"Depends on what that person has to gain by it." Quill was suddenly weary. "Money, perhaps."

"My puppies have to eat," Pamela said unhappily. She cringed. Quill hated it when people cringed. No self-respecting human being should ever have a need to cringe. "And Harland, I really think we need to be goin', now."

"Hang on a second, Pammie." Harland, clearly oblivious to the undercurrents of this conversation, cleared his throat in a marked way. His big leathery face was red. "We heard that you went to see Baranga at that warehouse of his and that he laid hands on you." The red deepened to puce. "If I'd had any idea. Well, you can bet if they catch the bastard, they'd better not let me get too close. We shouldn't have let you go over there all by yourself."

"I was menaced," Quill said cheerfully. "Not actually battered. And Harvey's back, so everything turned out just fine." She didn't look at Pamela. Pamela had eavesdropped on her conversation with Devon, that was clear. But what about the rats? Had the woman overheard Rudy and Harvey discussing the delivery of the rats? Had she let that drop into a "good gossip" with Harvey? And she'd obviously known where Quill was going; she must have listened in on that conversation, too. At least one of the questions peripheral to this case had been answered. Olivia paid for her information. But was it just from Pamela? Or did she find sources in other members of the IAPFP?

"Did you ever find out just how come Harvey beat feet out of town?" Harland asked. "I stopped by his house on my way over here, and his mouth was shut tighter than a clam at Christmas."

Quill snapped out of her reverie. It was more than likely that Harvey's woes were all due to Pamela's unruly tongue. A word to Harland would give him a disgust of Pamela that might even break up the relationship. And that would suit poor Marge just fine.

Pamela licked her lips nervously, and then buried her head in the Peke's fur.

"You know Harvey," Quill said kindly. "He's a jittery soul. And Rudy's a pretty scary-looking guy. He may have made Harvey nervous just by looking at him crosswise. Whatever the reason, it's over now."

"It surely is," Pamela said with a loud, nervous laugh. "And I surely need some tea, Harland. Or maybe something a little stronger?"

"Can we leave that dog in the car?" Harland asked glumly.

"Pookie? Pookie would be so sad!" Pamela linked her arm with Harland's and drew him toward the parking lot, leaving the rest of them behind. "I'm so glad that Millard and Rudy didn't grind you up into rat food, Quill!"

There was a ripple of agreement from the remaining crowd. Quill glanced at Priscilla Barnstaple. She'd turned an indifferent ear to the conversation and was checking items off on a clipboard. She didn't look like a woman whose husband was on the lam from a contaminated pet food scheme. But she hadn't liked Millard much, either, from what Quill had seen of their interactions.

And if Pamela's insinuations were true, she didn't much like men altogether. "I'm glad I wasn't ground up, too," she said cheerfully. "But thank you, everyone, for your concern."

Olivia had been standing dreamily alone, swaying slightly in the still air. "Ah," she said. "They're here." She nodded toward the school parking lot. A van marked MIND DOESN'T MATTER, O. O. PRODUCTIONS braked to a stop. The "O's" had little eyes in the middle. Several technician-looking types spilled out onto the asphalt. Olivia waved majestically and moved toward them. The crowd followed her like a flock of geese correcting course in midair.

Quill put her hand out and touched Priscilla lightly on the shoulder as she passed by. "Can I speak with you a moment?"

Priscilla cast a contemptuous eye over Max, who was chasing a flea behind his ear with his hind leg. "If it's about entering that dog in a class for tomorrow's show, I wouldn't recommend it."

Quill's attention was momentarily diverted. "He understands practically everything I say," she protested. "I think he'd do very well in the vocabulary class."

Priscilla shook her head. "This is such a crock." She looked up at Quill. She was a plain woman, whose weathered skin showed the effect of too much sun and too little care. Her graying hair was skinned back in a tight knot behind her head. Her nails, Quill noted, were well cared for, and the half boots that she wore were old, but polished and of excellent quality. "Have you ever attended a real dog show?"

"By a real dog show you mean an AKC show?"

"Professional shows aren't just limited to the AKC, although they, of course, are the better known. This amateur stuff . . ." she made a movement of disgust.

"Are you judging this show, then?"

"No." She clipped her pencil to the clipboard with an air of finality. "Not me, not anymore. Olivia's judging that idiot 'Dog Votes for Dog' thing. And there's a costume class, if you can believe it. She's judging that, too. The ordinary classes are being judged by that guy over there." She nodded in the direction of the bleachers. An elderly man and his daughter stood talking to Elmer and Adela. He was of slightly less than medium height, wiry and fit despite his age. His daughter, whose proportions were queenly, was taller than he, with a wild corona of mahogany hair that exactly matched the coat of the collie at her side.

"That's Austin McKenzie."

"I know of him," Quill said in mild surprise. "He's a vet from Summersville. And that's not his daughter, that's his wife. Madeline? Isn't that her name?"

Priscilla nodded, a little wistfully. "And doesn't he think she's hung the moon. He's primarily a large animal practice, but somebody talked him into coming over and judging this damn thing. Olivia, probably. Although I've forgotten more about dogs than McKenzie will ever know."

Quill took this with a gain of salt. The McKenzies' collie was magnificent. He sat at his mistress' side in a perfect sit. At a sign from McKenzie himself, he promptly dropped to a truly noble-looking down. Priscilla sighed. "Never mind."

"You care about dog shows?"

"I care about good dogs, yes. If it hadn't been for Kittleburger I'd still . . . forget it." She looked resentfully at Quill. "Is there something you wanted?"

Quill bit her lip. "What did you hear about what happened this afternoon?"

"To you, you mean?" She shrugged, "Just that you went chasing after Rudy because of some *contretemps* over this local ad man. Rudy lose his temper with you?" A mean smile crossed her face. "Not one of nature's gentlemen, our Rudy."

"Rudy," Quill said bluntly, "was involved in a scheme to provide an illegal product to Pet Pro and Vegan Vittles. Rudy thought Harvey Bozzel, our local ad man, as you call him, was on to it. When I went to Rudy's warehouse this afternoon, I discovered the scheme by accident."

"Illegal product? To my company? And to Pet Pro? What sort of illegal product?"

"Rats."

"Rats?" Priscilla's stare was disbelieving. "Are you crazy?"

"Nope. Rudy got the carcasses from the Pest Control people in New York City, ground them up into sort of a mouse meal, I'd guess you call it, and sold the meal to Maxwell Kittleburger. And to you."

"Rat meat?" She gave a sudden shout of laughter. "You have to be kidding. And Rudy sold this stuff to Vegan Vittles?" Her face darkened. "You mean to Millard. Millard was involved in this?"

"I'm afraid so."

Priscilla went very still. "Well," she said after a long moment. "And you know this because Millard was at the warehouse this afternoon, too?"

"Yes. He was."

"Rudy seems to have escaped to parts

285

unknown, as they say. I'm to take it that Millard went with him?"

"I'm sorry, Priscilla."

A cool breeze had sprung up as the twilight drew in. Priscilla hugged her cardigan closer to her thin chest. "Vegan Vittles was my father's favorite project," she said, so softly that Quill had to bend to hear her. "He had other companies, other businesses, but this was the one that reflected his own philosophy. His own principles. He loved animals. Not," she jerked her chin contemptuously toward the parking lot, where Olivia Oberlie's crew was setting up the cameras, "that kind of exploitative crap. But he had a real appreciation for who they are. How they relate to the rest of us." She bent over and ruffled Max's ears. "He would have had a soft spot even for this guy." She straightened up. "As for Millard. Well, I was fooled, at first, by the wire-rimmed glasses and the ponytail and all that blather about our animals are our brothers and how material things didn't matter. But he turned out to be just like the rest of them. After my money." Her mouth drew downward in a bitter curve. "What happened, exactly?"

"Rudy and Millard were pretty upset that I'd discovered the freezers full of . . . umm . . . product. Rudy's solution was pretty straightforward. If they got rid of me, they got rid of the problem. But Meg and Jerry burst in, and for a few seconds, there was a free-for-all."

"Millard actually hit somebody?" Priscilla said with mild interest.

"Well, no," Quill admitted. "Actually, he ducked out the door and jumped into Rudy's Cadillac. Rudy jumped in after him. The last I saw, they were headed north on I-80."

"Toward the Adirondacks?" Priscilla's odd laugh barked again. "Millard hates trees."

"I did overhear something that puzzled me, Priscilla. Millard said that he'd paid the last five hundred thousand to Kittleburger Monday morning?"

"The last five hundred thousand what? Dollars?"

"To complete the purchase of Pet Pro. Yes."

"Nonsense. I was in the process of buying Pet Pro. Max and I had an agreement in principle, but nothing had been signed yet." Priscilla's face was set in ugly lines of anger. "Five hundred thousand, you say? The only way Millard could have gotten that kind of money was to borrow on his stock. Where's Victoria?"

Quill looked around the field. "There she

is. It looks like she's just leaving."

Victoria, trailed by a sulking Robin, was halfway down the trail to Peterson Park.

"Hi! Victoria!" Priscilla shouted. "Come here!"

Victoria said something to Robin, and then headed across the field toward them. Robin turned and disappeared into the green of Peterson Park.

"What is it, Priscilla?" Victoria's face was flushed with annoyance but her tone was polite. She'd made a bright print scarf into a headband to hold back her dark hair; the effect made her look gaunt.

Priscilla thrust a long finger at her. "What was Maxwell on about, selling Pet Pro to Millard behind my back?"

"Maxwell wasn't doing any such thing," Victoria said. "Who told you that?"

"I did." Quill frowned a little. "I'm afraid I have proof."

"Proof?" Victoria's lips thinned. "What kind of proof?"

Quill felt herself blush. One of the unpleasant parts of being a detective was that you had to snoop. And in the process of solving the case, sometimes other people would realize that you were a snoop. It was very embarrassing. But nothing would be gained by backing away from the current situation, so she said: "I overheard Millard tell Rudy Baranga that the last payment of five hundred thousand dollars had been made to Maxwell Kittleburger on Monday. It was the final earnest money for the purchase of Pet Pro."

"What Millard said and what Millard did could be two different things entirely," Victoria said. "That isn't proof."

"Five hundred thousand dollars had been deposited into Lila Longstreet's money-market account Monday morning," Quill said. "She supervised the bookkeeping for Pet Pro, didn't she?"

Victoria shook her head slowly. "This makes no sense to me at all. And how did you get access to that information anyway? You aren't with the police."

"Um. No. But we were, ah — doing a credit check," Quill improvised, "and we sort of ran across the information accidentally."

"At the least," Victoria said icily, "you've obtained that information illegally. And I want to see it."

"And I," Priscilla was equally angry, "want my five hundred thousand dollars back."

Chapter 12

"It was there this morning," Devon said. "I saw it. Agent Quilliam saw it . . ."

"Agent Quilliam?" Victoria stared at Quill. Quill in turn stared accusingly at Marge. Since Marge had the sensitivity of a charging rhino, she merely said, "Shut up, Devon. And how long are you two planning to tie up my consultant? I want to know where to send the bill."

Victoria gave Marge a brief flash of teeth, "Not long. And I'm sure that you wouldn't want me to make public the fact that your genius consultant here," she laid one hand on Devon's shoulder, "is committing at least three federal offenses. If not more."

It was Marge's turn to glower accusingly at Quill.

"You're sure you saw my money, young man," Priscilla said.

"If that five hundred K was your money, then yeah, we both saw it."

"Then where is it?"

Devon clattered away at the keyboard for a moment. "It got moved to an offshore account," he said. "And let me tell you, even I can't hack into those Cayman Islands files. And if I can't do it," he added with simple pride, "no one can."

"So you don't know who has it?" Victoria said. "If it even existed, that is."

"Oh, it existed all right." Devon clattered away at the keyboard again. "There it is. The account history." Devon stretched his arms over his head and yawned. Priscilla gave a howl of rage. Victoria leaned over his shoulder and stared at the scene intently. "It looks as if close to two million dollars has moved through that account in the last few weeks."

"That's how much Maxwell wanted up front," Priscilla said. "We'd agreed on that in principle last week."

Victoria pulled her cell phone from her purse. "I'm going to punch in a call to the bankers. I wonder if they know anything about this." She thumbed the phone, looked at it, and said, "Damn it all to hell." She tossed the phone onto the floor. Without thinking, Quill bent and picked it up. "Maxwell's been dead, what, two days? It didn't take them long to cut off the company phones."

Quill looked at the cell phone in her hand. It was a Nokia, an expensive one. "Did everyone at Pet Pro have a cell phone like this?"

"What?" Victoria had grabbed the handset of the landline next to Devon's computer.

"You're not making long-distance calls on that phone," Marge said. "Hang it up."

Quill repeated her question.

Victoria threw the handset into the rest with a clatter and a nasty look at Marge. "Yes, we all had phones like this. Why?"

"Mr. Kittleburger had a Nokia, just like this one?" Quill persisted. "And Lila Longstreet, too?"

"What of it?" Victoria snapped. "Max got a volume discount." Victoria glared down at Devon. "Can you print that bank statement out for me?"

"Not without getting the bank on my tail," Devon said cheerfully.

"Not on your life," Marge said. "I've had it with this hacking business. Close it down, Devon."

"I can bring it up on someone else's computer, though," Devon offered. "If you want to print it out, it'll be your problem. As a matter of fact, Mrs. Schmidt is right, I should get out of there right now." He bent forward and punched several keys. The little spinning icon that had driven Trooper Brookes to distraction replaced the data on the screen. "Don't want to hang out there too long, or they'll be knock-knock-knocking on my door."

For a moment, there was silence in the room. Quill was absorbed in assessing the significance of the Pet Pro cell phones. Provost had told her Kittleberger had been found with a Minolta. The Minolta was on the evidence list. The time of Kittleburger's murder was wrong. It had to be.

Devon broke the silence with a loud yawn. "Guess I'd better be going. Got a hot date. See you tomorrow, Mrs. Schmidt. Watch your back, Quill." He gave her a thumbs-up, grabbed his briefcase and shambled out of the room.

Victoria watched him leave. She looked at Marge. "Can he keep his mouth shut?"

"I don't know," Marge said testily. "Probably, yeah, if I ask him to. But I didn't exactly have this kind of crap in mind when I hired him on."

"And what kind of crap would that be?" Victoria asked silkily.

"Money laundering?" Marge folded her arms under her considerable bosom. Her jaw was at a truculent angle. "Illegal transfer of funds? Theft?"

Victoria's smile combined superiority and condescension in equal parts. "We've been watching too much television, Mrs . . . Schmidt — is it?"

"M.E. Schmidt," Marge said. "Yeah. That would be me."

"M.E." Victoria's smile faltered. "You wouldn't be related to the M.E. Schmidt Corporation of Allentown, Pennsylvania?"

"I'd be the owner, yeah," Marge said.

"Mrs. Schmidt." Victoria, Quill noticed, fawned like an expert, "If anything I've said has offended you at all . . ."

"You breathin' my air has offended me. If you've finished your business in here, you can beat it."

Victoria scrabbled in her briefcase. "Just for emergency purposes, Mrs. Schmidt, here's my card. I'm licensed to practice in the state of New York, and compared to that, the Pennsylvania bar is no . . ."

Marge narrowed her eyes to steel points. Victoria adjusted her hair band, gripped Priscilla by the elbow, and left, trailing "good-byes" and "real pleasure to meet you's."

Quill leaned against a filing cabinet. "Marge, do you mind if I make a call on that landline? It's to Ithaca, so it will be a toll call."

"Help yourself."

Quill dug Simon Provost's card out of her purse and keyed in the numbers. He answered on the first ring, which was good, but he sounded extremely testy, which was bad.

"It's Sarah Quilliam," she said. "You said to call if I had any new information for you?"

"Yeah," Provost said warily.

"Well, I might. But I need to know what kind of cell phone was found on Maxwell Kittleburger's body. I think you said it was a Minolta? 'We checked out the Minolta' — those were your exact words?"

"That's right, Mrs. McHale. Now what . . . ?"

"Thank you!" Quill hung the phone up with care. "Yes!" she said. "The first break in the case."

Marge looked at her glumly. "Can you maybe forget the darn case for just a couple of minutes?"

"But, Marge . . ."

"Hey!" Marge blew out her breath in a long whistle. "I thought maybe you could give me a hand with something right now."

"But Marge! The case has opened up. The whole thing is making a lot more sense to me now."

"It is?" Marge said without much interest. "This thing I want you to help me with can't wait. Those dead guys can. C'mon. I'll tell you about it over Betty's pot roast."

Max had abandoned his spot by the lamppost outside Marge's office for parts unknown. Quill called his name to no effect.

"He'll be rummaging in somebody's Dumpster," Marge said.

This was true. Quill tried unsuccessfully to suppress her guilt. "I should train him better."

Marge tramped halfway down the sidewalk and turned impatiently. "C'mon. There's usually a run on the pot roast Friday nights."

"I'd just like Max to enjoy staying home," Quill said a little wistfully.

"Then you'd have to get another kind of dog," Marge said unfeelingly. She snickered, "Like a Pekinese, maybe. D'ya see Harland with that damn little dog of hers?"

They were passing by Pamela's Pampered Puppy Palace. The windows were dark, the CLOSED FOR NAPPIES! sign prominent in the window. Pamela herself was nowhere in sight. "I did," Quill said. "And he didn't look too happy about it, Marge."

"That little pink leash? That rhinestone

collar? You can bet old Harland's going to hear about it." Marge's satisfaction was short-lived. She sighed, and they trudged along in silence. "You know about men, Quill. All the experience you've had."

"Me?" Quill said in indignation.

"Musta. Men seem to like the beautiful ones."

"On a first date," Quill admitted, "that's true. But men stick with the good ones, Marge. Looks don't matter a whole lot after the first infatuation's over."

"So you say," Marge said bitterly. "Well, hang it. There's his dually. He's in my bar right now. What d'ya want to bet it's with her?"

Harland's familiar red pickup was parked right in front of the bar. Quill followed Marge in, and yes, there he was, the bozo, sitting at the bar up front, a beer in one hand, and Pookie's pink leash in the other. Pamela herself was nowhere in sight.

Marge behaved as if he were invisible. Quill said, "Hello, Harland."

" 'Lo, Marge. Quill." He eased himself off the bar stool and thrust the leash in Quill's direction. "I was wondering, Quill, if maybe you'd hang on to this for a little bit."

"Well, sure, Harland. But . . ."

"Just till she gets back from the ladies."

"Ol' Harland's gonna start using the ladies, too!" Geoff Peterson, another member of the far-flung Peterson clan, shouted out down the length of the bar. "Coeee, sweetcakes!" A roar of laughter swept the room. Pookie yapped in excitement. Harland, Quill noticed, seemed to have spent most of the afternoon in embarrassment because of the Peke, and it looked as if this evening was going to continue the trend. The blush crept up the back of his neck and seemed to suffuse his eyeballs.

"Anyhow," he rumbled, "I gotta go somewhere." He thrust the leash at Quill again. This time she took it. "And Margie?"

Marge, nodding to various acquaintances, affected deafness. Harland scraped his feet. "You tell her, Quill. I'll see her around." He shouldered his way out the door.

Quill looked down at the Peke, who had lifted his leg against a bar stool. "Cut that out, you."

"Pookie!" Pamela's long red nails flashed in front of Quill's eyes. The leash was snatched from her hand. "Hello, Quill. What are you doing with my dog?"

"Harland had to go somewhere," Quill said, scrupulously exact. "And he left the dog with me. Until you got back from the bathroom."

"Oh." Pamela looked disconcerted. "What about dinner?" She flashed her teeth at Marge, who'd turned to give her a scathing stare. "I've heard Betty makes the best pot roast in the county. It's funny though, the Big Guy didn't seem to like it all that much. He wanted to take me all the way to Syracuse."

"Dog's not allowed in the bar," Marge said gruffly. "State health rules. And we're out of pot roast."

"But I just saw Betty serving some!"

"You coming, Quill?" Marge turned her back and marched down the center of the dining room to her usual booth. Quill gave Pamela a little wave and followed her.

"Well," she said, as she settled herself across from Marge, "I'd say that was quite encouraging."

"Yeah?"

"Nothing like embarrassing a guy in front of his buddies," Quill said with satisfaction. "And did you hear him? He said, 'Tell Marge I'll see her around.' "

"Hm." But Marge looked a little more cheerful.

"So. The motives for murder seem to be flying thick and fast, Marge. Once we find out who moved that money out of Lila's account, we'll have the murderer! And I can pretty much tell you who it's going to be. It had to be someone who had access, one way or another, to the financial records of the company."

"Robin Finnegan," Marge said flatly. "He was the lawyer for Pet Pro before he got disbarred. He's broke and not happy about it, and he was having an affair with Lila Longstreet."

"We're thinking absolutely along the same lines. The problem all along has been the time of Kittleburger's death. But Marge, the cell phone on Kittleburger's body wasn't his."

"Huh?" Marge looked blank.

"Wait a second. The police checked the phone records. There was a call to Pamela at the right time. But Robin could have made that call from anywhere. He was close to the Inn on that hike. He could have gone up the fire escape — we don't keep it locked, you know — gotten Kittleburger to open the door and then, whack."

"And Lila?"

"He could have conned Lila into giving him the acess numbers to her account, killed her, and moved it to his offshore account."

"That I can see. But he didn't have time to kill her. You said Nate saw him leave the bar for half an hour, maximum."

"Time enough to arrange to meet Lila at Horndean Gorge, drive down to the Croh Bar here, take Harland's dually, and then . . ." Quill leaned back. "He left her there. There's nothing to say when the body was moved after her death. It could have been hours. No one's checked alibis for the middle of the night. And Marge, we threw away that note!"

"Harland's dually?" Marge said in dismay.

"He leaves his keys in it," Quill said. "We all do."

"If Robin's done all that, then why hasn't he left town yet?"

Quill waved both hands in the air. "I don't know. Maybe he thinks that it'll look more suspicious if he takes off in the middle of this investigation. The person that did this has to have nerve, Marge."

"But there's still a bunch of stuff here that isn't adding up."

"That's just because we haven't sat down and put events into a logical order," Quill said confidently. "If we do, what doesn't make sense at the moment will fall into place. It's pretty clear that something very funny is going on with the purchase of Pet Pro."

Marge's attention had been caught by

something over Quill's left shoulder. She was staring, totally indifferent to the conversation.

"Marge?" Quill said with some exasperation. "I said . . ."

"Hush." Marge swiveled her head like the turret on a tank. Quill knew that look. Someone was about to get the full force of Marge's considerable artillery. "C'mon." She slid out of the booth, and crouching, grabbed Quill's hand and pulled her out of the booth. "Down, darn it!" she snapped. Quill obediently dropped to a crouch, too. The surrounding diners paused briefly in their consumption of Betty's pot roast, and then continued eating.

"Follow me!" Marge crouch-walked down the narrow aisle between the booths. Directly ahead was the bar, crowded with the usual Friday night custom. Quill saw a lot of feet. Marge jerked her to the left and through the swinging doors to the kitchen. Quill recognized Betty's feet, which were shod, as usual, in nurse's shoes. (Betty's bunions troubled her, she said, something fierce.)

"Hey, Betty."

"Hey, Quill."

Marge got to her feet with a groan. Quill followed suit.

"Bet," Marge said. "I'm goin' out for a while. You can handle things here okay?"

Betty nodded. "Comin' back?"

"I'll be late." Marge grabbed Quill's hand and dragged her toward the back door to the parking lot.

"Where are we going?"

"You saw her following Harland like a cat in heat?"

"You mean Pamela?"

"Ssh!" Marge pushed the exit door open slowly and peered out. "Coast is clear. C'mon."

Quill followed her into the lot, which was filled to overflowing with parked cars. Marge ducked down behind her Pontiac. Quill ducked down beside her. "Marge, are you thinking of following Pamela to her house to see if Harland's there? Because, believe me, this is not . . ."

Marge clamped one meaty hand over Quill's mouth. Pamela came around the corner of the building, the Peke at her side. Both were trotting, the dog scrambling to keep up. Pamela tossed the dog into a Dodge Caravan. Quill was facing the passenger door, which trumpeted the name of Pamela's shop in foot-high pink letters. Pamela hustled around to the driver's side. There was something different about her.

Quill frowned in concentration. It was her walk. She'd dropped the rather languorous Southern belle shuffle.

The van rumbled to life. Pamela backed out of the lot — rather erratically — and pulled into the street. Marge shoved Quill toward her own passenger door, jumped into her car on the driver's side, and before Quill knew it, they were out on Main. Pamela's taillights were three blocks away. Her left turn signal was blinking. Marge put her foot on the accelerator and followed.

"Marge," Quill said firmly. "This is not a good idea. Believe me, you don't want to see Pamela and Harland together."

"I'll tell you something," Marge said between her teeth. "Miss Molasses-wouldn't-melt-in-her-mouth is up to something. And we're going to find out what it is."

By the time Quill had exhausted the reasons why they should be calling Provost to arrest Robin Finnegan for the murders of Lila Longstreet and Maxwell Kittleburger instead of chasing after Marge's rival in love, she and Marge were parked at the lip of the junction between Hemlock and Horndean Gorge, staring down into the darkness. Pamela's taillights had disappeared down the narrow road that led to the foot of the gorge. Far below, Quill saw the steady glow of lights from a house or a barn.

"She's up to something," Marge repeated stubbornly.

Quill had a lot of sympathy for women who had been dumped. She'd been dumped herself, not all that long ago, and the memory still stung. So instead of jumping out of Marge's Pontiac and marching down to the Inn — which was only a mile and a half away — she said in a reasonable tone, "By 'up to something' do you think she has the brains to pull off two fairly complicated murders?"

"Course she doesn't," Marge said abruptly.

"Well, do you think that Robin, who *does* have the brains to pull off a theft like that, has Pamela as a partner?"

"Course I don't."

"Well. Gee. Nuts." Quill tugged at her hair in exasperation. "So why are we parked at the edge of the gorge in the dark instead of getting Robin arrested? I know, I know. Because she's up to something."

Marge opened the driver's door. "You comin'?"

"Sure. Of course."

Neither one of them had taken the time

to pull on a coat, and the air was frosty. Shivering, Quill followed Marge down the rutted gravel. Many of the smaller country roads in Tompkins County were unpaved. This helped maintain the delightfully rural feel, but the roads were a pain to drive on, and Quill was discovering an even bigger pain to walk on in the dark. Especially in her good boots. On the other hand, the effort to stay upright was warming her up, so that the autumn chill was welcome.

The lights they had seen from the top of the gorge proved to be those of a large house trailer. Two house trailers, Quill realized, as she stood in shoulder-high brush next to Marge. The first was clearly occupied. Light shone from the kitchen windows. Quill made out a figure moving behind the thin plastic blind that covered it. The other trailer was a rusted hulk. Quill could see very little of it. It loomed ominously in the shadows.

Marge sniffed. "You smell that?" she whispered.

Quill nodded.

"That dog poop?"

Quill nodded again. The door to the first trailer opened. Pamela emerged with a five-gallon pail in each hand. The Peke danced around her feet. "Back inside!" Pamela kicked out sideways. The Peke yelped and raced back up the shaky aluminum steps. A torrent of barks and howls from the rusted trailer responded either to the sound of Pamela's voice or the injured Peke. Perhaps both.

"My god," Quill breathed. "It's a puppy mill. She's running a puppy mill!"

"I could use some help out here!" Pamela waddled awkwardly forward. One pail seemed to contain water, the other smelled of raw meat. Quill suddenly thought of the twenty pounds of pork loin missing from the Inn's refrigerators. "Goddamit," Pamela shrieked, "come and give me hand before I spill all this stuff."

A second figure came down the steps. The light from the trailer illuminated silver-blonde hair, and silhouetted a voluptuous figure.

Lila Longstreet.

CHAPTER 13

The Peke charged down the steps, raced across the scrubby excuse for a yard, and planted itself in front of the stand of scrub pine where Marge and Quill stood flattened against a tree. It yapped with monotonous, high-pitched regularity. Lila Longstreet whirled and raced into the trailer. Pamela set the pails down and walked toward the brush.

"Pookie? You find a skunk in there, Pookie?"

Marge raised herself on tiptoe and whispered in Quill's ear: "We can take her."

Quill shook her head, and backed carefully away from the tree, deeper into the brush. She tugged Marge along with her.

"Scat, you!" Pamela stamped her foot on the ground. "It's just a polecat, or a woodchuck, or something, Lila," she called out. She bent down, grabbed the dog by the scruff of the neck, and hissed, "Just shut up!" The Peke stopped barking, mostly because Pamela had a choke hold on its neck. The volume of barks from the trailer increased.

A door slammed in the distance. The howling stopped. The silence was immense.

Quill held her breath and stood absolutely immobile. Marge was just as quiet and still, although she stared steadily at the clearing where Pamela stood with the Peke dangling from one hand.

"You give them all that pork?" she called out. "It's too rich for them, Lila. They're going to vomit it up all over the pens, and I'll be damned if I'll clean it up."

She hauled the now-silent Peke to the trailer steps, tossed the dog inside, and returned to the five-gallon pails. She picked them up and headed for the makeshift kennel, water sloshing over the top of the one in her left hand. "Lila? Where the hell you get to, anyways?"

"Right here," said a breathy voice in Quill's ear. Quill felt the cold muzzle of a gun in the back of her neck.

Instinctively, she ducked away from the gun. Lila's long nails dug into her arm. Quill stumbled forward, tearing away from Lila's grip. She tripped and went down, crashing against Marge's sturdy hip. Marge cried out. A tremendous roar in her ear sent her rolling desperately into the brush. Deafened, she struggled to her feet. Lila's eyes were wide, staring straight into hers. The light from the trailer turned her silver-gilt hair to orange. She looked demonic, and Quill, the least superstitious of women, flung her hands in front of her face as if to protect herself from a devil. Lila swung the gun up and trained it at Quill's chest. Her lips drew back from her teeth in a snarl. Then she swung the gun down and trained it on the ground at Quill's feet. Confused, dazed by the gunshot, Quill looked down. Marge lay there, curled up in a ball, her hands folded into her stomach.

"Don't *move!*" Lila's voice was a mere thread of sound in the roar of silence in Quill's head. Quill knelt. She put her hands over Marge's eyes, as if to keep her from the sight of Lila and the gun. She became aware that someone was screaming, and hoped it wasn't she, herself. Pamela, her mouth open, her eyes glazed and mindless, ran to Lila and simply stood there. Lila gripped the gun with her left hand, and slapped Pamela with her right. The screaming stopped.

". . . Kill her," Lila said. She turned the gun sideways with a rapid, competent flick of her wrist, jammed the magazine home, and pointed it at Marge's head. Quill nodded comprehension. She rose to her knees, slipped one arm around Marge's shoulders, and tried to tug her to a sitting position. Her hands were wet and sticky. She looked down, and in the dim light from the trailer, she saw dark splashes across her palms.

Quill was rocked with a sudden, consuming rage. "Help her!" she shouted. "Help her!" Her voice was muffled and dim to her own ears.

Lila jerked her head curtly at Pamela. The slap seemed to have brought her back to her surroundings. She squatted next to Quill. Together, they tugged Marge upright. Marge groaned. Her eyes opened, shut, and opened again. The lack of awareness in them struck Quill to the heart, and the reckless rage swept over her again. Somehow, they got Marge to her feet. Once upright, Marge seemed less vulnerable, more present, Quill thought, and the dread that Marge was mortally hurt ebbed a little.

Lila and the deadly gun in her hand directed them to the house trailer. But by the time Pamela and Quill got Marge inside, Quill's hearing had come back, and her own adrenaline-fueled rage had crystallized into a cold anger.

"Put her on the couch," Lila said.

"She'll bleed all over it," Pamela complained.

"Shut up!" Quill said fiercely. One arm supporting Marge's back, Quill lowered her onto the couch with as much care as she could manage. She sat down next to her, aware that her legs were trembling so hard that she couldn't have stood up any longer. She took several deep breaths.

"What in the Sam Hill?" Marge said huskily. She cleared her throat and tried again. "What's going on, here?"

"You've been shot, I think." Quill kept her voice calm. "If you'll just let me see where you're hurt?"

Marge nodded in a bewildered way. That, too, cut Quill to the heart. In all the years she'd known her, Marge had never lost that bluff self-confidence that was such an appealing — and occasionally aggravating — part of her personality. She ran light fingers over Marge's arms and chest. Her chinos were soggy with blood; Quill patted her legs lightly and Marge said in surprise, "There, I guess." She moved her right leg with difficulty. Quill looked carefully. There was a hole in her chinos, in the middle of her thigh.

"It's not really bleeding much," she said.

"But we've got to get help." She looked up at her friend. "Does it hurt much?"

Pain was replacing shock in Marge's face. Her lower lip was between her teeth. Her face was pale. "Guess I didn't feel it all that much at first," she said with difficulty.

Quill turned and snapped at Pamela, "Get me a towel. And a wet cloth."

Pamela looked at Lila, for permission, and Quill fought down the impulse to slap her silly. Lila kept the muzzle of the gun trained steadily on Quill, and said, "Yeah. Get it. We don't want any evidence here, if we can help it."

"These days," Quill said rigidly, "there's always evidence. You're in a world of trouble, Lila."

Lila laughed. "Tough cookie, aren't you?" Then, to Pamela, "Go on. What're you, stupid? Get the towel."

Pamela snuffled, then walked heavily to the rear of the trailer. She reemerged with a stack of bath towels and a dampened washcloth. Lila sank into the armchair next to the couch, her face amused.

And she never lowered the gun.

Quill muttered "sorry, sorry, sorry" under her breath as she wrapped Marge's leg. Her friend's face was very pale. She lay slumped back on the couch with closed eyes. Quill cleaned her face with the washcloth, then rose and went to the sink in the tiny kitchen and washed the blood from her hands. "Evidence," she said as she ran the tap and watched the pink water whirl down the drain, "all over the place. You may think you can kill the both of us, but you're not going to get away with it."

"I wouldn't be too sure about that," Lila said agreeably.

Quill walked back to the couch and sat down next to Marge. "Let's see if I can get the events in order, here. When Maxwell Kittleburger decided to sell Pet Pro, you decided to steal as much of the purchase price as you could."

"She'd already taken the old fart for a bundle," Pamela said proudly. "But with those accountants coming in to check things over, we would have been in the soup, wouldn't we, Lila?"

"So you had a deadline? The attorneys were coming in to start the discovery process, and you would have been caught with your hand in the till." Pamela nodded. "That helps makes sense of the timing of the murder, I guess." Quill crossed one knee over the other. She felt an eerie calm. "But why kill Maxwell? I take it you're planning on leaving us for a country that doesn't believe in extradition? And surely being sought for grand theft, or whatever the charge would be, is a lot less risky than being a fugitive from a murder charge."

"I never did figure out why we had to kill Mr. Kittleburger," Pamela said.

Lila's eyes flickered — so briefly that Quill almost didn't catch it. Abruptly, her calm disappeared. "Pamela! You were going to pin Maxwell's murder on Pamela!"

"Don't be ridiculous." Lila raised the gun. "There's so much blood around here that a little bit more isn't going to matter. I was planning on a less messy way of getting rid of you two, but this will have to do."

"Wait a minute." Pamela's watery blue eyes wore a baffled look. She grabbed Lila by the shoulder. "What do you mean, pin that murder on me?"

Every nerve in Quill's body was on alert. "You're a bit of an inconvenience, Pam. To somebody like Lila, at least. You know that the time of Maxwell's murder was supposed to give you a cast-iron alibi. Did you know that the cell phone that Maxwell supposedly received the phone call on at nine forty-five wasn't his cell phone at all? That when Lila went in to kill him at ten thirty, a time when you didn't have an alibi, she replaced his own phone with the one police now have in evidence? And that the cell phone in evidence was purchased by you?" This last shot was what Quill's business manager, John Raintree, would have called a "Wild-Ass Guess." But unlike Quill's own business plans, the WAG worked. It was clear from Pamela's shock that she had purchased the cell phone, undoubtedly at Lila's suggestion. Ruthlessly, Quill pressed on. "And guess how long it's going to take Simon Provost to track the purchaser of the phone? They have serial numbers, you know." Quill didn't know if cell phones had serial numbers or not. But it was clear that Pamela didn't know, either. "Simon Provost has that phone. I saw the evidence report myself." Quill leaned forward. "Have you ever known Lila to be faithful to anyone? You know what Olivia always says: character is destiny. Destiny is character. Just look at Lila's history." Quill brought her feet under her so quietly that neither one of the women could have noticed. "She's been through how many guys since you've known her?"

"That's different," Pamela flared. "Men are different!"

"And what about Priscilla? She dumped Priscilla, too."

Pamela's face was red with temper. She screamed, "Shut up! Shut up! Shut up!" But the screams weren't directed at Quill. They were directed at Lila herself. Lila shrugged, brought the gun smoothly around, and shot Pamela through the heart just as Quill and the Pekinese sprang at her.

CHAPTER 14

"She is just the most beautiful baby," Quill said. "Truly, John."

John Raintree smiled at all four of them. His wife Trish, Quill, Meg, and his first child, Sarah Margaret Raintree, all sat in Quill's office late Saturday afternoon, as promised. Quill held the baby in her arms with a feeling that was both achingly new and as old as time. The baby's soft cheek pressed into her throat; her breath was as light as dandelion down.

"Can I have a turn?" Meg whispered.

Quill handed Sarah Margaret over with a strange reluctance.

"So you've solved another murder," John said. A broad grin creased his bronze cheeks. He was half Onondaga, and one of the handsomest men Quill had ever seen. His business acumen had kept the Inn afloat in its early years. Once Quill and Meg were firmly on their feet, he left to pursue more substantial clients. And he had married Trish, who was both beautiful and calm.

"And now the baby," Quill said aloud.

"Did you say something, Quill?" Trish was keeping a slightly anxious eye on her month-old offspring, but she was keeping up with the conversation.

"Yes, we did wrap the case up yesterday." Quill blushed. "Sort of. I was convinced that the murderer was someone else entirely. But I think we would have worked it out. I mean, once we realized Lila wasn't dead, everything fell into place. Lila knew about the rat meal, for example, because she was part of the inner workings of Pet Pro. She told Pamela, probably because it amused her. Pamela fed the information to Olivia. Hence the prophecy."

"Hence," Meg muttered. She and John exchanged grins. "She's still upset, no matter what she says to the contrary. Remember how she gets wordier when she gets upset? She still does it."

Quill continued with cool dignity. "There were other clues I ignored or overlooked. The fact that Pamela identified the body that was supposed to be Lila. The fingerprints on Lila's purse didn't match the fingerprints on the body, for example. Not to mention the fresh bleach job on whomever the corpse will turn out to be."

"The woman hiker that was missing," Meg said quietly. "Davy said they would have identified her correctly within a few days, but by then Lila was planning on being out of the country." She gave Sarah Margaret back to Trish. Quill saw the same reluctance on her face that she'd felt herself. "I must say it was brilliant of you to shake Pamela up like that, Quill."

"Not so brilliant." Quill looked out her office window. The serenity that she'd felt holding the baby was rapidly disappearing. "She's dead. And it's my fault."

"You didn't have a lot of choice," John said.

There was a confident tap at her office door. Quill knew that tap. It was Jerry Grimsby, and he would come in whether she said to or not.

Jerry poked his head around the door. "They're here," he said. He caught Meg's eye and smiled warmly. "And the party's ready."

They rose and followed Jerry into the dining room, where, at Harland Peterson's request, five tables had been set with the Inn's most festive tablecloths and flowers.

Quill, Meg, and John and his family took a seat at the largest table. Marge, her leg in a bright blue walking cast, hopped to the head of the table, followed by Harland.

"You feelin' okay there, Margie?" Harland tucked his hand under her elbow and helped her into the chair. He placed her crutches neatly against the far wall and settled into the chair next to hers.

"Stop fussing, you old fool," Marge said gruffly. Her face was pink with pleasure. She shot a glance at Quill. "Think he'd never seen a person on crutches before."

"Thank goodness he's never seen *you* on crutches before," Quill said warmly.

"And may you never be on them again." Jerry Grimsby smiled gallantly at Marge, and then wrapped one arm around Meg, who was seated next to him.

Quill looked around the room. They were all there, Dina with Davy Kiddermeister, Doreen and her husband Stoke, the mayor and his scarily competent wife, Adela, Howie and Miriam. Quill changed the color of her dining room every few years — whenever the carpet in the dining room needed to be replaced — and the new cloths had just arrived. They were a clear crystal pink, a color that shouldn't have worked, but did. Autumn roses held pride of place in the centers of the tables; the beautiful bronze of Oregold, the passionately red Mr.

Lincoln, the creamy perfection of Peace. The flowers set off the perfection of the china Helena Houndswood had designed for the Inn so long ago. Quill lightly traced the rose-breasted grosbeak in the middle of the dinner plate and sighed with relief.

Lila Longstreet had been arrested for the murders of Maxwell Kittleburger and Pamela Durbin late last night. Olivia Oberlie and her TV crew had departed that morning for the Seattle zoo, where she planned to translate messages of unity and peace from the giant pandas. The Finnegans had hired divorce lawyers. Rudy Baranga and Millard Barnstaple had been stopped at the Canadian border and arrested. Priscilla Barnstaple had made Rudy's bail, but remained stern in her desire to press charges against her hapless husband. Quill had hopes that she would relent. And Esther West had rescued thirty-two puppies from the rusty trailer behind Lila Longstreet's hideout, which she now referred to as the Trailer of Death. So far, Carol Ann had failed in her attempts to double the taxes on West's Best Dress Shoppe. It was two businesses now, Carol Ann alleged: a pet store and a dress shop. Harvey Bozzel had created a new slogan for Esther: "West's Best! Dogs and Dresses." She'd ordered t-shirts and coffee mugs with her new logo — Pookie the Peke in a trouser suit.

"Your champagne, Mr. Peterson." Cassie Winterborne set the largest of the Inn's wine buckets at Harland's side with truly professional flair. She wrapped a white napkin deftly around the neck of the first bottle, poured a taste for Harland, who sipped, nodded gravely, and waited while the rest of the table was served. Then he stood and raised his glass:

"To old friends."

"To old friends," they echoed.

Harland grinned. "And me? I'm gonna kiss the bride."

"Go on, you old fool," Marge said, with unmistakable pleasure.

Quill looked at the achingly beautiful Sarah Margaret, and made plans that would please Myles very much.

BEST-EVER POUND CAKE

With Quill in a maternal mood, she is doing quite a bit of home baking. If you bake this cake in a deep-sided, 9-inch round pan, you will get terrific results.

1 cup salted butter
1 3/4 cups sugar
4 eggs
2 teaspoons baking powder
2 cups flour
1 cup heavy whipping cream
2 teaspoons vanilla

Beat the butter and sugar together until fluffy. Add one egg at a time, beating well after each addition. Add the baking powder to the flour, then add 1/2 cup of the mixture to the egg/butter/sugar mixture. Beat well. Add the heavy cream. Beat well. Add the last 1/2 cup of flour and the vanilla. Beat until mixture turns satiny, at least three minutes.

Bake about one hour at 350 degrees.

Toppings for this pound cake range from berries to mousse. Take your pick!

ABOUT THE AUTHOR

Claudia Bishop is the pseudonym for Mary Stanton. *Ground to a Halt* is the fourteenth in the Hemlock Falls series. Look for her new series, *The Casebooks of Dr. McKenzie,* which will feature some of your favorite characters from Hemlock Falls. (The McKenzies live one town over.)

As Mary Stanton, Claudia is also the author of fourteen other novels. She is the senior editor of three successful mystery anthologies, *Death Dines at 8:30* (with Nick DiChario), *Death Dines In* (with Dean James), and *A Merry Band of Murderers* (with Don Bruns). Claudia divides her time between a working farm in upstate New York and a small home in West Palm Beach, Florida. She loves to hear from readers, and can be reached at claudiabishop.com.

We hope you have enjoyed this Large Print book. Other Thorndike, Wheeler, and Chivers Press Large Print books are available at your library or directly from the publishers.

For information about current and upcoming titles, please call or write, without obligation, to:

Publisher
Thorndike Press
295 Kennedy Memorial Drive
Waterville, ME 04901
Tel. (800) 223-1244

or visit our Web site at:

www.gale.com/thorndike
www.gale.com/wheeler

OR

Chivers Large Print
published by BBC Audiobooks Ltd
St James House, The Square
Lower Bristol Road
Bath BA2 3SB
England
Tel. +44(0) 800 136919
email: bbcaudiobooks@bbc.co.uk
www.bbcaudiobooks.co.uk

All our Large Print titles are designed for easy reading, and all our books are made to last.